# LET'S TELL THIS STORY PROPERLY

# LET'S TELL THIS STORY PROPERLY

## An Anthology of the Commonwealth Short Story Prize

Edited by Ellah Wakatama Allfrey
Foreword by Romesh Gunesekera

## DUNDURN
### TORONTO

"Grandmother" by Yu-Mei Balasingamchow appeared in *Starry Island: New Writing from Singapore*, the summer 2014 issue of *Mānoa: A Pacific Journal of International Writing*: manoajournal.hawaii.edu.

"Antonya's Baby Shower on Camperdown Road" by A.L. Major appeared in *Subtropics*, Issue 16, Spring/Summer 2013.

"Let's Tell This Story Properly" by Jennifer Nansubuga Makumbi first appeared in *Granta* magazine online, June 2014.

"The Sarong-Man in the Old House, and an Incubus for a Rainy Night" by Michael Mendis first appeared in *Granta* magazine online, May 2013.

"The Ghost Marriage" by Andrea Mullaney first appeared in *Granta* magazine online, May 2012.

"The Night of Broken Glass" by Jack Wang first appeared in *The New Quarterly*.

Editor: Allison Hirst
Design: Laura Boyle
Printer: Webcom
Cover Design: Sarah Beaudin
Cover Image: Peter Whiddon

Library and Archives Canada Cataloguing in Publication

Let's tell this story properly : an anthology of the Commonwealth Short Story Prize / edited by Ellah Wakatama Allfrey.

Short stories.

Issued in print and electronic formats.
ISBN 978-1-4597-3055-7 (pbk.).--ISBN 978-1-4597-3056-4 (pdf).-- ISBN 978-1-4597-3057-1 (epub)

1. Short stories, Commonwealth (English). 2. Commonwealth fiction (English)--21st century.
I. Allfrey, Ellah Wakatama, 1966-, editor

PR9088.L48 2015          823'.01089171241          C2015-900561-2
                                                    C2015-900562-0

1   2   3   4   5        19   18   17   16   15

 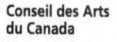 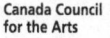   

Conseil des Arts du Canada   Canada Council for the Arts   Canada   ONTARIO ARTS COUNCIL CONSEIL DES ARTS DE L'ONTARIO an Ontario government agency un organisme du gouvernement de l'Ontario

We acknowledge the support of the Canada Council for the Arts and the Ontario Arts Council for our publishing program. We also acknowledge the financial support of the Government of Canada through the Canada Book Fund and Livres Canada Books, and the Government of Ontario through the Ontario Book Publishing Tax Credit and the Ontario Media Development Corporation.

Care has been taken to trace the ownership of copyright material used in this book. The author and the publisher welcome any information enabling them to rectify any references or credits in subsequent editions.

*J. Kirk Howard, President*

Printed and bound in Canada.

VISIT US AT
*Dundurn.com | Definingcanada.ca | @dundurnpress | Facebook.com/dundurnpress*

Dundurn
3 Church Street, Suite 500
Toronto, Ontario, Canada
M5E 1M2

# CONTENTS

# THE COMMONWEALTH SHORT STORY PRIZE

The Short Story Prize was launched by Commonwealth Writers in 2012 as an award for the best piece of unpublished short fiction written in English from across the Commonwealth. It is one of the few international prizes open to published and unpublished writers alike and to stories translated into English.

Commonwealth Writers is the cultural initiative of the Commonwealth Foundation, an international development organization based in London. It was set up to inspire and connect writers and storytellers across the world. We believe that well-told stories can help people make sense of events, engage with others, and take action to bring about change.

This anthology comprises some of the strongest entries to the prize between 2012 and 2014, selected by the Chairs of the judging panels: author Bernardine Evaristo, broadcaster and journalist Razia Iqbal, and editor and critic Ellah Wakatama Allfrey.

Each year the international judges select five winning writers from five different Commonwealth regions — Africa, Asia, Canada and Europe, the Caribbean, and the Pacific — one of whom is chosen as the overall winner.

We receive thousands of stories from almost every one of the fifty-three countries in the Commonwealth. As well as more established writers, the shortlists each year include many new and emerging writers, often from countries with little or no publishing infrastructure.

It's our aim to bring writers from around the world to the attention of a wider audience. *Let's Tell This Story Properly* is one way to achieve this.

We would like to thank our judges from 2012–14: Tash Aw, Doreen Baingana, Urvashi Butalia, Craig Cliff, Elise Dillsworth, Marlon James, Billy Kahora, Oonya Kempadoo, Cresantia Frances Koya, Michelle de Kretser, Nicholas Laughlin, Lisa Moore, Courttia Newland, Jeet Thayil, and D.W. Wilson. We also wish to thank Kirk Howard and Beth Bruder from Dundurn Press, the seventeen authors featured in the anthology, and the thousands of writers who enter the Prize each year.

Lucy Hannah, Programme Manager
Commonwealth Writers

# FOREWORD

Sometimes you can wait for months, even years, for a story to turn up. You wait, sheltering by the side of a library, or at a bus stop where once you had taken a magical ride that changed your life, and peer into the failing light, desperately looking, hoping one will turn up before the light goes completely and it is too dark to see. You begin to wonder whether you just missed the last one. Maybe you no longer know what a story looks like and it has passed by without you recognizing it. You try to remember what a story is, what it was, what it meant. You panic because you can't be sure what moved you most. What was that thing that lit up your life? Made you think it was all worthwhile. Just to read it was to make the day worthwhile. You look at a story you started to write and think, no, that can't be it. Then, even that disappears like the invisible lemony ink of your childhood. You wonder why the clouds are moving across the sky. Or are they? You begin to wonder, does anyone write stories anymore? Are there any stories left in this world that is so gridlocked with the debris of instant gratification. You wonder whether you will ever see another story like the one you can't remember that set you on this road on which you are now stranded.

And then something turns a corner and you see a story coming. Then another, and another, and another. You see a whole anthology bringing you a whole new world in one amazing parade. The relief is indescribable. The best thing you can do is to turn the page and read. Then, you will remember everything: why you write, why you read, why you are who you are.

Romesh Gunesekera

**Romesh Gunesekera** was born in Sri Lanka and moved to Britain in the early 1970s. A Fellow of the Royal Society of Literature, he is the author of eight books of fiction. His novel *Reef* was shortlisted for the 1994 Man Booker Prize. His new collection of stories set in postwar Sri Lanka, *Noontide Toll*, was published by Granta in 2014 along with a twentieth-anniversary edition of *Reef*. Romesh is the Chair of the 2015 Commonwealth Short Story Prize.

# EDITOR'S NOTE

Late this summer, the team at Commonwealth Writers gathered together the last three Chairs of the Commonwealth Short Story Prize judging panels: me, Bernardine Evaristo, and Razia Iqbal. We had the daunting — and hugely pleasurable — task of choosing our favourite stories to publish in this anthology. During our deliberations, we looked for writing that evoked a strong sense of place. After all, the adventure of reading away from one's own immediate environment is the promise of instant travel, the possibility of immersion in another reality. We also looked for writing that was ambitious, stories that offered surprise, stories that made us think, and stories whose characters stayed in our minds long after the pages were turned.

The result is an eclectic mix of genres and settings — both in time and place. The voices you will find here are as varied and individual as the countries from which the authors are writing. Each story brings us news from another land: there's the hunt for a giant squid in New Zealand; a chronicle of hard times in Singapore; a baby shower and a lost boy in the Bahamas; an English woman and her spectral lover in China; and adventures in taxidermy in South Africa. Each story is written in English, but the language is inflected with the cadences of locality and a host of native tongues: Ganda, Chinese, patois, Afrikaans. Several of the writers appearing here already have a significant body of work to their credit. A couple appear with the first stories they have ever written. In casting its net across the globe — bringing stories from around the world to readers around the world — the Commonwealth Short Story Prize is unique in allowing such a range of writers to appear together in one volume.

Ellah Wakatama Allfrey
London, November 2014

## DANIEL ANDERS

# Hummingbird

The old man awoke with a start. He checked the time. 07:13. He jumped out of bed and went to the window where a bird cage perched. His hummingbird lay on the floor of the cage. He took it out and held it, realizing then the cause of death. He confirmed his suspicion by going over and checking the radiator. It was set to low but was stone cold, like the creature in the palm of his hand. He kicked the heater and cursed his building superintendent, his boss, the party. He dressed clumsily, having to re-button his shirt to align the buttons with the holes. He left the bird on the table so he could bury it when he returned from work.

On the train, songs which his bird would normally sing to wake him echoed in his memory. He wept. "What a stupid old man I must seem to my fellow travellers. But I cannot help my feelings for my bird."

He arrived at work after nine. *Three hours late*, he thought, though any lateness was too late for his superiors. Along with the other "recalcitrants," he now filed into a room off to one side, furnished with a long table and benches all around, and supplied with cheap paper and pens and, of course, for cross-referencing purposes, the "handbook," or, to give it its official title, *A Guide to Managing Misconduct and Unsatisfactory Performance Reviews,* which was required reading — even if it did run to eight hundred pages — for checking the tone and style of one's letter of apology against the rules that abided precisely for these situations. He took a seat across from a pair of young lovers, who were now flush with embarrassment after the passion of their encounter the night before had subsided and cost them the shame of unwanted tardiness, and spent the morning penning his submission to his superior.

2008.08.08

Dear Madam Acting Deputy Superintendent, Third Class,

I am grateful for the opportunity to condemn the personal disgrace of my failure to attend this place of employment pleasure.

I mean no abnegation of responsibility for my depravity when I say that due to the calamity of the premature loss of my hummingbird, I did not awake punctually and therefore missed my shift.

I would be honoured if you would allow me to do five shifts without pay.

And, due to the demise of my hummingbird, I humbly beseech you for the opportunity to accommodate my purchase of a replacement bird. However, as this will necessitate my absence for a half day, I implore you to dock my wages for another week.

Thanking you in bountiful esteem for your unwarranted consideration in advancement of your conclusive and binding dictum, and being yours in everlasting gratitude,

Acting Deputy Superintendent, Fourth Class:
Crystallization Manufacturing Process, Post-Production Division, Hard Waste Disposal: Plant #14, Block #5, Unit #39, Office #610; Employee #44014.

He read over his composition, noting smugly that he had managed to keep the letter within the band of obsequiousness and officiousness expected. His support person agreed with this analysis: "An appropriate response."

Having waited all day, he was granted an audience with the disciplinary board after the shift he should have done — had he arrived on time — was due to finish at 18:30 hours. He entered on his knees, eyes lowered, hands clasped. The board substantiated his recommendations and, given the difficulty of filling his position at short notice, offered him his job back provided he accepted a cut in pay and swore never to undermine his boss again.

"There are no second chances for superintendents fourth class at this hard waste disposal unit. Do you understand?" He nodded his assent while continuing to look at the floor.

"Most benign fortune," the old man's support person said once outside. "Your letter's transparent contrition was a welcome respite from the disputations which some of your less fortunate comrades fall prey to. May your fortune continue in your endeavour for a hummingbird to replace the old one."

◆

When he arrived home it was dark and the utility shed was locked. The bird had thawed out during the day and started to moult and rot. He lightly rubbed its beak with his thumb. He couldn't bring himself to throw it away like leftover rubbish. He cried and resolved to write a note asking the building supervisor to leave a shovel out tomorrow so he could attend personally to a tribute for his bird.

The next day he went to the hummingbird district. From the moment he departed the train he heard the tones of the morning song sung by a choir of birds. He cried, recollecting that his bird had been preparing for that song yesterday.

He went into a shop and was greeted by a sales assistant. He gave his rank and the assistant informed him, consulting a catalogue, of what he was entitled to: "Standard issue brown hummingbird, of no more than five inches in stature, with a home tone of C if a male or C sharp if a female; weight, no more than three hundred grams."

He asked where amongst all of the birds on display he might find this classification.

"Nowhere. They're not in stock. Currently we have a three months' waiting list of back orders."

A higher-up superintendent, wearing insignia that distinguished him as of the first class, entered the establishment. The salesman promptly went over to the higher-up, showing him the birds he could select from. He pointed at a plump, bright yellow fellow, which was dutifully caged, paid for, and taken away.

A young assistant, pretending to be busy dusting while wiggling her hips and backside to music coming from a device attached to the waistband of her leggings, came around the corner. She tapped the old man on the shoulder and smiled before asking him to move. The old man moved aside, hesitated, then went over to her. "Excuse me?" She removed one ear bud and feigned listening to him. He gestured with his thumb at the departing higher-up: "Why is his bird more impressive than the ones I can have?"

She looked over her shoulder to the superintendent, first class, then witheringly eyed the old man. "Stupid," she cooed at him, batting away the query with a dismissive wave of her hand, causing her plastic bangles to jangle; but, seeing his nostrils flare and his eyes boggle, she tempered her response. "Don't be silly." She reached out to pat his elbow. "He pays more for his." This information didn't seem to allay the old man.

She paused and from some recess where it had been tucked away, she pulled out a prescient quote, the fortuitousness of which made her blush: "'From each according to his ability, to each according to his need,'" she quipped, her head nodding as she completed the text, her bob of jet black hair flouncing as she smiled.

Another assistant piped up: "Go, girl." The salesman who had handled the higher-up came over and, seeing the girls tittering, directed them to go sort some new stock.

The old man accosted the salesman: "Why do you have birds for him and not for me? I have another two years to go before I can retire at eighty-four and six months. I must have a bird."

The salesman looked round the shop. It was deserted. "See here, I can't give you one of those canaries: there's one type for your class and another for the next up, and so on. I can't do it." He bobbed his head upwards and back down again. "Now look, I probably shouldn't even be telling you this, but you wouldn't want one of the higher-ups' birds anyway, even if I could sell it to you. See, the latest thing for the higher-ups is a portable transistor radio. You need a reliable supply of electricity, which rules you and your kind out. But their birds are just for show. We can keep them supplied only because the birds don't need to know the songs. He'll wake up to pop music on some station his kids have tuned it to. Count yourself lucky, chump. Your bird makes beautiful music. The problem with that is it takes time." He dug into his pocket and pulled out a fresh pack of cigarettes. He unwrapped the plastic shell and then the foil lining and, inverting it, tapped on the top of the pack with the palm of his hand before offering one to the old man. When he declined, the salesman extracted one for himself. "Still, you can't rush beauty. You have to let it happen naturally." The salesman reached into his back pocket for a packet of matches and was in the act of striking one when the old man grabbed him.

"Do you understand? I can't wait. I'll lose my job if I miss another day of work. I must have one by tomorrow."

The salesman shrugged off the old man's hand. "So it's *serious*?" the salesman suggested.

"Yes, of course it's serious," re-joined the old man. "I wouldn't be here if it wasn't."

"My mistake, sir. I didn't realize you were *serious*." Then, leaning in and lowering his voice, the salesman cooed: "Hey, look, I want to show you something." He motioned behind him, cuffing the old man's arm at the elbow and hoisting him out back. "Just come along, okay? I can help you with your problem."

Outside, chained up along the back fence, a row of men squatted in soiled rags, many of them with blotchy, discoloured skin. "Choose one," the salesman advised.

"What for?" queried the old man.

"For the songs, of course. These men can sing them." The old man was confounded, so the salesman kicked the chained man nearest and demanded he sing the song of the morning smoking break. The man sang as the salesman puffed on his cigarette nodding appreciatively and the old man wept, remembering his humming-bird's rendition of the same song. Then the salesman dropped his cigarette, butted it out, and kicked the singer to stop him.

"But how?" the old man questioned the salesman.

"The songs that the hummingbirds sing were taught to them by men. These men have been conditioned and are now under-going reform and re-entry into society. We have trained them to learn the songs because of their sweet natures. They deserve a chance to return to the society of men, don't you think? For they had been men, but were turned into dogs by the camps and will now be like birds in order to someday be reborn as men."

"But how can you offer me a man to act as a bird? Surely if there aren't enough birds there can't possibly be enough men?"

"No, you're quite wrong. First of all, there are more men in the world than hummingbirds. And anyhow, it's easier to train a man than a bird. After all, men are smarter, so it takes them less time to learn. And these men are more docile than the birds. No. It is better to use men than birds, much better!"

The salesman had the bird-singing-men, or birdmen for short, disrobe, so the old man could determine which one he most pre-ferred. "Just as you would appraise a hummingbird's plumage, so take a look at these birdmen." The old man saw that many of them suffered from discoloration of the skin, with blotches in various dark hues, from dark red like wine to deep purple, almost black. While he observed each of them in turn, the salesman went up and down, kicking and prodding the birdmen to coax them to sing. The old man settled on one with crimson markings, whose chirping, while faint, seemed sweet and pleasant.

Aboard the train home, the old man felt embarrassed hanging on to the lead that was tethered to the birdman's neck. "A pair of idiots we must seem to these fellow travellers," he muttered.

Once they were in the old man's room, and he had removed the lead, he felt at ease. He absentmindedly asked the birdman if he wanted a cup of tea. "I could certainly use one." For a reply he heard a plaintive song coming from the other end of the room. He saw the birdman standing in front of the window, cupping the dead hummingbird in his hands, and singing a song of mourning for it. The old man wept.

Later, he noticed, as the birdman undressed before retiring to bed, his "plumage," which looked like bruising and scarring across his back, chest, and arms. There were a series of welts crisscrossing his spine. "Did you stand too close to the fire or something? Didn't they teach you that flames can be hot?" The birdman did not respond.

♦

Weeks passed, with the old man enjoying having a birdman to sing to him. Each morning he awoke to the song of the sunrise, inviting him to start the new day. He ate his breakfast hearing the song of gracious thanks, and he came home to the sounds of the evening greeting.

He was proud of his birdman and decided to display him. So, on his stroll in the park on his rostered day off that fortnight, he took his birdman along with him, tethered on a lead. The old man sat down on a bench, beside another old man, whose eyes were closed, his head slumped on to his shoulder, the birdman squatting in the space between them. He took out his pipe and, seeing this, the birdman began to sing the song of the pipe, which would segue into the song of the smoking break. As the birdman sang, the other old man lifted his head and opened his eyes.

When the old man had stopped smoking, and the birdman's song had trailed off, the other old man spoke. "He reminds me of my old hummingbird."

"Me too. My poor fellow passed. Because those bastard higher-ups turn off the heating in my building overnight, he froze to death, poor thing." The old man spat.

"Mine flew away. I left his cage door ajar, so he could fly around, but when I went to leave, he escaped. Really, I have only myself to blame. I felt sorry for him, cooped up in that tiny cage all day. But now I miss him dearly." He turned away as the tears welled up. Bocce balls could be heard clanging and the men playing made comments to egg one another on, while children, further in the distance, squawked and hooted as they jumped and climbed and slid while their mothers cheeped at them to be mindful of the perils of the playground.

The birdman began a vigorous whistling that startled the two old men. He kept it up in a round: repeating the chiming whistle, pausing, then repeating it again; as he did so, hummingbirds began to appear, flying down to land near until it seemed more than two score had descended. The hummingbirds called and cooed and jumped and fretted about. The two old men turned and looked at one another in amazement.

"Now, I suppose you need to establish which one of these is yours," declared the old man to his companion on the bench, who laughed as he watched the display of birds.

Soon after, the old man entered his birdman in a singing competition, thinking he could show him off in front of other superintendents, fourth class. However, there had arisen a demarcation between those who still had hummingbirds and those who had moved on to birdmen. Many of the owners of hummingbirds were upset that the owners of birdmen had muscled in on their competition.

"This is not fair. The judges will be biased against the birds and for the men. Go off and compete on your own. Leave us to our birds."

Others disagreed. "Our birdmen are better singers than your stupid birds. Face it. Men can hum better than hummingbirds."

Some claimed that the higher-ups wouldn't accept the birdmen and would disband them. "I hear that we are to go back to cockerels: one per building, the responsibility of the building superintendents."

"Please no," spoke up another. "I am a building superintendent and I love my hummingbird. Why should I have to get rid of it, just because of your birdmen?"

"There are rumours that a birdman has escaped from his owner and set about freeing others," another suggested.

"That's just a rumour," yelled a fellow from the back, "to justify a purge."

2008.11.11

TO: ALL EMPLOYEES OF CRYSTALLIZATION MANUFACTURING PROCESS, POST-PRODUCTION DIVISION, HARD WASTE DISPOSAL: PLANT #14, BLOCK #5, UNIT #39

FROM: MADAM ACTING DEPUTY SUPERINTENDENT, FIRST CLASS

MESSAGE: DUE TO EARLY ATTAINMENT OF THE REQUISITE QUARTERLY PERFORMANCE QUOTAS, THE AFORESAID ARE TO BE PUT ON LOW ACTIVITY, EFFECTIVE IMMEDIATELY

The old man, however, was called in to work his gratis shifts. He spent most of the first day sweeping outside the front office so the higher-ups could see how dutiful he had been. As it was approaching dusk, trucks arrived with containers that the invoice stipulated were full of "work clothing." The old man was directed to keep the containers fully powered until the goods were collected tomorrow.

As he undressed for bed, the old man mused, "Funny, I can't remember if I checked that the power was on for the third row of containers." He checked his watch: 00:44 it read. "They told me it was only work clothes — they'll probably come to no harm: so what's going to waste in there?" He turned off the light, then walked through and turned on the light in the bathroom. His birdman was drying himself off after a sitz bath. The old man studied his birdman's legs and lower back, and noticed that the discoloration was greatest here and also on his hands. "How did you come by those marks? Crushing too many grapes, were you?" he croaked with laughter. His birdman made no response.

The next day, as he went to leave, he hesitated, then retrieved the lead, and, attaching it to his birdman, he muttered, "Come along, might as well make an outing of it."

Inspecting the third row of containers, he noticed that a lock on one of them had started to rust. He squeezed the shaft and it pushed in and, with a twist, the prong came out. Opening the lock and removing it, he then pulled open the door and peered inside. There was a tiny recess of wriggle room just behind the door, so he stepped into the darkness. He thought for a moment that he could hear exhalation of breath coming from within the container, but the impression ebbed. Then, turning on the headlight mounted on his helmet, he ascertained that the container was full of boxes. He took a pen knife from his jacket pocket and slashed a box, cutting a slit into it. He stuck in his fingers and, grabbing what was inside, pulled out a red woollen vest. Rubbing his fingertips along the inside of the collar, he felt the ribbed texture of the fine fibres and pulled out the entire garment. On the left breast was a patch of a small green dragon. The old man traced his thumb over this patch.

He stepped out of the recess at the back of the container,

closed the door, and removed his jacket and then donned the vest. He looked from one breast to the other and back again, before putting his jacket back on over the vest. Proud of his discovery, he waddled off to find a spare lock.

However, when he returned, he found a team of men fitting the containers to trucks in order to haul them away. A young man, waving a wad of paper in his face, accosted him. "You there, what's the idea of not being ready? We've had to cut the lock at the gate to get in. Don't think for a second that we're paying for that."

Another man came running up to the first. "The third row was without power."

"Eh?" inquired the first.

"Dead."

"But I checked them just before. The vests were fine."

The first man rounded on him. "How did you know what was inside?"

The old man looked down, from his flaccid left pectorals adorned with the green dragon to the lock in his hand.

The first young man seized the old man and turned him round, propping him up against a truck and using his back to write on, scribbling on the pages in his hands.

Then he turned the old man to face him and thrust the paperwork at him. "Sign here." He stuck a greasy pen in the old man's hand, and then, having procured a signature, scurried away.

◆

It wasn't until all the trucks had gone and the old man had returned to the office that he realized his birdman was missing. He trekked back to his room and got ready for bed. As he was about to put out the light, he looked over at the old bird cage. He went and opened the cage door, swinging it back and forth in between his fingers, before leaving it wide open and going to bed.

The next morning, the old man awoke calmly. It was 07:44 hours. He got up to begin making himself a pot of tea and started cleaning out his pipe. He was busy with this task when he heard a knock at the door. "It's open," he said, feeling strangely torn as he realized that he was hoping that the birdman had returned. Instead, a young uniform policeman wielding a charge sheet sauntered in.

"Slave #42014-12, you have been found guilty of aiding and abetting the unlawful escape and liberation of a 'humming-bird-trainer-in-lieu-of-actual-bird.' Your hummingbird-train-er-in-lieu-of-actual-bird, which you obtained illegally, has been found guilty of unlawful escape; therefore, you, Slave #42014-12, will be released when he is apprehended: when he is caught so might you be set free."

The old man looked across the quarry and saw the sun setting and sang the plaintive evening song that reminded him of putting the pot on the stove and setting it to boil and preparing his pipe for a tranquil smoke, in that time when he had just come home from work.

He had only gotten through the refrain when he felt a hard thrust in the small of his back. He heard the guard right behind him: "Insubordination: no singing outside of the requisitioned periods in accordance with Ordinance 610/8, Paragraph two, Subsection eighty-eight."

On hearing the song, a superintendent, fourth class, took pity on him and filled in bogus paperwork, ostensibly to have him transferred to another camp, but actually to take him home as his birdman. However, this fraud was uncovered by a superintendent, first class, who agreed not to report the fraud on condition that more bogus paperwork was completed to show that en route to another camp the truck had broken down along the highway and that Slave #42014-12 had attempted to escape but was shot dead.

The superintendent, first class, then bestowed the old man as a house-warming gift on a "friend," a self-styled gentleman, who, despite being on a party member's salary, had moved into a splendid villa with views of the city from his newly planted cherry blossom garden.

"His voice may lack strength and the quality of his timbre may not be the highest, but there is an aspect of his plain manner that I am entranced by," the gentleman said, on reflection, after the old man had sung to him the song of the sunset.

"There is a beauty in the flaw that perfection shall never match," offered the superintendent, as they admired the old man in the cool of the evening.

"Yes, well spoken." The gentleman's white linen suit pants whooshed against the lavender as he walked past. He bent over and picked a bud, holding it up to his jaundiced face and crushing the flowers to release their fragrance.

With a choir of voices crying in climax to Beethoven's "Ode to Joy," the gentleman's phone announced that he had a call. "What?" the gentleman asked the caller. "You say you have another one. And you're sure we're compatible. Yes, yes, blood type AB positive, that's right. When can you take possession of it?" He could hardly wait for the response: "And the operation? How long will I have to wait for the transplant?" Once again he butted right back in: "Just remember, no dye workers: that shit doesn't just mess up their skin. I've already had one cock-up, I don't need any more. Understood?" The gentleman held the phone to his ear and tried to listen to the disclaimer coming from the other end of the conversation.

A butler in formal attire bowed and gestured toward the rock pool. "Tea is served, sir."

The gentleman gestured for his guest to precede him, but he shook his head and deferred to his host. "Do you smoke?" the gentleman queried his guest.

"When I get the chance," the superintendent replied.

"Good. I want you to try a Churchill from my latest shipment of Havanas."

The butler poured the tea and struck a match in order to light the cigars of both men. Down the embankment, panting against the retaining wall, the old man closed his eyes. He remembered the taste of tea and the smell of tobacco. In pain, he wiped his mouth and went to stand, but instead fell back and collapsed against the wall, where he was found by the gardener, later, as he came out, ostensibly to finish the evening watering, though he was looking forward to listening to the old man's extraordinary rendition of the evening song, which he was eager to hear once more, as it reminded him of his hummingbird, which he had recently lost and had yet to replace.

## EVAN ADAM ANG

# A Day in the Death

*Lim Oh Kee kills himself in the early hours on the 12th day of December 1921.*

*His last meal is rice and nothing. His last words are that by tomorrow (by today), he'll be gone. He dies by hanging. He cannot afford to buy rope for an occasion like this. Instead, it's a scavenged piece of cord that's wrapped around his neck when his son finds him, suspended from a door along the five foot way. He's blocking foot traffic but it doesn't matter, because the route itself is barely used.*

*No one knows whether he aimed to be considerate, even in death, or if he simply picked the nearest available option. His son (little, eleven, and living with his friend Chuan) was not the first to discover him, only the first to recognize him. In the very short, very brief report on Lim Oh Kee's death made by the Coroner, it's noted that he has been out of work (like so many people have been out of work) for some time. It's noted that he's been ill (like so many people have been ill) for longer. He has — he had — nowhere to live. The door he hung from wasn't even his own.*

*He looked starved. He was starved.*

*Lim Oh Kee was not the first person in the area to die like this, and he won't be the last. Plenty of people have beaten him to the proverbial punch. The day before his death, another man hanged himself. A week before that, a woman drowned herself in the river. A month before that, another slit her own throat. Six months prior and there are more crimes, more murders, more deaths. Some are caused by fights between gangs. Some are cheap, stupid ones. Others are planned, deliberate, and carefully orchestrated.*

*No one of any importance cares about Lim Oh Kee's, though, because no one of any importance knew he even existed.*

◆

This is Singapore.

Crime has gone up, but crime is always going up. It's bad, but it's not as bad as other, more important things, like the price of food, going up. That's bad too, but not as bad as the price of opium going up. That's *really* bad.

It's hard to tell if the reason everything is going to what seems a whole lot like hell is because more people are reporting things to the police and everything is getting recorded in greater detail or if it's because things are actually worse in general. The truth is, things are worse in general.

Seventy-nine years from now, at the turn of the next century, the leaders of Singapore will honour the hardworking men and women on whose aching backs their glorious nation-city-state was built. They were very good people, the leaders will say, who came from their hometowns in China chasing some glorious dream. They were entrepreneurs who planted pineapple farms; they were brilliant doctors who were willing to sacrifice everything they had before (which was next to nothing) for all the opportunities that Singapore afforded them (still next to nothing). They came from every walk of life, besides the ones that Asians weren't allowed to tread. Museums will showcase exhibitions about their lives and the hardships they faced. Children will be asked to interview their grandparents about them. Their lives will form an integral part of the Singapore Story™.

Unfortunately for Lim Oh Kee, this is not seventy-nine years later. This is not even forty years later, or thirty.

This is now, when even *opium*, desirable as it is, is starting to be a hard sell at sixty out of the eighty cents that the average coolie earns each day.

◆

*Lim Oh Kee does not qualify for the Contingency Relief Fund, the Destitute Seamen's Relief Fund, the Indian Coolies Fund, the Tamil Immigration Fund, the Widows and Orphans' Pension Fund, or any protection ordinances. This isn't actually a serious problem for him, because even if he did, he wouldn't have applied for them anyway.*

*It'd be difficult to do something like that, when he doesn't even know that they exist.*

*He does know about the Societies, though, and the various clan Hway Kuans that provide help to people in need. He's heard of a free hospital for people like him but he doesn't trust hospitals and he doesn't think they will help. Sure, a lot of Chinese people go to hospital, he tells his friend Chuan, who has come over with his son, but they're a different type of Chinese people.*

*Chuan, sitting next to Lim Oh Kee, listens, nods, agrees, and then asks him: What about the free one?*

*It's still a hospital, Lim Oh Kee replies. And he's not Cantonese, he says, because this explains everything.*

*It doesn't, actually — not everything, but there's enough in there that his friend (whose wife passed away in a hospital a month back, who didn't understand why, only that she did, who says he wasn't angry with her and who genuinely never understood why she tried to kill herself) nods and says that he understands. They're Hokkien, not Cantonese. This matters. He gets it.*

*Besides, people die in hospitals. That's not so good. A lot of people die outside of hospitals, too, but that's natural. That's different. If they were going to die or if they wanted to die or if they had nothing left to do but to die, then the death houses on Sago Street would have been happy to welcome them, for the price of what they had left. But hospitals ... hospitals are different. Since they were introduced to Singapore*

*by Europeans, they will always be different. The only thing that mat-*
*ters is how, and why, and whether people can afford to be different.*

*Right now, not many can.*

*Lim Oh Kee shakes his head at that, says he heard of a family*
*that ran a store selling paper goods to people who wanted to pay*
*their respects where two uncles and a son died in short succession.*
*It bankrupted them, to pay their respects to the various deceased*
*properly. This, he says, is a bad time to die if you're rich. It'll cost*
*you, he says. But if you're poor and you couldn't afford anything to*
*begin with, you lose nothing. It's a better time to die if you're poor.*

*Chuan says it's always a bad time to die.*

*Lim Oh Kee isn't so sure about that, but he pats his son on the*
*head and gives him a brief hug before he goes.*

*He's hungry.*

*He's not quite starving, but he will be soon.*

◆

The thing about Singapore in 1921 is this. If you're the average
person (Chinese, male, somewhere in your twenties or older —
but not too much older if you're going by the median), then
you're probably working an average job that pays you barely
enough to get by.

This is not actually a bad life, or a bad salary.

You could live on it, probably. You could maybe raise a family
on it. A small family with not too many children. But here's the
thing: the way prices have been looking, the way the cost of *every-*
*thing* — from rental and lodging to coffee to night soil — has
increased; you won't be doing much more than just living on
your salary. There's no saving, there's no sending home, there's no
maybe doing something else in the future.

You have to work because you came here to work. You probably can't read, but that's fine, you can find someone to read things
out loud for you (for money). You sometimes dream about wanting
to go back to where you grew up, but if you don't have the money

then you can't, and if you did have the money, why would you ever want to? If you have the money (you don't), this place is quite nice.

If you were an average person and had the money, you wouldn't worry so much about your life. You'd be able to pay for the opium that you need but can't afford. You'd be able to pay for something that would make a real difference or that you really want — maybe a generator — because you have the money. Maybe an expensive raincoat, just so you don't get wet outdoors. Maybe chicken, for once. You haven't eaten chicken in months.

But you don't have the money. What you are is — you're a coolie, a physical labourer. You wake up at five sharp every morning and are out of the door by a quarter to six. Your life is drudgery, mostly, there's very little thinking involved. You get by, because you've always got by. You don't like to think about what would happen if you lost your job or if you fell ill or if you couldn't work, because every other person you see on a regular basis is a hell of a lot like you, and all they want is the work you're doing and all they need is half a chance to take your job. If something like that happens, you think, maybe you'll kill yourself.

Find some rope, loop it around your neck, tie the other end to a doorframe, and drop yourself right down. Suspension hanging, as opposed to the long drop method practiced in the prisons. It's easier to do and there's less chance of an accidental decapitation. Either way, though, you'd still be dead at the end of it. A miserable corpse for someone else to find.

Meanwhile, you're still thankful for what you have.

You should be. You're one of the lucky ones.

You still have a door.

◆

*Lim Oh Kee's son doesn't want to leave.*

*It's not as if there's much of a choice, though. His son can't stay with him, not because he doesn't want to be with the boy, or because he thinks the boy is worse off around him. It's not like that. His son can't stay because there's nowhere for his son to stay.*

*It's a simple enough problem. Their savings have run out and even the rent for a room shared with five (or six, or seven) other men is too much for someone like him and a child who can't even earn money yet. Maybe if he had another year, if his son was twelve instead of eleven, someone would hire him.*

*There isn't another year.*

*He pats the boy on his head. This is simple; it's a matter of priorities. Lim Oh Kee doesn't expect his son to understand, but that doesn't matter. Right now what matters is keeping his son alive and as well as is possible for him. Paying rent means money that he can't afford to spend, and what's the point of having a place to stay when you don't have food to eat? Even that is limited right now because he can't work. And assuming he could, who would hire him? There are younger and stronger men with no jobs and no sons.*

*Sure, there are the triads and the societies, but if he's too sick then he's not much use to them either. In any case, he can't even claim to be able to read or write. His main asset was his strength. Right now, he doesn't have that.*

*So he ruffles his son's hair and sends him off with his friend Chuan and tells him to come by every evening to see him. His son promises he'll do that. Chuan promises to send the boy over and to come over himself if he can. For a while, Lim Oh Kee gropes for something to say to his son. There isn't much that comes to mind. He's already told the boy not to be a bother.*

*Drink milk, he says, finally. It'll keep you healthy.*

*Chuan says, when he comes by a few days later, come live with me, it's better than out here. Your son already does. You're not working anyway; don't you want to be closer to him?*

*Lim Oh Kee looks at the money he has left. There's not much.*

*I can't pay for anything, he says.*

*You pay for opium, Chuan replies.*

*Opium's different.*

*There's a pause and Chuan sighs.*

*Opium's different.*

◆

Of course life isn't like that for everyone.

This is the early 1920s. What an exciting time it is! Newspapers, previously the domain of the Western colonial, are starting to be written and set up by Asians. The *Fookien Times* in the Philippines and the *Malaya Tribune* in Singapore. "For Asiatics, *by* Asiatics" is the slogan, and all across the region there's never been anything like this before.

Somewhere in there is a story starring Dr. Lim Boon Keng as he struggles to set up a paper that caters to the English-speaking Asians. He faces challenges and difficulties of all sorts, but with the support of the Chinese community behind him, he successfully challenges the way newspapers cater only to Europeans with his new publication. This fledgling start-up, the Europeans who believed in it and worked for it, the negotiations they had to undertake and the audience they had to please, all of that makes a good tale.

Somewhere in there is another story about the colonial subject who struggles with his ethnic identity and his place in a society that calls him second class and will allow him to rise above that due to his birth, and which expects him to fit himself comfortably into the social order. Writers in the future will touch on the strange dichotomy that exists between creating a sense of belonging and forging a national identity where none existed before. They will expound on the slow realization of the inherent injustices that lie at the core of colonial society.

This is all very important to the future. When countries are created based on the legislation and nationalist arguments that the colonial powers have inadvertently introduced to the region, narratives have to be constructed, stories have to be told of the past, linking the people and places and joys and sorrows to the present. Everything that happened built up to this. The nationalists were *our* nationalists, the coolies were *our* coolies, their stories are *our* stories.

It's all very dramatic. But that's good, people like drama, especially when it's drama about themselves and it makes them out to be the heroes, or the sons and daughters of heroes — which definitely sounds better than the children of people who never really thought about the future because just getting past the day was good enough for them.

Of course, the important thing to keep in mind is that while all of this is unquestionably important, whether or not the people of that era were aware at all that they were labouring away in someone else's story is another matter altogether.

The thing about caring is that it doesn't always go the whole way. Coolies, that's one thing. The coolies, the people who came, who worked, who suffered so that future generations could survive, those hardy belaboured, labouring men. They're easy to care for.

A coolie?

That's another thing entirely.

◆

*Lim Oh Kee is not a rich man, but he's doing well enough. He's a normal man in many respects — no wife, but a child he feels responsible for and takes care of as best as he can. He doesn't earn much, but there's enough for him, his life, his child, his child's life, and his opium habit.*

*It's not a bad habit, he thinks.*

*Before he came to Singapore, he'd never smoked opium. It wasn't as if he hadn't heard about it, of course he had. It was a big issue that important people talked about using big important words. But it was a big distant issue, not one that ever really affected him. Not until he came to Singapore and started working every day until he was tired to the bone, and finished working every day only when he was tired to the bone.*

*The first time he tries smoking opium, he's not overwhelmed. It's a bad drug, he's heard a lot about how it ruins lives and ruined a country (or helped it along its way to ruin, but that isn't much better). And yet, all he feels is … mellow. Good. Comfortable. All right.*

*That's it, he asks, leaning over and looking at his friend. That's all?*

*That's all, his friend says. It's good.*

*He can't disagree with that. Opium isn't a scary drug; it's sooth-ing. It doesn't make him want for things, or put himself in danger, or have visions and bad dreams; it doesn't scare him or lure him into believing he's fine when he isn't, it just calms him. That's all. And the next day when he wakes up for work he doesn't hurt as much — it's not like that one time he got drunk and couldn't walk straight the following morning — all he feels is okay.*

*And "okay" is better than "normal."*

*It isn't even that expensive, really. Just a few cents here and there, he still has enough of his daily pay left over to buy food and supplies and to save a bit of money. And what else is there for him to do? He has to work hard, for the sake of his son. He never touches alcohol these days. Hasn't even thought about it for a long while. Opium, though, opium is all right.*

*He works better on opium, rather than worse. He doesn't feel sad, doesn't feel tired, doesn't hate his life, he's okay. He can wake up in the morning and go to work, he can come back and smoke opium and tell himself that he can get up the following morning. He can smoke opium and go to work and come back and smoke opium and he's okay. He can love his son, and opium, he can live like this —*

*And he's okay.*

*Then the few cents worth of opium isn't working anymore, and he needs money, but it's no problem. It's no problem at all. He can afford this. It isn't that much of an increase, not yet. It will be, in another two months, another three months, but not yet, and when it increases then it's not going to be that much of an increase com-pared to what he would be paying by then. It's not much.*

*He's just a normal man, anyway, no wife, one child, enough money, some savings, and maybe he has to dip into them now and then but it's fine if he has opium, everything's fine, he thinks.*

*Everything's fine, he says, when his son asks him how things are. Don't worry.*

*We're okay.*

◆

The thing about the past is this: no one is really special, unless someone makes them out to be.

At the very start of 1921, a man murders another man over a pot of curry. The case is notable for the detailed investigation that went into it, all of which was recorded in the Coroner's report on the man's death. It's very exciting. It has all the elements of a good tragedy. People coming to Singapore to work, the struggles they face in their lives, the hopes and dreams they had and all of that shattered by a senseless, reckless act of violence.

The thing is, that's it.

Looking over the reports and cross referencing them to several other sources reveals a few things. The first is that there isn't mention of it in any of the papers. It's very exciting, but at the time no one wants to read about it, or wants to read about it enough that anyone else would want to write about it.

No one is even sure how old the victim is, or how his name should be written. No one is entirely sure whether the murderer was drunk at the time or not or whether or not it mattered. Time passes, and all that remains is the crime and the records.

It's a good crime, as crimes go. Saucy, dramatic, tragic, exciting, but there really isn't much more if it that has been recorded since then. If Gopal (or Gobaloo or Gopaloo or Gobalu) is special in any way to anyone alive now, it's because he died in a spectacular way over a pretty stupid thing. No one can reasonably claim to know for sure what he dreamt of, or what he wanted to be, or what he hoped for, or what he loved, or if he ever loved, at all.

… Unless, of course, someone starts to lie.

◆

*Lim Oh Kee comes to Singapore in the early 1900s with nothing but a small package and the clothes on his back. In the package is everything he owns and once he steps ashore he finds friends and* contacts and societies that will help him find a job and find a home. *The process isn't easy, but he works hard, he makes friends, he survives. Some years pass, and he finds love, he has a wife, he has a son. He's happy.*

*Lim Oh Kee comes to Singapore in the late 1900s with some money and a letter in his pocket that he can't read. He knows what it says, though, it's an introduction. He's supposed to pass it to a person his family knows and they'll help him find a job and find a home. After a long while, during which he's young and foolish and does stupid things and makes up for them, he finds love, he has a wife, he has a son. He's happy.*

*Lim Oh Kee is born in Singapore in the mid-1880s into a moderately well off family. His parents are merchants. They have him as their son and they're happy. He knows the basics of reading and writing. When he's young, one of his uncles dies, then his father dies, then his cousin dies. The family is bankrupted by the expense, and his mother takes him and leaves. He struggles to support her, then, when she dies, he struggles to support himself. Eventually, he forgets everything he learned, remembering the past only in vague terms. Eventually, he finds a new home, a new life, a new job. He even has a wife and a son of his own. He's happy.*

*Lim Oh Kee is …*

*Dead, and it's sometime in December in 1921.*

*That's about all anyone can be sure of.*

*It doesn't matter how his story starts. This is how it ends.*

♦

Lim Oh Kee isn't special.

He could have any one of a dozen different origin stories, each of them dramatic in their own way. It's hard to say which would work best for the sake of plot.

Maybe he's the Struggling Independent Coolie who Dreamed of a Better Life, or the Bearer of his Family's Dreams who Dies Alone, or even the Tragic Once Rich Son who on His Deathbed

Thinks About Everything He Could Have Been. The last one is definitely the most dramatic, the first the most tragic, and the second the most bittersweet.

None of that is ever recorded.

The only facts about Lim Oh Kee's life that are known for sure is that he was forty-five years old when he died, had a son, was starving, and hung himself by tying a cord around his neck then tying that to the door of a house on the five foot way where he slept. He was sick when he died, and starving. He had a friend called Guan Chuan who offered to let him stay with him, but refused because he was too ashamed — or so his son says. He worked as a coolie, when he was still healthy. He had a wife, but she died some years before he did.

We don't even know if he was ever happy at any time ever. I just made that bit up.

I like to think he might have been, once. It makes for a better story, for him to have been happy once and then to lose it all. If his whole life had been miserable, that would just have been a bore to read through. A societal tragedy; not a personal one.

But everything about him here was made up (right down to the opium addiction). It's not real, but here's the thing: it could have been. For some people, it was. Maybe not the part where he was married, or had a son, but maybe the part where he had a friend whose help he turned down. Or maybe not that part, but the part where he faced the choice between food and shelter. Or even the part where he had to plan his own death and genuinely thought that it was the right choice.

Lim Oh Kee isn't special as himself. As someone who symbolizes destitution and poverty, though, he does a decent job, but lots of other people and lots of other stories would do good jobs at that, too. His story doesn't even have to be set in 1921. Lim Oh Kee could be thirty, in America, in 2012; he could be twenty, in Singapore, in 1980; he could be fifty, in London, in 1840.

But as himself? He's a man whose last words to his son were "Tomorrow you will find me gone."

So here's the real story of December 12, 1921.

*The weather is (more likely than not) rainy. It's the monsoon season, after all, so people who sleep out on the streets are miserable. Early in the morning, people are struggling with questions of identity and nation, furiously writing down their thoughts. In some places, they're waking up before 6:00 a.m. to head out to get to today's work, which is exactly like yesterday's work, which is exactly like the day before yesterday's work. A man starts on his real breakfast, which is not the same as his morning tea or his tiffin lunch.*

*As the day rolls on into afternoon, newspapers are sold for five cents and ten cents to a small group of readers who are automatically set apart from the vast majority of people for the sheer fact that they're buying newspapers. A woman heads to the market to buy food for her family and then instructs her Cookie on what to prepare and how exactly to do it. As the day rolls on into evening, another man tries opium for the first time, and feels good. A movie theatre puts on the latest show, preceded by a few minutes of newsreels. Hawkers pack up their stalls and head home, if they have homes, and to their families, if they have families.*

*And Lim Oh Kee looks at the cord in his hands, ties it to a doorframe, and decides to kill himself.*

## YU-MEI BALASINGAMCHOW
# Grandmother

Hui Yen's grandmother was smoking again. She wasn't supposed to, for the usual health reasons, but she had told the doctors that she had been smoking for most of her life and wasn't about to stop now. Hui Yen's mother didn't like the smell of cigarettes in the flat, so her grandmother smoked at the bus stop downstairs. She sat perched on the edge of a dull grey plastic seat, one leg elegantly crossed over the other despite her age and her weakened, thinned-out limbs, puffing languorously on her cigarette as if drawing every last gasp of flavour from it. She cut a cryptic figure in the neighbourhood, with her salt-and-pepper ringlets of tightly curled hair, her out-of-fashion *samfoo*-style pantsuits in a discreet dark green or dark blue print, and her soft black canvas shoes, the kind more likely to be worn by a kung fu master in an old Hong Kong movie than a wiry, sun-faded woman in a sleepy, sallow Singapore housing estate. The only splash of colour on her was the crimson packet of cigarettes, clutched in one hand with a rumpled handkerchief.

It was against the law to smoke at the bus stop. Hui Yen knew this from assembly talks in school, when cheerful policemen in stiff, sweaty uniforms warned them about the dangers of smoking and dutifully listed all the public areas where smoking was banned.

Hui Yen didn't know if anyone, policeman or otherwise, had ever tried to reprimand her grandmother for smoking at the bus stop. Probably not, given the crinkled, sour expression her grandmother typically lapsed into when she was by herself. It was the same expression that had intimidated Hui Yen into petrified silence whenever she visited her grandmother as a child, back when her grandmother still lived on her own, in a little flat in Chinatown.

Hui Yen was fourteen now, old enough not to be so easily spooked by her grandmother, and also old enough to know that the way the ends of her grandmother's lips disappeared in that downward twist, the deeply etched arches of skin that appeared between her nose and her mouth, merely meant that her grandmother was preoccupied with her own thoughts. "Ah Ma is used to living alone," her mother had told Hui Yen when her grandmother moved in with them. "You try not to disturb her. If she wants to be by herself, it's okay."

Hui Yen didn't often see elderly women by themselves in the housing estate. Most had grandchildren in tow, or they huddled with friends at the ground-floor "void decks" of the apartment blocks, trading in gossip or furtive games of *chap ji ki* (although it was also against the law to gamble in public areas). In comparison, Hui Yen's grandmother was alone whenever she was at the bus stop. Sometimes Hui Yen saw her there when she came straight home from school, around 2.00 p.m. Other days she was there when Hui Yen got home close to dinner time, after spending the afternoon at band practice or dawdling at the neighbourhood McDonald's outlet with her friends.

At first Hui Yen pretended not to see her. After all, her mother had said not to bother her grandmother unnecessarily. After a couple of weeks, though, as the cool of the northeast monsoon was superseded by the relentless middle-of-the-year heat, Hui Yen began to feel uneasy that her grandmother seemed to be exiling herself to the bus stop during the worst of these scorching, sweltering afternoons. One day after band practice, when Hui

Yen's white school uniform shirt was sticky with perspiration and clung greasily to her back, and her black-and-white-checked skirt felt curtain-like and dank against the back of her knees, she spotted her grandmother's lone figure at the bus stop and, instead of going upstairs to their flat, continued straight toward her.

"Ah Ma," she called.

Her grandmother turned slightly to look at her, then nodded and turned back, exhaling cigarette smoke away from Hui Yen.

Hui Yen hovered uncertainly, shifting her weight from one foot to the other. "Ah Ma, you always come here to smoke, right?"

Her grandmother glanced over again. "You always watching me, *issit*?"

"No, no, no, I just meant ..." Hui Yen slid her thumbs under the straps of the backpack that drooped limply against her sweaty back. "Ah Ma, if you smoke at home in the afternoon, Mummy won't know. By the time she comes home, the smell will be gone already."

"Telling me how to bluff your mother *ah*?" Her grandmother's quizzical expression deepened.

Hui Yen shrugged one shoulder awkwardly. "Not really ... but it's very hot and you sit at the bus stop so long. It's cooler upstairs in the flat. Can turn on the fan also, blow away the smoke."

Her grandmother took another drag on the cigarette and when she blew out the smoke, it surged forward in an enthusiastic, ephemeral tangle. "You very clever to think of these things. Just like your father."

Hui Yen felt a tingle along the side of her neck, as if a bead of perspiration had just snaked down from her hair to her collarbone. Her father, Ah Ma's son, long vanished from their lives, whose face she knew more from photographs than from memories. Her mother kept the photographs in a battered biscuit tin and had solemnly passed the tin to her a few years ago, telling Hui Yen to keep them, look at them, do whatever she wanted with them — but don't ask any questions. That her father was her grandmother's son seemed improbable — this short, taut, serious woman, that loose-limbed, athletic-looking man in the photographs. In the decade since he had disappeared, Hui Yen had gotten so used to not asking any questions about him that she didn't know how to respond to her grandmother now. She let the silence drag out between them, like the years that stretched between the present moment and the last time she had seen her father, when he and her mother had dropped her off at the childcare centre before they went to work.

Her grandmother didn't speak either, until she finished her cigarette and flicked the butt onto the ground. "I stay in your mum's flat. I'm only a guest," she said to Hui Yen as she stood up. "Mustn't make life difficult for her."

"Okay, but I won't tell her anything," Hui Yen volunteered as they headed toward their block. "I didn't tell her I saw you smoking before."

Her grandmother looked bemused again. "*Wah*, what other secrets are you keeping from your mum?"

"Don't have *lah*, Ah Ma," Hui Yen said impishly. "I help other people keep secrets only."

◆

Hui Yen's grandmother had come to live with them after she slipped and fell at home and broke her left leg. Once her injury had been set in a cast, the hospital wanted to discharge her but insisted that she couldn't be allowed to live alone. At first Hui Yen thought this meant her grandmother would live with Auntie Ruth, her grandmother's only other child, who had studied business, met and married a doctor, and now lived in a grand house in Bukit Timah with three children, two maids, and a Siberian husky. But after a few hurried phone conversations between Hui Yen's mother and Auntie Ruth, Hui Yen's mother said Ah Ma would come to live with them in Bedok instead. "Auntie Ruth has too much to manage already," was all she gave Hui Yen by way of explanation.

"Then Ah Ma's flat in Chinatown — how?"

"Your auntie will rent it out. We have to help your grandmother pack and move her things here. With the crutches, it'll be quite difficult for her to move around for a few months."

Hui Yen, who liked her grandmother well enough for someone she saw only at Chinese New Year and her birthday, thought that having her grandmother live with them meant that there would always be someone to talk to when she got home from school. She was growing into the kind of teenager who enjoyed jabbering away with her friends for hours or prattling with her mother on weekends when she wasn't worn out from her secretarial job at the bank. But her grandmother stumped her with silence. Unlike her mother, her grandmother didn't seem very interested in what Hui Yen did in school, what instrument she played in the band, or what she was doing with her friends over the weekend. Her grandmother was so quiet that Hui Yen barely even knew if she was home unless she heard, in the first month, the tap and rattle of her crutches and, subsequently, the sounds of chopping and cooking in the kitchen (her grandmother, without being asked, had started cooking all their meals once her leg had recovered, relieving Hui Yen's mother of having to buy dinner after work). After a few months of this, Hui Yen hazarded to ask her mother if her father had been like that too, reticent and keeping to himself. Her mother only shook her head, then made an excuse to leave the room, looking as if she had been about to cry.

The other telltale sign of her grandmother's presence that first month was the whiff of cigarette smoke. Hui Yen caught it several times, usually drifting out of her grandmother's room, until her mother said something over dinner about how the smoke made her throat itch and she didn't want the smell to get into the curtains or the mattress. After that, Hui Yen thought her grandmother had stopped smoking altogether — until she started seeing her at the bus stop.

The bus stop was deserted most afternoons, when it was too hot to go anywhere, too hot to think. Once every ten or fifteen minutes, the lone bus service that plied this road appeared, discharging a hodgepodge of passengers who dispersed almost as suddenly as they arrived, shrinking like frenzied ants into the expansive shade of the surrounding blocks of flats. Mostly, her grandmother had the place to herself.

The next time she saw her grandmother there, Hui Yen was with her classmate Prem, who lived nearby, and they were nursing ice-cold bubble tea drinks. After saying goodbye to him, Hui Yen drifted toward the bus stop, slurping loudly from her plastic cup. "Ah Ma," she hailed, "you got try bubble tea before?"

Her grandmother had just lit a cigarette and waved it to decline Hui Yen's offer. "All the drinks nowadays, too sweet."

"Nice what." Hui Yen slid onto the bus stop bench beside her grandmother.

Her grandmother smoked silently, silkily. Eventually she said, "Just now, that boy, is your good friend, right?"

Hui Yen was surprised that her grandmother had noticed. "Friend *lor*. We're in the same class since last year. Sec One." She didn't have the words to explain her friendship with Prem, how she found him so easy to talk to, how they found the same things hilarious, how they text-messaged each other every day, all day.

"He's Indian, right?"

Hui Yen nodded.

"Last time I had an Indian good friend also, when we joined the police together. A woman *lah*." Her grandmother nudged her cigarette against the edge of the bench, letting the ash scatter to the ground. "*Donno* know what happened to her now. She became an inspector, then later assistant superintendent or something."

Hui Yen's mother had told her that her grandmother had retired from the police force around the time Hui Yen was born. Hui Yen had seen old photographs of her grandmother as a young woman wearing a stiff police uniform, a diminutive figure whose face seemed to vanish below the dark-blue peaked cap. "Were you an inspector also?" she asked.

"No *lah*," her grandmother said dismissively. "No proper education, how to become inspector?"

She lapsed into silence again, puffing on her cigarette intermittently. A single tendril of smoke meandered up from it.

Hui Yen pondered what was left of her drink. She wanted to make it last and lowered the plastic cup to her lap, cradling it with both hands. "Ah Ma, why did you join the police?"

"Needed to earn money, after your grandfather died," her grandmother said matter-of-factly. "I had to take care of your father and your auntie by myself."

Hui Yen had heard her mother say as much and she felt reassured that the stories lined up. "But you can do a lot of different jobs what. How come you decided to join the police?"

Her grandmother snorted. "Cannot study, cannot do office work. Police work I thought: the money is not bad, not so much funny business for a woman, and I already know how to fight. Last time I got three older brothers in Malaysia, you know — of course I know how to fight."

While Hui Yen knew that her grandmother, like her mother's family, had been born in Malaysia, she had never given much thought to what other families they had come from, belonged to — left behind. She imagined the small, faceless woman in the dark-blue uniform brandishing her fists or a gun, barking down cartoonish men twice, three times her size. "You really used to fight? Fight with the criminals?"

"Not fight because want to fight," her grandmother corrected. "It's my job, *unnerstand*?"

Hui Yen had seen lots of police dramas on TV, American cop shows with wisecracking characters and convoluted plot twists, and extravagant Hong Kong or Singapore series that alternated between solving horrendous crimes and resolving contorted questions about loyalty, morality, and duty. "Ah Ma," she began, then pulled up her thoughts in a halt.

It was her grandmother's turn to prompt her. "What you want to ask?"

Hui Yen rotated her cup in her hands, the tepid plastic crackling with every twist. "Ah Ma," she tried again, "did you ever kill anybody before?"

Her grandmother didn't answer for a long while. A bus pulled up and a few passengers got off. Hui Yen thought the bus driver was frowning at her grandmother with her cigarette, but he drove off without comment. To fill the silence, Hui Yen sucked up the last mouthful of her drink and got up to throw the cup into the bin. Then she didn't know whether or not to sit down.

"Hui Yen." Her grandmother patted the space on the bench beside her, as if Hui Yen were a little girl again.

Hui Yen sat obligingly, her schoolbag slumping heavily against her back.

Her grandmother took a drag on her cigarette, the smoke she exhaled clouding her face before she spoke. "Hui Yen, some things we can tell you now. Some things, not yet *lah*." She sounded, uncharacteristically, like Hui Yen's mother, laying down some unconvincing boundary when Hui Yen asked if she could go to a midnight movie with her friends or buy a slinky tank top or a pair of impossibly high heels.

Her grandmother went on, "Doing police work, I got kill people before. Because if I didn't kill them, they will kill me. Last time all the gangsters, you know, not scared of police one. So sometimes, no choice ..."

Something in her grandmother's tone made Hui Yen think she should apologize for asking the question, or at least stop her grandmother from saying any more. But her grandmother seemed to have found some kind of rhythm — inhale on the cigarette, exhale away from Hui Yen, then talk.

"I never say kill a lot of people. But sometimes you have to. To protect yourself, protect other people."

Hui Yen stared at the space between her feet, clad in well-scuffed, once-white school shoes. Now that she had the answer to her question, she didn't know what to think of her grandmother. *She's killed people before,* she thought and snuck a glance at her grandmother's rough, bony hands, one clutching the cigarette, the other resting inert in her lap. *She took a gun or a baton or something, and she ...*

"I try not to think about it too much," her grandmother said, raising her cigarette to her lips and just holding it there. "But sometimes I ask forgiveness from God *lah*, Guan Yin *lah*, whatever god — sorry that I had to take away a life."

Abruptly, Hui Yen asked, "Do you think my father is dead? Do you think someone killed him?"

Her grandmother lowered her cigarette without having taken a drag, holding it with her arms folded. It would have been an imperious gesture, if not for the softening crow's feet around her eyes, the gentle droop at the edges of her lips. "Why you ask this kind of thing?"

Hui Yen shrugged. "Nobody knows what happened to him what. So many possible reasons." She had discussed numerous permutations with Prem, usually after they had compared notes on the latest episode of some crime show on TV. Prem had a more vivid imagination and dreamed up scenarios in which Hui Yen's father was leading a dramatic, glamorous but secret life somewhere; Hui Yen leaned toward the more straightforward possibilities. She went on casually, "If he's dead, maybe it was an accident, or maybe someone killed him."

"You think so?"

"Ah Ma, I know you retired from police a long time already, but when my father disappeared, did you ask your friends in the police to help find him?"

Her grandmother resumed smoking; her cigarette was almost burned down to the end. "Ya, I tried to ask for help. But a lot of the people I knew, they retired from police around the same time as me."

Hui Yen nodded. "So weird — that someone can just disappear like that."

"Not that difficult," her grandmother mused. "Last time, if you know how, you can get over to Malaysia without passport. Anyway, your father was always quite playful, like to *kaypoh*. Not only a busybody about other people's affairs, but like to get involved also. Lucky your mother is very different."

"She is?"

"Anyway, if your father is here, *donno* whether he will let me live with you all or not," her grandmother said, then took one last drag on her smouldering cigarette.

◆

Hui Yen wanted to pick up the conversation when they were at home, to find out more about what her father had been like, and what could have become of him. But it was harder to find an opportunity to talk to her grandmother in the flat. Hui Yen offered to help her cook dinner, but she declined, telling Hui Yen she should be doing her homework. At other times her grandmother bustled purposefully about her room, and even though her door was always open, to Hui Yen it felt like a threshold that she couldn't cross unless she was invited. At nights and on weekends, her mother was at home, which made it difficult to have a private conversation in their compact flat.

The next few times Hui Yen saw her grandmother at the bus stop, she happened to be with Prem and preferred to linger with him in the cooler air of the void deck at the foot of her block, while they recounted something funny that had happened in class that day, or listened to music on his smartphone to see if she liked the same songs he did. He was one of the few friends she had who was always where he said he would be, whether it was waiting for her in the canteen after school, going to the library to work on a school project, or meeting their friends at the cinema on the weekends. Hui Yen liked to test him sometimes, text-messaging to ask where he was in school or at the town centre, then walking over to see for herself that he was there.

Prem couldn't fathom that Hui Yen didn't have to go up and greet her grandmother every time they saw her at the bus stop. He lived with his parents, two brothers, grandparents, and an aunt, all in a flat only slightly larger than Hui Yen's. He was used to having family members around all the time, at home and in the neighbourhood. "If that's my grandmother and I don't say hello and then she sees me," he said one afternoon as they loitered at her block, "I'll *really* get it from her when I reach home."

Hui Yen toyed with the straps of her backpack. "My grandma's quite relaxed about these things *lah*."

"Ya, okay, your grandma *is* quite cool. Smoking at the bus stop some more," Prem added admiringly.

Something in his tone made Hui Yen consider her grandmother anew. She chatted with Prem until he had to leave for a tuition class, then went over to join her.

"Ah Ma," she greeted. It had been several weeks since the last thunderstorm and there was a kind of unremitting hostility in the air, as if it would never rain again.

"Talking so long at the void deck *ah*," her grandmother said.

Hui Yen wasn't sure what to make of that. "A while only."

"Is he your boyfriend?"

Hui Yen was flummoxed. "No *lah*, Ah Ma — friends only."

"You two always talking. But he looks all right, not the trouble-maker kind."

Hui Yen tried to redirect the conversation. "Prem said your smoking is quite cool."

"Cool," her grandmother repeated, as if she was unsure what the word meant. She held her cigarette lazily, with all the loose confidence of someone who had been smoking for most of her life.

"Ah Ma, how old were you when you learned how to smoke?"

Her grandmother shrugged, her slender shoulders twitching quickly. "Last time everybody smoked. Never think about what age."

Hui Yen demurred, "Can I try?"

"You want to try smoking?"

Hui Yen tried to downplay it. "A lot of people in school smoke also, but I never try before." She didn't mention that her mother had expressly forbidden it several years ago.

To her surprise, her grandmother handed the cigarette over, just like that. It was Hui Yen who was left fumbling, her thumb and forefinger arched in unfamiliar positions as she took hold of the cigarette. "Just … breathe in?"

Her grandmother nodded. "Inhale. Sure cough one. But never mind, just try."

Hui Yen gingerly edged the cigarette to her lips and sucked on it as if she were sucking up the last drop of bubble tea from a cup. The acrid sensation that coursed through her mouth and snaked down her throat made her gasp, cough, and shiver. She blinked furiously, seeing her grandmother watch her intently. When her paroxysm passed, her grandmother said, "Can try again if you want. First time is the worst, or the first time after you never smoke for a while, like after I stayed in hospital."

Hui Yen's tongue tasted thickly of charred carbon and nicotine. Instinctively she wanted to hand the cigarette back, but there was also something oddly reassuring about the foreign sensations in her mouth — a promise of new flavours and undreamt-of revelations to come. Without thinking further, she inhaled again, very quickly, from the cigarette. It burned again, but not as much as before, she told herself.

Her grandmother admitted a small smile. "Like it already *ah*?"

Hui Yen swallowed, tasting to the full extent the stinging warmth before it flickered down her throat. She attempted a few more puffs, in between a few stuttering coughs, then returned the cigarette to her grandmother.

"Do you feel sick?"

Hui Yen shook her head, though her throat was still scratchy.

"If you don't feel well later, you tell me. Better not let your mother know."

"Of course not!"

"And don't get into trouble in school with any smoking *ah*. You go to school to study, not to learn this kind of thing."

"Learn from you, Ah Ma," Hui Yen teased.

Her grandmother snorted. "I got nothing to teach you *lah*."

"Got," Hui Yen said readily. "Maybe about my father?"

Her grandmother had reassumed the straight-backed, seated posture she favoured while smoking. As she raised the cigarette to her weathered lips, the crook of her wrist stiffened and when she spoke, she sounded disapproving. "You — really always thinking about your father."

Hui Yen plunged ahead. "I just want to know something, anything. How can there be no information at all, not even stories or rumours?"

"Of course got rumours, but ..."

"What rumours, Ah Ma?"

Her grandmother looked away from her, exhaling cigarette smoke, which bloomed and wilted rhythmically in front of her face. Finally she said, "There are some stories I heard, I didn't tell your mother or your Auntie Ruth."

Hui Yen perked up.

"I heard your father was in Ipoh, so I went there to check. Some people told me he got mixed up in some funny business with gangsters, from Singapore all the way to Malaysia. But hard to get information, you know, this kind of underworld thing."

"Did you see him?"

"No," her grandmother said, too quickly. She looked squarely at Hui Yen. "I'm telling you this because I *dowan* you to think he will come back, or that he's having a good life somewhere."

"But you also *donno* what," Hui Yen pointed out. "You said yourself, this is just a rumour. Maybe he figured a way out ..."

"No," her grandmother cut her off, "this kind of gangster thing, it's very complicated. Your father is *not* coming back." She closed her eyes, as if the heat and the words had all been too much for her.

"Ah Ma, what did you see? How do you know?"

"I didn't see your father," her grandmother began, a line both reassuring and well-rehearsed. "I saw a lot of things, cannot tell you. Things were very messy up there, very difficult to know who you can trust."

Hui Yen waited.

"I didn't see him," her grandmother repeated, as if trying to convince herself, "but I saw enough to know what I had to ... what happened to him." She opened her eyes, her gaze sterner now. "He's dead, okay? Just like the other day, what you said."

Hui Yen felt cheated, yet again, of a fuller answer. It was no better than her mother telling her, when she was in primary school, that her father had gone away "just for a while," or changing the television channel whenever a *Crimewatch* episode about missing persons came on. "But how do you *know*?" Hui Yen insisted.

"He's dead," her grandmother intoned. "I got no evidence to show you or to report to the Singapore police, but I know what I had to ... I know what I saw. He died already."

Something in her leaden tone and hardened posture made Hui Yen hold back further protests and questions. There was a firm religious conviction underlying her grandmother's words, more resolute than her usual stubborn independence — a certainty of knowledge that opened a world of stories and sealed them shut all at once.

They sat together in the shade of the bus stop, her grandmother smoking steadily to the end of her cigarette, Hui Yen wishing that she could lean against something, anything for support. She now knew more than her mother did, it seemed, but it felt like less than she had known before. One mystery unfolded into another, while her father became a more inscrutable figure than ever.

She would talk it over with Prem. Maybe Prem would figure it out — or at least come up with a good story for it. She would text him as soon as she got home. She knew he would answer, as soon his tuition class was over.

Hui Yen slid off the bus stop bench. "Ah Ma?"

"Hmmm?"

"Will you tell me everything one day? When I'm grown up."

"I *donno*." Her grandmother tossed her cigarette butt onto the ground, as usual. "It won't really matter what age you are. I cannot ..." She let the sentence trail off.

Hui Yen knelt to retrieve the cigarette butt and threw it into the bin. "Cannot anyhow litter, Ah Ma."

"Ya, okay." Her grandmother got to her feet, straightening her *samfoo*. "Nowadays everything also must do properly, follow the law. Not like last time."

"Ah Ma, you always break the law. Throw things here, smoking at the bus stop ..."

Her grandmother waved her hand dismissively, the bright red of her cigarette pack flashing like a warning sign. "Must know the law, then you know how to go around it."

"Just *dowan* you to get in trouble."

Her grandmother clasped her free hand on Hui Yen's shoulder as they started to walk toward their block of flats. "You don't worry. I managed to avoid trouble for many years already."

## HAZEL D. CAMPBELL

# Devil Star

It was the first of times. It was the last of times. It was even the first time at last; and some were saying, "Cho! Jamaica nuh sweet again." There was looting and there was shooting. There was pillaging and there was rummaging. There was ravishing and despoiling. Some wined and dined; some could only lick their lips and pine. Some dipped their fingers in voting ink; blood-red, not blue. Some dipped themselves in healing streams which had no power to "put it back." It was deejay time. It was dance hall time. It was slack lyrics time. It was mayhem, noise, and corruption time for it seemed that Satan himself (herself?) had taken up permanent residence in shack, shanty, concrete nog, and high rise.

In hard times, the Church prospers more than Satan, for the sinful can easily be convinced that they're being punished for sins of commission and omission; so the church benches full-up on Sundays and the balm yards pack-up on Tuesday nights for some think that if they pray loud enough or shout loud enough or trump hard enough or get the right set of tongues to communicate to the unknown, something bound to break the drought, the famine, the bad luck, hard times, and the waywardness — all of which, as we know, worse than any obeah.

◆

Devil Star had received Devil of the Month award, again — eleven times in a row. Now, all he needed was to bring home to hell another ninety and nine souls to win the coveted Devil of the Year award. He scanned the globe and shook his head. There were so many places ripe for picking; so many places in which he could find the required ninety-nine in a moment of time that he yawned in boredom.

Eventually, he spun the globe, having decided that wherever his finger pointed when "eeny, meeny, miney, mo" ran out would be the chosen spot. The last "mo" found his finger pointing at Jamaica.

"*Aahh!*" he exclaimed. "Wicked! Wicked! Nice warm place with a lot of sinners." He wiggled his hips and grinned. "Piece a cake!"

He practised a few steps of the popular old Bogle and Gully Creeper moves, and made Usain Bolt's "To the World" gesture before his full-length mirror. "Unoo see me, though? Cho!" He giggled.

"Let me see," he said, as he examined his reflection. "I don't want to be conspicuous, so ..." He snapped his fingers once and looked at his mirror image. He was dressed as a devil.

"Naw," he said. "Them don't have Halloween, and is not Jonkunnu time yet. And this little too realistic, even for Jonkunnu."

He snapped his fingers twice and looked at himself dressed in a business suit. "Eenh-no! Them wi run me. Too much chickeeny business going on up there."

He snapped his fingers three times. "*Ahhh!*" he said with great satisfaction. "Ah bad! Ah bad. Ah reely, reely ba-a-ad!"

He turned and twisted, admiring himself more with each move. The hem of his baggy jeans rested on the top of his luxury priced sneakers. The waist rested comfortably on his hips exposing the top of his multi-coloured boxer shorts. He was wearing a short, bright-green merino under a long orange fishnet vest. A gold chain of the cargo variety hung from his neck.

He patted his head, very pleased with the haircut, a fringe of a blonde topknot with the very closely shaved sides etched with the inscription "devil star."

"Whee whoo!" he whistled to himself. "Mi own modder woulden know me. See how me trash an' irie. Me is the Don of dons. Me a tek life, mon!"

◆

A streak of lightning hit earth and the loud thunderclap awakened those still asleep in their foreday morning beds.

"Lord! Please don't let it rain," Mother Cassie prayed. She was in charge of food and drink for the group gathered in the square waiting for the bus which would transport them to a Portland beach for the day's outing.

Elder had decided to top off a very successful week's membership recruiting campaign with an outing which would provide both worship and relaxation for his fledgling flock.

Elder believed that the best way to worship was to be out of doors. He was already regretting the time when the church would be able to put up a building and stop meeting under the tent. He liked the exposure to the stark reminders of God's power, like the intense clap of thunder which had just caused people to huddle together in fear and exclaim, "Lord! Have mercy!"

The outing was also a fund-raising event. At one thousand dollars a head, food and drink provided, it wasn't a bad deal for city dwellers starved of healthy entertainment. So good a deal that many who had no intention of joining Elder's church had paid their money and were anxious to be off.

Mother Cassie was worried. She had provided food and drink, with a little to spare, for seventy people, the number the bus could comfortably hold. However, motherly soul that she was, she wondered if there would be enough food for everyone. "Sea breeze have a way to mek people hungry," she fretted.

Shortly after the thunderclap, a group of some twenty or more people suddenly turned up in the square. They were coming directly from their Friday night session, gloriously bedecked in all their dance-hall finery — underwear turned outerwear, indeed almost "no-wear" for some. Colourful costumes matched even more colourful hair, curled and crimped and gnarled by wondrously skilled stylists.

"Hail, Sista! Dis a de tent church outing?"

"Yes?" Elder replied, before the sister addressed could answer. He suddenly sensed trouble.

"We a come wid you. Whey de @%#** (expletive deleted) bus? We tiad. Up all night a dance. We ave fi ketch a shut eye pan de way."

"I don't understand," Elder said sternly. "This is a church outing."

"Hmn -hmn. Me know. We pay we money. See de ticket dem ya. Sista Webb sell we ..."

Sister Webb, who was in charge of ticket sales, came forward reluctantly.

"Eld ... Elder, de bus did have more space, an we did need more money fi make a profit, an some a de people say since we a PNP dem not coming and mi brother say him an him fren dem did in ... interested, an dem pay dem money an ..."

"Sister Webb!" Elder raised his voice. He was truly astounded. "We? PNP? What kind a nonsense is that? We don't belong to any political party! We are God's people! That's the only party we know!"

Sister Webb looked duly chastened. "*Me* know dat, Elder, but ..."

"You sold tickets to these people?" He made it sound as if she had invited faecal matter, called doo-du in Jamaica.

But before he could say anything more the bus arrived with a great noise of grinding gears and air-assisted braking.

"Raaay!" The dance hall group shouted as they noisily boarded the bus ahead of the church people. Elder turned his head away from the sight of the women's posteriors, skimpily encased in their "batty riders," saucily mocking him as their owners boarded the bus. There was nothing he could do now. Sister Cassie was in a state of great confusion. With the driver, she would now have to feed — she counted quickly, more than ninety people — she would need a miracle. She didn't have that much food.

The last dance-haller to board the bus grinned broadly at her. She glared back at him and frowned at his back. His head had something written on it, but in the light of the early dawn she couldn't clearly read what it said.

◆

Elder prayed silently that the day would soon end. What a day it had been!

First, many of the church people had to stand in the bus since the dance-hallers took all the seats they needed. As the journey progressed, when those standing got tired, they started cotching three to a seat or sitting on the floor. To elder's distress, instead of the sober hymn-singing outing he had imagined, there was much hilarity and chatter as the bus swayed around the corners of the often winding, narrow road, throwing the passengers against one another. He tried to raise a hymn, but nobody but a few older sisters took him on, and the dance-hallers grumbled because some of them wanted to sleep despite the overcrowded situation. Elder's seat was on the side that gave him a clear view of the steep precipice beside the road. Instead of singing, he began to pray for safety.

Then, he had hoped that once they reached their destination the dancehall group would have gone their way and left him in peace, until it was time to go home. Or (and this was a very private prayer for he didn't want to look foolish if the prayer wasn't answered), that somehow he and his group would be able to win even a few of them to salvation.

Not so. First, it was a secluded beach with no nearby entertainment. The dance-hallers therefore proceeded to provide their own fun with loud, sometimes competing music from their electronic devices. Bluetooth amplification reigned.

Sister Webb had an old-time boom box on which she tried to outplay them with gospel music cassettes, but she could not compete with the temptation of dance hall volume and slackness.

Then, in an effort to protect his flock from temptation, Elder led them away from the sinners onto a little hillock overlooking the beach. There they tried to spend time in meditation and worship. In the midst of Brother Max's very loud prayer, however, some young people began to giggle. The giggling soon developed into the kind of laughter that gets more uncontrollable in the face of disapproval. In vain did the sisters screw up their faces trying to silence the young ones. Indeed, when they themselves identified the source of the laughter, they had to press their mouths shut to prevent any sign of mirth from showing.

Elder stopped the prayer and gave the youngsters a severe lecture, but the more he talked, the more they laughed, and when he, in turn, discovered the source of their mirth, he was momentarily at a loss for words.

On the beach below them, the dance-hallers had decided to go for a swim. The cause of the laughter was a gloriously fat mama rolling slowly toward the water. Layers of fatty folds jiggled around what seemed to be a naked body.

Elder was outraged. He rushed down the hillside and accosted the woman.

"Lady," he began, "this is a church outing. We are decent, God-fearing people. We cannot have this kind of wanton behaviour in our midst. What will people think? I rebuke you! You'll have to go elsewhere with your indecent exposure."

Fatty stared at him in amazement.

"Ah who you a chat to? Me?" she asked. "Hindestant exposure! You no see me well cover up inna me bikini?" She lifted a fold of flesh to reveal a bikini bottom stretched so tight it provided little covering for the main point of interest. When she released the fold you couldn't see anything but flesh. Likewise, the bra was a string enclosed by fat with two petals barely covering her nipples. No wonder the church people had thought she was naked.

"But, anybody ever see my dying trial?" Fatty continued, arms akimbo. "A mussi wife you a look!" She was now fully incensed.

Her voice grew louder with each phrase and the fatty folds shook with indignation. "No bodder wid me. Me like me man dem look like man! Me nuh romp wid mirasme baby!"

Laughter washed the beach. Elder's face burned. Fortunately, his flock could not hear the exchange. He ground his teeth in frustration. This was enough provocation to make a saint start swearing.

"You coming for a swim, Parson? Tek off you clothes, nuh. Fatty want fi see what you have underneath."

"Yeah, Preach. Show we you stuff."

Elder fled.

The outrageous behaviour continued all day. Although the older church members tried their best to keep the groups apart, by late afternoon, some of the younger flock had drawn closer and closer to the dance-hallers. A few had even entered a very wild impromptu dance contest. When Elder saw the wining of the almost bare bottoms and the suggestive dance moves, he turned aside to pray even harder.

There were other problems, too. Having paid their money, the dance-hallers felt it was their right to eat as much as they wanted. They devoured most of the food and the church group had to be satisfied with very small portions. Tempers simmered. All manner of sinful things continued to happen. Smoke from cigarettes and weed floated in air already sweetened with the smell of rum. And it wasn't only the fried chicken and rice and peas which made Brother Joe smack his lips from time to time. Quarrels erupted and near-fights were barely pacified.

Finally, at five o'clock when Elder declared that it was time to leave for home, the bus wouldn't start and they had to wait for hours while the driver and two dance-hallers who were mechanics tried to fix the fault. Sister Cassie had to dip into the profits and send to a nearby district to buy bread and tins of bully beef and soft drinks to feed her charges.

"It's like Satan himself in our midst today," Elder told his people as they waited. "Pray that nothing worse happens!"

And strolling casually past him with a wide grin was a man he hadn't noticed before. He winked at Elder, who shuddered without knowing why. "Pray!" he repeated softly. "Pray hard!"

◆

It was past eleven o'clock before they could leave. The mechanics could find no reason why the bus wouldn't start, and just as they were about to give up, the engine had miraculously sprung to life. When they boarded the bus, Elder breathed a sigh of relief; the nightmarish day would soon end.

Two miles into the return journey, people had settled into the repose they expected to keep until they reached Kingston. Apart from their manner of dress, it was now difficult to tell the groups apart. Elder's followers were intimately mixed with dance-hallers as everyone tried to find a comfortable place. Just as before, they were sitting three in a seat meant for two; they squatted in the aisle and even sat in each other's laps, making the kind of flesh contact which Elder deplored. He knew too well where this could lead. In truth, surreptitious petting had already started.

Elder closed his eyes to say yet another prayer. He prayed that the bus would safely navigate the many steep winding places on the road and that they would reach home without any incidents. But, when he opened his eyes, he noticed the strange man with the big grin staring at him. The hair on Elder's head rose. Something was very wrong but he could not tell what it was. He looked away quickly.

Devil Star's grin grew wider and wider. It had all been so easy that he had decided to give himself an extra handicap — leading Elder's flock astray. He had until a minute before midnight to lead them to hell, thirty-five more minutes and five more souls to add to the lot on the bus. Excluding Elder, who might not succumb; that would give him his ninety-nine souls.

"Hmm-hmm," he shook his head, rejecting the immediate idea which came to him. "Too easy. I can get more fun out of this."

Just then, the bus swerved dangerously and there was a screeching of brakes. The sudden stop shook up the passengers and there was immediate consternation. Voices were raised in alarm.

"What de *&+%$# (more deleted expletives) idiot tink him a do!" the bus driver exclaimed. He dashed outside to see a car dangerously perched on the edge of the road.

"Help! Help!" Voices were screaming …

The bus quickly emptied and willing hands pulled five people from the car, which, as soon as the last person was out, seemed to rock gently and then ease itself over — almost as if someone had pushed it. There was silence among the people as they listened in awe to the crunching sound of the vehicle crashing from one rocky ledge to another on its way to the beach several metres below the road.

"Unoo fi say, tenk God!" a voice came out of the darkness.

It seemed to unleash the fury of the driver of the car. "Tenk God, mi headside!" He was almost weeping. "Mi jus buy de car an get dis job fi carry dese people go a airport. It don't even insure yet!"

"All we grip dem gone!" another voice wailed. "All the nice, nice roast breadfruit we was tekkin back!"

"But how you so fool-fool fi a try pass me pan dis lil kench a road. Me neva see unoo till de las minute. Good ting me brakes soun or else de whole a unoo would gone over."

Another little silence as they contemplated this near miss. Just the week before thirteen people had been killed in a road accident not too far away from this very spot.

"Ah mi unoo want tun inna h-accident statistics," a voice said humorously. A few people laughed but there was a general mood of sobriety and thoughtfulness as they returned to the bus. The driver had agreed to take the stranded travellers to the next town. There was no point in them standing by the roadside at that hour of the night, and there was nothing they could do about the car and luggage until morning.

Elder seized his opportunity. As they tried to settle down, he began to preach.

"We have just been delivered from a very close shave with the grim reaper," he began. "Many of us spent the day in riotous behaviour, forgetting to praise the Almighty who gives us life and health. Sometimes the Lord uses incidents like these to bring us back to the paths of righteousness." Elder felt himself growing warm as the words welled up in his mouth.

"True word! True word!" someone agreed, while others added loud *amens.*

"Preach it!" a screechy voice urged.

Elder was happy. Perhaps more good would come out of this than he had thought. All was not lost. Maybe he would return with more converts than he had left with in the morning. How many were on the bus? He did a quick check. With the additional five it must be about a hundred, he thought.

Suddenly his eye caught the grin that seemed designed to torment him. It made Elder's blood boil. He felt as if the man was challenging him. Devil Star looked down at his watch and nodded at Elder. Elder also glanced at his watch and saw that it was seven minutes to twelve. Time was running out, he thought, although he had no idea what this meant. Feeling cornered, he raised a hymn he thought suitable for the situation.

*There were ninety and nine that safely lay*
*In the shelter of the fold*
*But one was lost on the hills away*
*Far off from the gates of gold*

His followers, who had been duly chastened by the near accident, quickly took up the hymn, improvising different drawn-out harmonies around the tune.

*Away on the mountain wild and bare*
*Away from the tender shepherd's care*

Elder, with his hands clasped, did a slow rock to the rhythm, very pleased with the response.

Devil Star bent over with laughter.

Suddenly Fatty's voice broke into the song.

"Is a PNP song dat. We nuh want no PNP song in ere. Unoo hear me! Me tell unoo dem was PNP."

"My dear lady," Elder began, but Fatty was on her feet shaking off those closely packed around her. Perhaps she was still smarting from her earlier encounter with Elder and glad of another opportunity to embarrass him. She had a bottle raised menacingly in her hand. "Sing dat song an a better de whole bus did go over the cliff."

"Go way!" a voice challenged her. "What wrong wid a little Christian song?"

"Me is JLP an me no want fi hear no PNP song."

"You an who else?"

"Nuff a we a JLP. No PNP song nah sing in ere tinight!"

Someone with a sense of humour raised a new song

*Don't board de wrang train*
*Don't board de wrang train*
*De devil is the driver*
*Will take you down to hell.*

"Unoo stap de nize!" the bus driver shouted. "Unoo mek mi so confuse mi cyan even see where de bus a go!"

They ignored him. In no time at all it seemed the crowded bus had divided into two factions loyal to one or the other of the two main political parties in the country.

Quarrels were breaking out. Even Elder, beginning to lose his temper, pushed aside a drunk man who kept leaning against him. The devil had indeed taken over.

"Mek we see who is who," Fatty continued her tirade. "Stan up fi you position. Who is not fi me an de JLP is against mi." The bottle was still menacingly raised.

"Fight! Fight!" People began screaming as fists began to fly. "Stop de bus! Stop de bus!"

The driver braked and wearily placed his hands on his head as he bent over the steering wheel. He opened the bus doors, expecting the worst.

Devil Star suddenly jumped to his feet. "Drive! Drive!" he ordered in a thunderous voice. Round the next corner was the spot he had chosen for the bus to go over the precipice, thus giving him all ninety and nine cantankerous souls to take home to hell and win his prize. The driver *had* to keep going. It was almost midnight.

The bus grew silent for a moment as all eyes turned on him.

"Who you?" some of the passengers demanded as if they were seeing him for the first time, and, in the nature of crowds, glad to find a common enemy, Devil Star found himself isolated between both factions.

"Declare you han!" Fatty stood ready to pounce on him. "You a wear de two party colour, green fi JLP, orange fi PNP. State who you for, for you cyan be fi de two."

Devil Star looked around, bewildered. The grin had disappeared. He glanced at his watch, one second to midnight. They were going to spoil his plan. It had been such an easy, entertaining, perfect plan.

"State you position!" Both sides were now accosting him. "Head or bell, one or the other. Cyan be the two."

As they reached to grab him, ready to tear him apart, he disappeared in a puff of smoke. Intense heat and sulphuric vapours enveloped the bus. Surprised and panicking, the passengers tumbled out. As they stood outside coughing and trying to understand what had happened, something bright like a star seemed to streak out of nowhere and crash into the earth with a very loud thunderclap. Frightened beyond telling, many fell on their knees and began to pray.

**MAGGIE HARRIS**

# Sending for Chantal

My mother voice growing old over the telephone.

At first I thought was the line crackling, you know sometime reception ain good considering whether the voice have to travel under the sea or over the sky. Then there was also the business of her getting American. That one was a slow business. When pickney small is only so and so they does notice. Like how when Sunday come and we running up to Uncle Marcus house to hear the telephone and Granny complaining at me *slow* she say, *slow, your Granny leg ain fass like yourn.* And when we reach and the telephone ring *bringg! bringg! Bringg bringg!* and me one cyant control misself is climbing I climbing up high on Uncle Marcus kitchen stool. And when she sweet voice come tinkling down the wire like birdies singing or water down the drainpipe is the sound I holding on to and the words follow.

*Chantal!* She say, *Chantal! How's my sweetheart honeychile Mummy chocolate fudge eh?*

Sometime she so clear is like she was in the room and Granny say the first few time I drop the phone and was looking all round the house for Mummy and bust out one crying. Was like the time we puppy Smartie see he-self in the long mirror and start yapping and running behind the mirror for find the other dog.

Other time her voice ain clear at all, she sound like she shouting through the drainpipe or like the boys on the dam fishing, cupping them hand round them mouth and hollering cross the water. Uncle Marcus shake the phone then and blow down it, and put it to he ear and he face getting vex bad. He have to cut the line he say cos it na good but he don't cut it, he put it down and look at it and then it ring again after a long time when we getting fed up and then all of we jump and then laugh when Mummy voice come back on.

The other thing I remember about the first sound was happiness. Happiness come jumping through the telephone wire like sunshine running on paving stone. Mummy laughing and calling me her chocolate fudge and how she was going to eat me up and blow bubble on my belly like she used to. She even sing me song. She sing me song from movie pictures from flims she know I see, like *we off to see the wizard*. She know I see it because she send me videos. At school my fren them jealous bad when they see I have new videos that ain even in the store yet. She know all the word of them song so good Granny say is like she memorize them. And is true they sound same, same; maybe that was one of the times she start to sound American.

The thing that confuse me is this: Mummy happy voice. Because even though I happy hearing her voice dancing on the telephone line, even though Sunday was fill up with all the preparation for that, was still six other days to get through. And a day was a long long time from brekfuss to night. From morning light when other people mummy voice breaking through the jalousie to nighttime when them warning *yall come inside now before jumbie catch you.* I not happy. I want my mummy, the smell of her, the feel of her arm wrap round me even when she push me off she lap and laugh.

That day after my birthday when I was four, when I didn't realize what happening, when the house fill up with uncles and aunties and some cousins from the river and my god-sister who eye turn up funny, when car horn blow and Mummy come out her bedroom with a suitcase and heise me up and wipe ice-cream off my face with her kerchief and kiss me and squeeze me she say Chantal Mama gwine away for a lickle bit and Granny gwine look after you and Mama gwine come back soon and collect you … that day still clear clear in my mind. Before and After not so clear. Before mix up with mornings and sunshine and Granny flinging dust out with the broom. Before mix up with Mummy have the radio on and going outside with her church shoes on. Before was smelling Mummy nice talcum powder smell after she bathe. After was Granny use it up till it all gone. After was me hollering and not eating and vomiting and kicking Granny.

Was Uncle Marcus say Stop Crying! in he big man hard like rock voice. He say stop my stupidness as I nearing school time and they don't have babies there. He take me out with he in the Govment car and point out the beggars in the street. He drive past the marketplace where the women have their babies under holey parasols in the damblast midday sun while they selling one two mangoes. He drive up the country where the naked skin children playing under the stand-pipe and he akse me if I want to end up like them. Then he drive me by the seawall and buy me ice cream and tell me my Mummy working hard for send me to America.

In school was a white lady teacher. Her voice jump up and down the classroom like balloon when air fizzing out. She teaching everybody to read but some of we like me find it hard. No cat don't sit on no mat in we house. Smartie don't sleep like no log, he sleep like dead dog.

At home postman come with letters from America. Some have my name on them, I spell it out slow, with my finger. Granny read out the words inside and hearing Mummy words through Granny voice was a different experience to the telephone. She write the same things as she say about how she miss her chocolate fudge and how soon she gwine send for me. Sometime Granny slow down she voice and I feel she skipping what else Mummy say. Her lips move quiet then she say how Mummy working real hard, she have to scrub floors and lift heavy old ladies and she hardly don't get any sleep because of Beck and Call. I don't know who they is. She say how Chantal must write. She don't understand writing not for me, I prefer talk to she on a Sunday.

When I akse Granny when Mummy gon send for me she say soon soon. When I akse Mummy when she gon send for me she say soon soon.

Come a time we go to Uncle Marcus house and wait but no telephone ring. We sit down a whole afternoon and no telephone ring. That situation last a long time. I know because rainy season come and go and every Sunday we walk down the road rain flooding the road from the trench. Uncle Marcus say he ain driving no Govment car to get stick up in mud.

Day after day the postman ride past the house on he bike, raising he leg and cussing as Smartie take a liking to chasing he. Granny suck she teeth when he don't stop and under her breath she say people tiefing everything these days. Granny start for warn me things is hard, and food get simple, she lining up in the Govment shop for flour and rice. She taking in my uniform the same time she letting it down. Granny get job. She cleaning rich people house up by the lake. Sometime she take me with her, we get the bus and walk down a long road with big gate and button entry. The floor there not like we one. Them so shine I frighten meself looking down. The ice-box so big I can fit inside if I have a mind to. Granny point out lobster and clam in freezer bag she say come from Miami.

She assure me my mother is not in Miami.

In my bedroom I line up the things Mummy send me when the postman used to stop, dolly clothes and sweetie, pictures of she standing in snow with a woolly hat on. My finger trace she face with she short hair. The video she send stand up on the windowsill. I only see them one two time, because tiefman come in the house and steal the video-player.

The children them in the yard call me Sendtor. I dint know what that mean for a long time. They not nasty all the time. All o' we play catcher and hopscotch, skipping and dare. Two boy who did use to tease me boast how they really gwine soon and sure enough one day they gone. Granny say they uncle sponsor them to Canada. Somebody else in the yard they call Comeback. Was a girl who aunty take she to London say she would get her nurse job but she come back by Christmas and soon again sitting on the back-steps shelling peas.

By some foolishness there was also a boy call Fallback. They say he mother and father send he from London to learn education and respect back home because children don't listen to their parent there. I feel sorry for he more than me. People tease he because he so poshy poshy talk like English duck and quack quack is all we hear while we laughing until one day he cuff one of the boys so hard he knock he teeth out. After that they play nice and he larn for talk like we.

One day the postman bring not only letter but parcel. Granny hand shaking while she find the scissors and cut careful not to slice the stamps or anything that might be cuttable inside. When it cut, two bottle nail polish roll out. Follow by a pen and pencil set which had sharpener and eraser inside. It nice bad because it had Michael Jackson on it. Granny unfold the letter and go sit down in the rocker. I see words rolling way down the page. When she finish reading she hold it to she chest and start rock. I akse her Granny is what she say is what happen and she only shake she head. I akse she if we can go back Uncle Marcus on Sunday and she say wait and see.

Wait and see went on long. I start high school and Fallback start walking home with me. He tell me how he miss he mother too and I just look at he and look away and don't say nothing. I dint know that what it call, *missing*. In my bedroom I think bout this *missing*. I run my finger over the nail polish bottle and the Michael Jackson pencil set and I wonder if her finger touch them too. I put them to my nose and smell them. I wrap my arms round my old dolly and think about Mummy blowing bubbles on my baby belly.

At school they send me to special classes because they say I dyslexic. The saviour was the computer. I learn that thing so fast they say everybody got to watch out. As time went on computer start for do all kinds thing. Uncle Marcus lucky he still driving the Govment car; he say the best thing in this world is fa keep your head down and work hard. What that mean is that even when Govment change and one batch o' crooks get exchange for another he still got he job. Words he always say was like water and nobody must never waste them neither let them run away. Uncle Marcus buy computer then and so is how we get back in touch with Mummy, only this time instead of telephone go *bringg bringg* is the computer bringing Mummy voice. You have to wear earphone like pilot. The first thing I notice is how she voice changing, not only it not happy but it tired. The second thing was the time it take for somebody to talk and somebody to answer back. I imagine everybody words criss-crossing somewhere in the air. Musee like Luke Skywalker laser. Uncle Marcus say at least it free. Mummy akse me bout school and seem surprise I in high school already. The question I want to akse was trembling on my lip.

Everybody waiting to hear it too. But then Mummy said her papers taking a longer time to come through and lossing the job put her right to the back of the queue again. She akse me what I want she send for me and I think, *send for me.* Two week later a pile of magazine arrive. I look at the pictures.

I spect everybody wondering where my father is. Well he don't figure in the Before time. Nobody never call his name. But then come that time when Uncle Marcus get promotion. I remember he drive the Govment car up we road which eventually get fix with tar and stand there proud on the veranda telling Granny he going abroad. Me and Granny jumping up and dancing sure to Jesus is America we gwine see Mummy. But Uncle Marcus hold he palm and pressing it down and say, not we, he. He boss make Consul over in the islands and he say he want he safe honest same driver. He dint know if we can go holiday maybe. I jump up again. Airplane fly out same as Mummy. Bound for drop me somewhere near she!

Some say 'bout people crawling out the woodwork and that what my father did. Crawl out of some backwood and say nobody taking he chile out the country. Right on the doorstep there was ricketics carrying on and for the first time I like a bone in between. Between all o' them settle the agreement that this man who name my father go tek he turn look after he own pickney.

And so come Sendfor Chantal realize she have a father. I couldn't see no significance in that. Not everything got significance. And when he come fer me in some bruk down van I cyan hardly see Smartie tail dropping by the rocker whey Granny sit, me eye so fulla water.

There must have been dealings going on behind the scenes because after he turn up and Granny say I gwine stay the holidays with him I learn she get sick. I was fourteen then and couldn't carry on the way I did when I was four. Though I wanted to scream and shout and kick the way I did when Mummy left I know it would be unseemly. I look at my granny and realize I never even think of her with her own name. Rosa she name Rosa, not Granny. She look small small and her hair getting white.

Them holidays stretched to two year. Granny had to go hospital and then recuperate at her cousin house across the river. They let go we house. The man call my father live way up the East Coast with he wife Mena and three children. They had a farm with skinny cows and mango and jamoon which Mena sell at market. Was she I had to fight shame and tell when I see blood in my panty.

Them three children didn't make themself. That what I keep telling meself when they run tell lie how I tiefing the sugar, how I drop Mena best cup pon the floor. They tell me I lie my mother in America. They say I an got no mother. Mena vex that I cyant roll roti. The school they send me was more backward than me. They never see computer and everybody sharing exercise book.

Nobody round there had no telephone. I trying hard to keep Mummy voice in my head. Over and over I concentrate on how it sound, and how she laugh. Sometime one of the lil girls laugh jus like Mummy. I wake up foreday morning and imagine it was Sunday and me and Granny going up to Uncle Marcus house. I used to akse the man call my father if I cyant visit Granny, he say it too far and the van bruk down.

A line o' coconut tree run the back o' the yard. Behind that the land stretch flat and wild all the way to the ocean. When rain fall plenty it flood. Nobody don't go there. Ghost story fill everybody head when the radio not working or the man call my father cyant get work. He spit on the ground and say everybody abandon the country and if he had a choice he won't live near no slave logies. Mena catch another baby and school was done then for me.

The August I was sixteen Uncle Marcus come back. I hanging out the clothes and see the self same Govment car come driving down the road in a cloud of dust. The car draw up in the yard and the man call my father rouse heself from the hammock saying ah who dat. I know was my Uncle Marcus uncurling heself out the car. He get fat. A smile crease he face and I fly so fast I nearly knock he down. He say how I get big. I stick he in the belly and say how he get fat.

If money change hands that day I don't know. I only know that was one Big Head Queen sit down in that front seat and drive away. I only know that out the corner of my eye I peeping at Uncle Marcus like he's a jumbie. I dint cry at all when I leave the house with my one two things. Funny though all them children start bawling and the lil girl hold on to me tight.

Uncle Marcus house was same same; same kitchen stool which don't look so high. Same telephone sit up there. But pon the table a new computer. Uncle Marcus say we go visit Granny at she cousin but guess who send thing for me! Big box stand on the table. Inside was clothes and hand-bag, make-up and shoes. *You see she? You see she?* I akse. And Uncle Marcus bring out a envelope and show me photos of when he went America and visit Mummy. And there was Mummy in somewhere call New Jersey. She standing in a room at her godmother house. Her godmother old like Granny and can't walk. You see, chile, Uncle Marcus say, she cyant have you there. You still a dependent and she a dependent too.

But Uncle Marcus pick up the telephone and start dial. He saying hello hello, shake the phone and look in the receiver. Then he say hello hello again and he face break in a smile. He pass it to me. I say hello hello too and crackling over the line a *hello chocolate fudge* come over the line. My throat swell up all a sudden and I don't know what I saying. Her voice sounding so different like is stranger I talking to.

Uncle Marcus shake he head when he find out my education was rolling roti and minding chilren. He enrol me in college for learn computer and adding up.

My mummy head fill the Skype screen. At first nobody know what to say. She say I looking big like a proper young woman. I say she hair getting fine fine pon she head. Her voice sound real American now even slow and drawly. Only one two word coming through from hereabouts. Her cheek draw down and her hands fluttering like prayer flags. I want to akse her the question but I know the answer. I want to akse her something else too. I want to tell her 'bout the program I watching last night about all them Africans drowning trying reach Europe. We got TV here now and all the time I watching America though sometimes I get fed up with who boyfren do what to who girlfren and who uncle steal the money and car and gun and Hannah Montana singing and dancing and I switch to World News where water swallow up a whole island and terrorist blow up young people in a place call Bali. Instead I talk to she about Fallback. But she don't know Fallback. Only Granny know Fallback. I tell her 'bout Smartie, how he get drown jumping off the boat that take Granny. She akse me 'bout the man call my father how we get on and all I can say is all right I suppose. She roll she eyes.

It seem time past when Mummy can send for me. Rules say I now have to apply for visa on my own. But even Uncle Marcus can't find sponsor. He say left right and centre people jumping ship. He drive we by the seawall and say how this country never have no motherland, that why people stamping shooting killing each other. He say he sorry Fallback gone back how he know how I like he. He warn me must be careful now as man only want one thing. He say he sorry Granny depart this world and left me. Water come in he eye then, she his Mummy after all. We watch the water for a long time and I thinking how frighten bad people must be to fling themself in boat and plane and cross the sea. Then I think of them who reach and if that land really free and how much them really pay.

My mother voice growing old over the telephone. Her face grow old on Skype. Her hand grow old and shaky shaky on the paper she write me, which most times I can't read. But I shout the children, say come, you grandmother on the phone, tell she how people building concrete house now, tell she how yall working hard and maybe next year we can send for she.

## ALEXANDER IKAWAH
# Fatima Saleh

The night was just quieting down. Most people had obeyed the curfew the Kenya Police imposed after the murders of the Sudanese asylum seekers. Behind one of the tattered tents, Fatima Saleh was squatting in the patch she had cleared after the old one got messy. It still hurt from the night before but she was not going to see a doctor about it; word travelled too fast in the camp. Desert nights were cold and as Fatima stood, she let her jilbab fall to cover her legs. She spat and parted the thorn brush and headed for her tent.

Nights like this made her think of Jamal. The fool. Giving away his life for a cause that took and took without ever giving back. It was under a full moon like this one that he had said goodbye for the final time back in Kismayu. He had been smiling, confident he would return. Promising her a son, to be named after both his father and hers; Farah Saleh he would have been. Now the fool was lost somewhere. Dead in a foreign land no doubt. The enemies he had gone to kill had come and found her instead. When they began the bombing she had stayed, hoping the battle would bring her fighter back home. The men who came instead were fiends. Jamal would have shot them himself even though they claimed the same purpose for war. It was no place for a woman. She had packed up and left with the last groups of refugees that made it out of Somalia before the al-Shabaab took over. Now here she was in a foreign land. Even old friends and acquaintances were strangers here. They kept quiet in the night when monsters came; offering no help, not even a shout. Their silence was the ultimate betrayal. If Jamal had died for these traitors, he had died in vain. She would fight only for herself.

She didn't see Muhammad waiting behind the acacia tree halfway between the brush and her tent until he stepped out into the moonlight. He had been watching her as she approached.

"Salaam Aleikum."

"Aleikum Salaam," she replied, unsure of his intrusion. "What do you want?"

She looked him in the eyes. She was afraid, defiant.

"I heard what happened last night, Fatima. I heard everything. I'm very sorry."

She stared at him intently in the moonlight, watching for any sign of his true intentions.

It was dangerous that he knew. She could be cast out, treated like a pariah, maybe even killed.

"I'm fine."

"I won't tell anyone," he continued.

"What do you want?" she demanded.

"Their names," he replied. "I want their names."

She finally understood. She walked up to him, her lips quivering with rage.

"So just like that you are going to defend my honour? Is that it? Am I to have no choice in this matter too?" Her voice was getting louder, hot tears stinging her eyes as she spoke. "Is that your great plan? To have me indebted to you? Am I to fall in love with you and become your fawning wife after that? Is that it?" She was standing right in front of him now, her face an inch from his face, her breath hot with anger. "Answer me, Muhammad! Have I become a plaything that men fight over for their amusement? My hand worth only the blood of pigs?" And as he drew back to slink away, worried about the heads that were beginning to poke out of discreetly opened tent flaps, she drew back her hand and slapped him with all her strength.

◆

There was fire in his eyes. She saw his jaw clench and felt his breath come out in a short burst. For a moment, she was afraid. Then she steeled herself and glared back, and saw that his eyes had softened. He didn't strike her. Quietly, he turned around and began to walk to his tent.

"Muhammad," she called behind him. He kept walking.

"If all you can offer me is violence, leave me alone," she declared.

This time he turned, his eyes narrowing. She stared back at him, unflinching. The standoff held for just over half a minute, then they walked their separate ways. She entered her tent without a sound, the chill just as bad within the flimsy flaps of tarpaulin as outside. The pain was still intense, sharper when she moved. She swallowed one of the little pills, waiting a small eternity for the pain to ebb away.

◆

Her mind flitted as she waited, settling finally like a homing dove upon thoughts of Jamal. He had always kept an extra gun in the house, a pistol. Not for his own use but hers. He would take her to the desert, teach her how to aim, fire, reload. His firm hands taking the pistol apart, putting it back together with speed and ease.

She had reached under her pillow last night, a reflex. She had found nothing.

In the end, Jamal had taken even that last gun, her protection. He had promised to bring it back but she could already see the resignation in his eyes. She had let go of all the promises he had made that she had been clinging to like leaves in the desert wind. Now her memory of Jamal was like a dead tree.

A few hours after midnight, Fatima Saleh heard the rumble of the Land Rover truck outside her tent. She moved quickly, setting the plastic bottle of Coca-Cola just behind the metal suitcase, as if she was trying to hide it. She took the little bottle out of the wraps of her jilbab. The goat stew was still warm. She opened the lid on the saucepan slightly releasing its thick aroma into the tent. The rag she used to clean her only plate was lying on top of the pan. She grabbed it and soaked it in liquid from the small bottle then pulled up her clothes, dabbing each breast lightly with the cold wetness. She went to the tent flap, opened it a crack to see what was going on outside.

A cold wind licked the side of her face from outside the tent. There were three men near the truck, engaged in an argument. The two from the day before were there, and a third one now. A fat, ugly pig-like brute of a man; his belly bursting out of the blue uniform. Strains of Swahili from their argument filtered through, interrupted by the howling wind. They lit cigarettes and then laughed a bit, an agreement had been reached it seemed. A lump of hot lead shifted in Fatima's stomach, as if her fear had taken solid form. Her bowels felt loose as she turned into the tent. At least this time they didn't have the element of surprise. Behind her, the fat man put his hand in his pocket and pulled out a wad of notes, handing it to the other men. Then he turned and began to walk toward Fatima's tent.

She had returned to the bed and pulled the covers over her head, pretending to be asleep. Pretending not to hear as the tent flaps parted and the fat man entered, his hands already at his belt.

Fatima Saleh didn't scream. They took turns, tearing, grunting, eating, sucking, and drinking and, finally, the pig urinated on the side of the tent, his piss flowing back inside due to the slope of the land. They left at cockcrow, and the wind erased the trails of their sojourn from the sand as soon as the wheels had passed. There would be no trail behind them to lead back to Fatima Saleh. She got up only after the sound of the vehicle was no more. Her tears were streaming down her face as they had done all night. She took the pills out of her bag and swallowed two, washing them down with the half glass of drinking water they had left in her jug. One for the pain that threatened to split her in two, the other for the vile sludge the pigs had left inside. She took her aluminium pail and went outside.

The wind was cold, blowing her tears in wild patterns all over her face. It whipped puffs of sand at her legs and made her jilbab flap behind her with loud clapping noises. She grabbed the hem of it and rolled it up into a knot, leaving her legs exposed from the knees down. Now the wind changed tack, blowing into the jilbab from underneath and making it billow. She held its wraps tight with one hand and headed for the taps. The tent where women bathed was still far away, the path there winding between other women's tents. Fatima contemplated walking there, brushing past other early risers with the scent of pig on her. Instead she headed back to her own tent and moved the bedding and utensils to the side. There in the middle of her tent, she took off the jilbab and washed with the icy water, scrubbing her skin until one pain surpassed the other.

When she was finished, she put on fresh clothes and lit a fire outside. The red flames burned crazily, dancing like hungry demons in the morning half-light. She fed them; her jilbab, the plates, the sheets, the cleaning rag, the flimsy mattress, the soda bottle; everything that smelled of pig. The inferno raged, fanned by the wind whose temperature was slowly warming with the rising desert sun.

◆

When Fatima Saleh went to the marketplace with her wares at noon that day, it was impossible to tell that she had hardly slept. The painkillers were working fine and she had more in her coin purse. She greeted her friends and customers like every day, smiling. In the camp, every smile was pained. Nothing seemed askew.

"Aleikum Salaam."

"Salaam Aleikum."

They streamed to her mat.

"Have you heard what happened?"

"No, tell me."

"How much is this bunch here?"

"Three Kenyan policemen were found dead last night."

"Dead, wallahi!"

"One hundred shillings."

"Their car had rammed into a tree."

"Maybe they were drunk and had an accident."

"I heard there was vomit and blood inside, poison I tell you."

"Alhamdullilahi!"

"This is too expensive."

"The war has followed us here, wallahi."

"Things will get better."

"Shukran."

"But the security here is terrible, something is going on."

"Have a good day."

"I'll see you tomorrow."

◆

As Fatima Saleh put the coins in her purse, she took out a small pill from the box of painkillers and washed it down with water from a plastic bottle. Someone else was coming.

"Aleikum Salaam."

◆

Fatima stood up from the new patch she had cleared that evening, her jaw set against the pain. She was not going to see a doctor about it; word travelled too fast in the camp. She spat and parted the thorn brush and she knew he was there.

"I know what you did," said Muhammad, stepping out from the shadows behind the acacia tree.

She didn't even stop walking, brushing past him, making him follow.

"You are very brave."

She turned, the surprise showing in her eyes for a moment before she regained her composure. He had sounded exactly like Jamal, had spoken words straight from Jamal's mouth. His very last words to her. In the moonlight, Muhammad even looked and stood like Jamal.

"Thank you Muhammad. Aleikum Salaam."

"Salaam Aleikum."

She walked away from him.

## ANUSHKA JASRAJ
# Notes from the Ruins

### 1

"In 1906, my great-grandfather was steering the ship. Fifty tons of gold, fifty bales of cotton, three Bengal tigers, and two hundred passengers. The queen had asked for the tigers. My great-grandmother warned him. She said, the waters have been whispering about you. He said, I'm not scared of a few fish. Then, in '72, the remains of a shipwreck were discovered near here. My great-grandfather was identified by his teeth. The cat bones were never found. You know what they say: ten lives and smart as yogis."

The landlord took pleasure in telling this story to each new tenant of the Wanli mahal; a five-storey building resembling the wreckage for which it was named. Dahlia, whom the landlord had cornered in the compound, was unable to contain her amusement. The landlord looked hurt.

"I'm sorry, I'm sorry," she said. "I haven't laughed in a long time. I don't like wild cats. My mother passed away recently. It had nothing to do with cats though. I just don't like them."

The landlord coughed and coughed. "Excuse me," he said, and walked away.

Dahlia lied. Her mother was alive and as healthy as a kitten with all seventy-eight organs intact. It was her father who had passed away — years ago — and her mother had recently embarked on a pilgrimage of the northern cities. Dahlia was to stay with her cousin, Laldeep, who insisted on being called Lilya.

Back at Lilya's flat, which was now her place as well, Dahlia panicked when she noticed a slender young man lounging on the living room sofa. His grubby shirt suggested recent homelessness.

She had read about this in the *Newcomer's Guide to Mumbai*. They were called palathis, though they usually inhabited vacated building complexes. The guidebook had foregone a proper procedure for ridding one's living space of these squatters, simply stating: They are often delirious creatures and should be avoided. Dahlia stood paralyzed until Lilya emerged from her bedroom.

"This is Prakash. He lives here sometimes. Don't look so shocked. We're not doing it or anything. But please don't go and tell your sister or the entire khaandan will start talking about it."

Prakash, who had been watching Dahlia, introduced himself. "Struggling actor," he said, putting the word struggling in finger quotes. He taught workshops for eight-year-olds on weekdays, and spent weekends rehearsing with an experimental theatre group that called themselves mumblesnore.

"We met through mumblesnore," Lilya said. "Dahlia's an historian," she added, turning toward Prakash. "She just moved here from Jaipur."

"I'm not an historian," Dahlia corrected. "I study historical ruins. Elphinstone College."

## 2

Prakash offered to show Dahlia the Gateway of India, and she thought he was being hospitable; after all, he did live in her cousin's flat, rent-free. When he bought her a balloon from a young man selling them on the street across from the Taj Mahal hotel, Dahlia decided it was something other than kindness.

Prakash pointed at the Taj and said, "The architect planned it so the front would face the sea. But they misread the plans and built it backwards."

"Even your city's architecture is unwelcoming."

"My city," Prakash repeated, as if testing an incantation. "You live here too now."

"Maybe," Dahlia said. It was later that she noticed how Bombay was a place riddled with un-belonging; like cartoon illustrations in a novel of grave seriousness.

The *Newcomer's Guide* said, Mumbai has many beauties to be appreciated. These are also places where you are most likely to get robbed.

**3**

On their second date, which Prakash insisted was their first, he took her to Juhu beach and they wrote things in the sand with small pieces of driftwood. "It was exactly like that picture with Govinda and Madhuri," she said to her sister who lived in Dubai.

"You need to stop watching those duffer movies."

"He wrote me a poem. I don't understand what it means. Listen. I live on your lips. Next line. Like the silence of the ocean. Next line. Curled up in an empty conch. Next line. Waiting for the wind."

"Stay away from these types," Maggi said. "He won't pay your bills."

"I have to go. I heard a click. I think Lilya is listening on the other line. Have you heard from Mum?"

"No. She sent a postcard. Hold on. Here it is. It says: The unreal never is. The real never is not. That's from the Gita, I think."

"How cryptic. She and Prakash would get along."

"You're one to talk."

After the requisite sand-sculpting and feet-wetting, when even the flute-seller had retired, Prakash had led Dahlia to a part of the beach usually reserved for teenage couples or prostitutes and their clients. Prakash slipped his hand under Dahlia's skirt, fumbling like someone looking for a light switch in the dark. She smiled politely. This is what the *Newcomer's Guide to Mumbai* meant when it said: One must adapt to local customs and the speed of city-life. Try not to look surprised in order to blend in. His presence is irresistible, Dahlia thought, but his absence un-notable. An object bringing luck to the bearer. Five letters.

## 4

Date number four — Dahlia kept count — Prakash had cooked dinner. Daal and basmati rice. Under-seasoned but comforting, Dahlia decided. He claimed to know three jokes. "I'll tell you one. What did the apsara say to the man?"

Dahlia shook her head.

"Leave your shoes on the shore."

Dahlia smiled, unsure where the joke lay, feeling bad for the barefoot man, gill-less and beguiled.

"It's important to have jokes memorized," Prakash said. "Entertaining people get eaten last."

Wrong, she thought as she sprinkled salt into her bowl while he wasn't looking. It's not the jester who gets eaten last.

"I think we should get a cat," she said.

Prakash slow-zoomed his arm through the air and lightly punched her shoulder, giggling like a schoolboy. "This is what I love about you," he said.

"That which is a beggary, if measured. Four letters," Dahlia said.

They didn't have sex that night because Dahlia was menstruating. "Not even a blowjob?" Prakash had asked. "Just kidding," he added, too quickly.

## 5

Dahlia started attending Prakash's rehearsals, occasionally helping out with lighting effects and props. Mumblesnore met on Sunday evenings at the Bubbles auditorium, which was part of a nursery school owned by the director's cousin. All the furniture was child-size.

"I don't understand," she said.

"It's an allegorical exploration of bestiality," Prakash said.

The actors crawled around the miniature stage on all fours, snarling like lions in heat.

## 6

Lilya sometimes made breakfast for Dahlia, and brought her small gifts: A book about the Mughal Empire, a plastic flower that bobbed from side to side, a bottle of rose oil, a mug with "Know Thyself!" printed across it in large blue letters. What do these gifts mean? Dahlia wondered.

Prakash left for work before Dahlia woke up. He wrote Post-it Notes, which Dahlia collected. These, too, were gifts whose meaning she tried to unlace:

> *Won't be home for dinner.*
>
> *Out. Love, P.*
>
> *Morning! You snore like a train.*
>
> *Kisses & Waffles.*
>
> *We are like trees. XO.*
>
> *U rock.*

The three of them ate dinner together on weekdays, and sometimes, in their company, Dahlia felt like the child of too-young parents; a possible accident, and something they were obliged to love. Lilya offered to lend Dahlia her clothes, and Prakash asked if she had found anything in the ruins. "These kurtas are comfortable, but thank you for offering," Dahlia countered. "I'm not an archaeologist; I study discoveries that have already been made."

7

"You don't like to talk, that's fine. You could at least make some sound. It's like having sex with a cadaver. I can hear crickets," she said one night, having been introduced to the tongue-loosening qualities of red wine. It is not unusual for men and women to interact freely in public while under the influence of intoxicants, the guidebook proclaimed.

Prakash made an effort to be more expressive during sex. As Dahlia straddled him, doing most of the work as usual, he called out: Laila. This brought things to a halt.

"What did you say?"

"It's this play I'm writing. It's as if Majnun has inhabited my head. Laila was his other half. You are my Laila."

"What happens to Laila and Majnun?"

"In the original version, they can't be together, and Majnun goes mad and kills himself. But I'm re-writing it. Majnun won't go mad; he'll just pine briefly."

"Oh," Dahlia said. She reached for the iPod on her bed-side table. Asha Bhosle sang through the small silver speakers in Hindi: What thing is the heart? Take my life if you will. "It's okay if you don't like talking. We can play music to drown out the crickets." Prakash shrugged. The room was too dark for either to see the other's face.

"Isn't it strange," she said, "how we're constantly shedding dead cells? Thousands and thousands, every hour. This will all have fallen off in a few years. We'll be the same people, in new skins, but we won't have noticed."

"Keratin," Prakash said.

"What?"

"That's what we're made of. On the surface. Keratin."

"You smell like a grapefruit," Dahlia said.

"Do I? I borrow Lilya's shampoo sometimes."

## 8

Red Box — date twelve — the waiters looked reluctant to approach the table at which Dahlia and Prakash were seated. Can they see something, she wondered. The way she had seen it on Prakash's skin; on his arms and legs, but mostly in his desperation to please her, and in his puppy-dog eyes. The restaurant walls were lined with mirrors, to give the illusion of endless space. The reflections moved like synchronized dancers whenever she shifted in her chair. Dahlia looked at Prakash, wanting to squish his worm-like eyebrows.

She thought about the time when Prakash and Lilya had locked themselves in Lilya's room. "We're rehearsing," Prakash said.

"Slow processor," Maggi once said, when Dahlia punched her in response to an insult, twenty-four hours after the fact.

Dahlia wondered what her mother had meant. The unreal never is. The real never is not. Or was it the other way around? Perhaps everything that is real is disallowed from existence, just like that movie where the Fates are men in tailored suits whose job is to separate lovers.

"What was the second joke?" Dahlia asked.

"The second joke?"

"You said you know three jokes. You've told me one."

"A baby fish is swimming in circles on a warm July evening, and a grandpa fish waves out to him and says, aren't the waters lovely today. The baby fish says, what the hell is water?"

"Seven letters. Least likely to get it."

Prakash looked befuddled.

A waiter said, "Would you like a tour of the tomato garden? We grow our own."

"No," Dahlia said. "I'll just have the soup."

That night, Dahlia dreamed of a beach replete with shiny glass pebbles. "These used to be shards from broken bottles," a phantom stranger said. The waves crash against the shore and wear down the sharp edges. "That's the opposite of what happens with people," Dahlia said. "The sea is just the night, watered down," said the phantom.

"You were talking in your sleep," Prakash told Dahlia.

"Maybe I'm still asleep," she said, and pinched him.

"Ouch," Prakash said.

"They found a ship stranded at Juhu beach. It was in yesterday's paper. It was supposed to be taken to Alang to be scrapped, but the storm brought it to the shore, and now they can't move it."

"I heard about that."

## 9

Dahlia spread a rumour that Lilya's milky skin was the result of nightly rituals involving a pumice stone and Pond's Fair & Lovely. The girls who were part of mumblesnore's backstage crew laughed about this, spitefully, then went out and bought tubes of the lotion for their own use.

She watched Lilya and Prakash rehearsing. They crawled, along with the other actors, their animal noises beginning to resemble the braying of plump frogs. Dahlia noticed the largeness of Lilya's breasts relative to her own. Too bad she's not moneyed, Dahlia thought. There were things she could say about those melon breasts, if Lilya were rich.

## 10

A professor from Delhi University visited Elphinstone College. Dr. Ramnathan specializes in places that are no longer remembered, the posters claimed.

"The city of Prashta had a gift economy, and they had no concept of marriage. The men lived in groups, while women lived separately with their children and occasionally paid visits to the houses of the men. It was up to a woman to choose her mate and, naturally, the women were generally polyamorous. We cannot say whether or not they had any concept of love, though there have been findings of drawings that suggest they believed the afterlife to be a time of eternal monogamy, and perhaps they saw life as an extended expedition during which we are meant to find our mate for the next world. A theory that can be neither proved nor disproved.

"The Prashtians worshipped Indra, who is considered to be the Hindu counterpart to Zeus. Kama, the god of carnal love, is said to be Indra's slave within Prashtian mythology, suggesting that the qualities they valued included the ability to overcome primal desires. A philosophy that might seem contradictory at first, in light of their courting rituals or lack thereof. And as we can see from these images, Kama was depicted as having a phallic weapon —"

Someone in the audience whistled, and the lecturer blushed — he was young. Dahlia saw him in the cafeteria after the talk, sitting alone and drinking a coke. She handed him a paper straw and said, "Those things are covered in rat piss. I enjoyed your lecture. I was wondering —"

"You want me to sign a copy of my book?"

"No, I didn't know you had a book. I was hoping you could tell me more about the theory of —"

"It's all in my book, *Civilizations Besieged: A Chronicle of Forgetfulness*. You can buy it across the street. I'll sign a copy for you."

Dahlia walked away with no intention of returning. She was learning not to expect answers. Everything, and everyone, was always pointing at something in the distance: unidentified floating objects, bookstores, try harder next time.

"Thanks for the straw," he said, as she was leaving.

## 11

"What are you going to do?" Maggi asked over the phone.

"About what?"

"Dahl. Wake up. He's using you. It's been three months. You need to tell him to move his kabooze out of there."

"Don't call me that. I'm not some side dish. Have you heard from Mum?"

"Yes, wait. This one has a picture of a baby *haathi*. It says: 'Hope is the penalty for despair.'"

"That woman is hilarious."

"She didn't mean to — you know —"

"To withdraw; often in the face of danger or encroachment. Seven letters."

"I hate it when you talk like that."

## 12

Rehearsals for *Majnun's Life* began and suddenly everything seemed like a scene from Prakash's play; a series of borrowed motions. They were just miming the words. Dahlia was assigned the task of lighting director. The contact sheet stated: *Lightning director — Dahlia S.*

There were no other misprints. The part of Majnun would be played by Prakash, and Lilya would play Laila. "Such similar sounding names," the director said, as if that had clinched his decision.

## 13

MAJNUN. I slept with Laila.

TULIP. What?

M. I don't love her.

T. How did it happen?

M. I don't want to talk about it.

T. Why did you tell me?

M. I don't know. I'm sorry.

T. Why did you tell me?

M. I love you.

T. You expect me to forgive you?

M. I love you.

T. How —

M. I don't want to talk about it.

T.. Get out. I want you to leave.

M. For now, or for good?

T. Just go.

M. I can't live without you.

T. Then don't.

M. It didn't mean anything.

T. I don't want to hear it.

*(Curtain)*

*Majnun is alone. He holds a blue tulip.*

M. Life is like a circus that's left town, and you're left behind, burned by the world's most beautiful beard on a lady the size of a bear. The posters smile under your shadow, but soon the wind takes even that away, like a leaf folding and unfolding. You wish you had the trapeze artist's graceful nose or at least his ability to resist the forces of gravity. Madness is said to be the breakdown of negotiations between selves. I will eat my tulip, representative of eating my actions.

Dahlia read this while lying next to Prakash in bed. She kept her face still because he was watching her. Try not to look surprised in order to blend in. "I like it," she said. "Red tulips mean love. Yellow tulips mean love beyond hope. But there's no such thing as a pure blue tulip."

"And Dahlias?"

"Stars of the devil," she said, without meaning it. The same tone as when she'd said, "My mother passed away."

## 14

Opening night was a semi-success. "The auditorium is half-full," the director said in his pep talk. Dahlia climbed a ladder and positioned herself behind the key light. She watched Majnun and Lilya devour each other's faces before parting and wondered whether it counted as polygamy if a man was sleeping with one woman in reality and the other in a pretend universe. Maybe that's why Bollywood actors marry Bollywood actresses. This thought caused her to feel despair.

Prakash — or Majnun — was about to deliver his monologue. Dahlia slipped a colour gel into place and flooded the light. Prakash glowed red. Dahlia wondered how different things would be if she were named for some other flower; a more exotic variety like Orchid or Hyacinth. She increased the intensity of the spotlight and watched Prakash break into a sweat. Dahlia had never seen him naked; they had sex at night, in the dark, as if underwater. His thin shirt was soaked by the time he got to the finale, and Dahlia could see through to his murky skin. She wondered if his outfit was fireproof.

Lightning director, she said to herself, and smiled as the audience gasped. Connection of low resistance, established unintentionally. Twelve letters. Thick plumes of smoke left a layer of ash on Dahlia's arms and face.

The third joke, Prakash told her before going on-stage: "What did the gold fish say to the apsara?"

"What?"

"Nothing. He forgot what he wanted to say."

It was a riddle, and as with all things related to apsaras, she didn't think it was funny.

The smoke cleared and Majnun emerged looking charred but charming, like something accidental. The play did not have a second night. "This is inappropriate for children," the school principal said, even though there were no children in attendance. Dahlia rubbed the black dust on her arms and it flaked off like bits of dry skin.

Backstage, Prakash said, "That did not end where I'd expected."

"Denouement — no — you haven't told me how many letters," Dahlia said.

"I'm not blaming you, but I won't be home tonight. Drinks with the boys."

## 15

Dahlia wished life came with an answer key, like her Megasize Crossword Puzzler books, or at least an index to which she might refer. The closest thing, she decided, was Lilya's diary, which said:

*Poor thing poor poor thing. She loves him quite irrationally. Mother abandoned her. No other family here either. She can't leave him, and he won't leave. She thinks she's some tragic heroine from his play. I'm much better off, not loving. I tried to broach the subject with her, talk some sense into her. I even dropped hints that he and I were lovers. She seems to think love is like those ugly pictures in her textbooks — holding a hidden beauty whose appreciation requires an imaginative leap.*

## HELEN KLONARIS
# Cowboy

The first Saturday Mr. Lebreton came to work in our backyard I was in my room looking at a catalogue picture of the woodcraft construction kit my father said I couldn't have because I was a girl. With the kit I could build four miniature wooden houses, and I thought I could sell them to tourists and make a profit. My father said I had a good head for business, but girls didn't do that kind of work. Still, I wasn't giving up.

I don't know what made me notice Mr. Lebreton; maybe the fact that he was so tall he had to duck to cross the porch. Or, maybe you always remember what was there in front of your eyes in the moment you felt a certain longing. How the person — tall, lanky, brown skin — became confused with the feeling of wanting what you couldn't have. I sat at the foot of my bed biting my thumb nail and imagined hammering wooden walls together, pitching the tiny roof, adding a border of picket fencing, and then painting each house in colours I thought tourists would like: turquoise like the sea, yellow like the sun, all the little fences white like every picket fence I had ever seen. I imagined my father would forget I was a girl and be proud of me instead; I felt if I couldn't have that kit, I would never really know myself. And then I looked up. Through my bedroom window I saw Mr. Lebreton crossing the porch, something hesitant and gentle in his stride as he followed my father into the backyard. I had never paid much attention to the garden before. But now I wanted to be in it too. I left the catalogue lying on my bed and went to lean against the white porch banister.

My father was showing Mr. Lebreton around the garden, gesturing to the weeds, and the patchy grass that was already long and wispy and looked, my mother said, like people don't live here. Mr. Lebreton watched my father's hands and nodded in response. There had been two gardeners before him, but each had left one day and never come back. Police raids, my father said; they round them up and send them back to Haiti. A shame. But since my mother believed that having a gardener meant we were coming up in the world, my father hired another Haitian without papers and hoped for the best.

When my father was done showing him around, he said so, your name, how you call yourself? Mr. Lebreton's voice was raspy and soft and I couldn't hear his reply, but I heard my father's voice loudly, well, from now on, your name is Cowboy, understand? *Cow-boy*, my father enunciated. Mr. Lebreton nodded, yes, yes.

◆

I knew my father gave him the name Cowboy, just like he'd chosen new names for the first two gardeners, because it was a name he could pronounce, and a name, my father would have said, that might grow into something here in this new soil. My father took the name from watching John Wayne movies on American channels Sunday afternoons; we sat, all three of us, on the couch in front of the TV, me in between my father and mother, and when the movie got going, my father would repeat John Wayne's lines, imitating John Wayne's accent, the calculated drawl of his voice. Later, in the evenings after dinner, when he thought no one could hear or see him, Baba would walk the length of the back porch, his hips thrown forward, his legs turned slightly out, his arms loose and cocked at the same time. Watching from my window, sometimes I saw him pretend to draw a gun from a non-existent holster and aim it at an invisible foe. When he came back inside, he would clear his throat and ask my mother if it was time for bed. To which she always replied, I don't know, Van, is it?

Baba named the first two gardeners John and Wayne, and I suppose after a few futile attempts at fishing around for other names, nothing felt so right as Cowboy. After all, he had changed his names from Evangelos to *Van*, and Papagiorgiou to *George*, added a new first name, *Simon*, to the simpler syllables, Van George, making our particular strangeness less apparent to the English-speaking world.

◆

I pretended not to notice Mr. Lebreton, at first. Even though his arrival had inspired in me a new level of entrepreneurial yearning. If I could sell enough fruit, like the women selling dillies and carambola and sugar apples down at Potter's Cay market, then I could make my own money and buy the kit from Maura's Lumber Yard myself.

I sought out produce from the backyard: there were two mango, one sapodilla, one soursop, one key lime, and two coconut trees that had to be trimmed of their voluminous branches every June when hurricane season began. It was now mid-July, and the air was sticky and still. Heat rose up from red dirt in murky waves. I harvested the fallen coconuts and sold them for a dollar each to passing taxi drivers and their carloads of tourists. When I ran out of coconuts, I gathered dillies; fifty cents for a bag of six. The taxis would stop in front of our house, and the tourists would file out, snapping pictures of the white local and her wares. I was learning how to follow in my father's footsteps; I was on the road to becoming a good capitalist.

My father had left Greece thirty years ago, at the end of the Second World War, when communists wanted to take over the country. He said the problem with communism is that instead of only some people being poor, it gives everyone the freedom to be poor. At least with capitalism, you stand a chance at making something for yourself. Did he want to turn out like his brother? No. His brother who lived in a house the size of a bathroom and would never have a way of growing it any bigger? Communism makes you weak, he said, tapping his forehead. It makes you lose your passion to put something in the world that was never there before. Sometimes you have to take a chance, and in the new world, a man can take as many chances as he needs.

◆

I took to watching Mr. Lebreton from a corner of the porch. He was the colour of poinciana pods in summer, and had very large, graceful hands. Hands that might have played the piano or written novels, that paused for the briefest moment between moments, between tasks, as though some important thing had been forgotten and these hands were remembering. Hands that, in the aftermath of those brief pauses, stayed busy regardless of what Mr. Lebreton's eyes might have been envisioning, and it seemed to me they were envisioning tasks I could not see, tasks other than the pruning of lime trees or the weeding of bougainvillea hedges.

I found excuses to get closer when changes in his dress caught my eye.

It was, at first, just a hat, a brown leather cowboy hat with a leather cord dangling below Mr. Lebreton's chin, a red wooden bead at its tip. The following Saturday, Mr. Lebreton showed up wearing a brown suede vest over a dark blue shirt, sleeves rolled up to his elbows, and around his neck a twisted swathe of red bandana. The week after that, beneath the frayed hem of Mr. Lebreton's faded denims; I glimpsed the silver sheen of spurs, and at the other end, the thin filament of steel on the pointy toes of second-hand boots. When I had sold all the coconuts I found lying under the tree that morning, I hurried to the backyard to fill a basket with dillies, and then took my time so I could steal glances at Mr. Lebreton. On my way, something glinting in the dirt caught my eye. I squatted to look more closely and saw that it was a silver spur like the ones on Mr. Lebreton's boots. Finders keepers, is what I was thinking.

I pocketed the thing and hastened over to the dilly tree. Mr. Lebreton eyed me as I dropped my basket and surveyed the area for fallen dillies. I pretended not to see him as I fingered the spur in my pocket. I rubbed it between forefinger and thumb as if coaxing a new idea from an old one. I didn't yet know what the new idea was, but I sensed it involved getting Mr. Lebreton to help me. Instead of gathering the fallen dillies, I set my sights on those in the branches above. Seeing that I was too short to reach some of the higher branches, Mr. Lebreton came over and began picking the ones he could reach and dropping them one and two at a time into the basket. When it was full and heavy, he offered to lift it out to the road for me.

I suppose what happened next had its beginnings in the rubbing of the spur as if it were a magic lamp; just as we arrived at my TV tray for a table, and Mr. Lebreton was placing the basket on it, a beige Mercedes taxi full of Americans — all of them sun-burned pink — stopped, opened its doors, and let out its passengers to take pictures and sample the exotic island fruit. Their eyes latched onto Mr. Lebreton: Look, they shouted, a black John Wayne! And, without so much as a *May I …?* and *Would it be all right if we …?*, motioned me aside and began to take photos of him, directing him to stand legs apart, smile, stop smiling, tilt his hat, and so on.

· At first Mr. Lebreton was startled, a raccoon in headlights, but in a manner I would grow to become expert in myself, Mr. Lebreton took on each pose, became the face, the arms and legs, the body of the man they were looking for through the viewfinders of their Kodak and Nikon cameras. I stood in the grass, off the road, watching. When the tourists were done, they stuck U.S. dollar bills into an empty jar I had left on the table. And when they

pulled off, and the air settled around us, I looked over at the jar
of cash, then at Mr. Lebreton. He stood there, his arms unusually
still by his sides. He blinked, then gazed uneasily at the pock-
marked road. I picked up the jar, pulled out the crisp dollar bills;
eight in all. They smelled of tobacco and tin. Rapidly, I counted
off four, folded them in half and, without looking directly at him,
passed the cash over to Mr. Lebreton. He took it. The rest I folded
and slid into my pocket along with the silver spur and a greasy
feeling in my gut that I had crossed a line and could not go back.

◆

In this way, and without any verbal agreement, Mr. Lebreton and
I turned an accidental performance into a regular gig, with me as
financial manager. I must have been aware that there was something wrong with this arrangement because I did not tell my parents. I found a shoe box and used it to stash my dollar bills, which I
counted at night under the covers with a flashlight. I made sure my
parents were nowhere in sight when Mr. Lebreton and I took to the
front of the house, and the stretch of road that led to downtown.

Word spread amongst the taxi drivers and soon Mr. Lebreton
and I became a regular Saturday morning stop on the scenic island
tour, and our profits tripled. We lived on the outskirts of Over the
Hill, in a pink concrete house on Virginia Street where other Greeks
and a few Cubans had settled next door to whites who were not
quite as white as the ones who lived out east and out west. We were
an in between lot, a few city blocks of immigrants and light skin
blacks in the lower crease of the ridge that divided the island north
from south; the good beaches and coastal roads from the dense
Over the Hill settlements and soggy grey marshes; the shops and
hotels from the blacks who worked in them. Behind us and up the
hill, houses were no longer freshly painted concrete with porches,
but sagging wooden clapboards and dusty yards. Taxis driving west
to east could detour from the coast and show the tourists where
Bahamians lived, without making them uncomfortable.

♦

Every Saturday morning Mr. Lebreton arrived wearing something new. "Salvation Army," he'd mutter, a smile playing across
his mouth when I glanced over in admiration of the new belt
buckle in the shape of a horse, the shiny sunglasses that hid his
eyes behind tinted plastic, the new gun holster that hung, gunless,
at an angle around his waist. Word must have spread through the
communities of clapboard houses behind us, because people on
their way to work, all of them brown skin people, instead of taking the bus, walked so that they could slow down and take a good
look at the cowboy.

Among these onlookers were other Haitians who lived in
patches of clapboards in the alleys in between and on the fringes
of settlements. At times they stopped completely, on the opposite
side of the road, their eyes widening, then hastily dropping their
gaze. I didn't know what to make of the heads bowed seconds
later and the hurried steps across uneven asphalt. Mr. Lebreton's
eyes narrowed as he watched them flee.

Once, a group of women passing by yelled out to him. The
only word I heard and remembered was *macoute*, and though I
recognized it, I had no idea what it meant. The woman who had
spoken this word glared at Mr. Lebreton. Her face shone with
sweat and fear and something deeper: the particular texture of
the presence of loss, how someone carries around the dead in
their eyes, in the clenched rigidity of a jawbone, in the frayed
edge of hysteria in a voice. The other women hushed her, pulled
at her arms, patted her face, encircled her, reasoned with her in
soft tones, and they too hurried past. A cloud descended over Mr.
Lebreton's eyes and took up residence there; his face hardened
and I recognized the mask he had pulled on.

The mask was part of the costume Mr. Lebreton was wearing when a red minivan stopped in front of our stall, and a man
whom I first took for a hacker, since there was no evidence he was

a licensed taxi driver, got out and began talking with Mr. Lebreton in the same language I had heard yelled from across the street. Mr. Lebreton's voice was low, stilted; his face and body, turned askance, had stiffened. The man's voice rose, his hands gesturing urgently toward Mr. Lebreton, and then angrily at me. I took a step back. Mr. Lebreton crossed his arms and refused to look the other man in the eye. The man spoke again and waited, as if for an answer, but none came. He shook his head, got back into his car, and drove away.

I looked at Mr. Lebreton.

Boss lady don't have to worry.

◆

Soon after, I began noticing more changes in Mr. Lebreton's appearance. His clothes seemed larger, or he seemed to be shrinking inside them. His shirts ballooned around his waist, his pants bunched at the hips where his belt seemed pulled tighter. The leather cowboy hat hung too loosely on his head, swivelling left to right when he bent down to pull weeds or chop grass, so that he had to put his machete down, fix the hat straight again, tightening the drawstring under his chin. He saw me examining him and walked to another part of the yard. I followed.

Why do those women yell at you? Why did that man talk to you like that the other day? I sat cross legged on the grass beside him.

Mr. Lebreton sighed, squatting opposite me, holding his machete in both hands. They don't like cowboy.

They used to be your friends?

In my country, cowboys *pa bon*. Very bad.

Were you a cowboy there too?

Mr. Lebreton did not answer. I looked at his hands. They held the machete reverently.

I wanted to know more, but the softness of his fingers against the machete's blade made me stay quiet.

I reached into my back pocket and pulled out the spur. I handed it to Mr. Lebreton. He took it, rubbed its surface with his thumb, and this time it wasn't a magic lamp, but a mirror that showed the past and the future; I could not tell which Mr. Lebreton was looking at, but for a moment the mask slipped and his brown eyes shone wet.

◆

The following Saturday Mr. Lebreton arrived in full gear with an added prop that rounded out his attire: a black plastic revolver. Soon after, six taxis arrived at once, parking in single file all along the roadside. The tourists spilled out, their cameras eager and poised before they reached our stall. They jostled each other to get good spots in front of the main attraction. On the opposite side of the road a small contingent of Haitians gathered and seemed to have arrived at some decision; they regarded us with hard eyes.

The taxi drivers acted now as if they had set up the whole thing. They ordered Mr. Lebreton around.

Haitian, stand with your hands like so, they motioned for him to stand arms akimbo. That's it, now go for your gun, yeah, you got it.

The tourists clicked, shutters opened and closed in rapid fire. And then one of the tourists, a large white man in a Texan hunting hat, hollered over at Mr. Lebreton: Get her. Get the girl. Go on, Cowboy, act like you gonna shoot her. Someone grabbed me by the arm and pulled me into the centre of the crowd, next to Mr. Lebreton. The man in the hunting hat hollered to his companion, Joe, Joe, go on, you save the girl! Get in there Joe. Joe laughed, turning red in the face, and egged on by the others, jumped onto our makeshift stage.

Mr. Lebreton shakily aimed his gun at me, blinking; I froze, my hands half way between up and down, and then Joe, transformed into the protagonist, seized Mr. Lebreton from behind, his right arm around Mr. Lebreton's neck, in a sleeper hold. You got this Dave? You got this?

The shutters flew — open shut open; the crowd pressed in on us, enthralled. The taxi drivers smiled, but the smiles did not reach their eyes. They put their hands in their pockets, fingered their keys, glanced at their watches and away from the scene playing out before them. I sought out Mr. Lebreton's eyes. I wanted him to know I knew we were just play acting. But when he did lock eyes with me, I looked away; I knew we were play acting, but even so, I felt my heart skip and start, sweat bead on my upper lip. I was afraid of the man in the hunting hat, his loud drawl, the crowd snapping pictures. Still, there was something in all this that reminded me of the tone of my father's voice when he warned me not to play in the streets after dark. The thin desperate texture of my mother's voice when she ushered me out of the car after a night out, scanning the darkness before darting up the steps and unlocking the front door.

The hunter turned director yelled at Joe, now, knock the gun out of his hand!

Joe reached around and gripped Mr. Lebreton's wrist, shook it hard till the plastic revolver clattered to the ground, cracking along its middle seam, so that it lay broken and useless on the ground.

When I found Mr. Lebreton's eyes a second time, his mask had slipped and I saw him breathing shallow, as if inside the triangle of Joe's fleshy arm, and in this space between me, the tourists and the taxi drivers, he felt himself trapped painfully in a too small place with no air. His hat drooped on his head, his shirt sagged, sweat-soaked across his narrow shoulders. He watched me watching him. Something like a spasm crossed his face. I gasped. And then Joe let go of him, and it was all over and Joe and Dave and their buddies were whooping and high fiving; Dave was slapping Joe's back and the men and women from their respective taxis were shoving dollar bills and five dollar bills in the glass jar till it was stuffed. The men joked about Dave being the next up and coming Hollywood director. They said they'd come back and hire us for their first movie. Did we want to be famous? Their voices ricocheted off the pink and yellow walls of the houses.

They put their cameras away. They dropped cigar ends on the road and crushed them with their sneakers and brown boat shoes. The taxi drivers left without hailing us, their heads bent as if deep in thought. The gathering of Haitian men and women across the road disintegrated, scattering in different directions as if the scene had confused them and whatever decision they had been certain of was no longer certain.

I counted out the money from the jar more slowly than usual. A yellow dog trotted past us and didn't stop to look. Flies hovered over the sapodillas and limes. And a heaviness settled in my arms and legs that made me want to weep. I gave Mr. Lebreton his share, and did not look at him as I sank my hand and the wad of cash into the back pocket of my shorts.

◆

That night the greasy feeling in my gut turned into ocean swells inside my belly and I knew I could no longer take from Mr. Lebreton the money he earned being Cowboy. The money I had collected, one hundred and sixty-five U.S. dollars, lay secret and useless in the cardboard darkness of the shoebox inside my closet. I retrieved the box and by the glow of my flashlight counted the green and beige bills, turning all heads north, unfolding creased corners, straightening and stacking them into three neat piles. My hands felt hot. I smelled on them the slick residue of other people's hands — the storytelling Texan, Joe the saviour, their camera wielding believers all stuck to my clammy fingers like tar. I hid the money back inside the shoe box. I closed the lid. In the bathroom I scrubbed my hands with Ivory soap and a wash cloth, patted them dry on a clean towel. In bed, I sank down and floated up, over the oily swells, so that by morning I awoke hunched and clutching my gut on the way to the toilet.

When I had relieved myself, I took the wad of dollar bills out of the shoebox and folded it into my back pocket. That was when I heard a knock at the door. Through the living room window

I saw a dark blue van in the driveway. The knock came again. I opened the door. Two men in khakis were on the front steps. One of them stuck a form in front of me. He pointed to the second line. "Jean Lebreton." You know this man? I shook my head. We have reason to believe he is your gardener.

Cowboy. I had never asked him what his real name was.

The men looked at me, waiting. I knew Cowboy — Mr. Lebreton — was already in the backyard; I had heard the chop-chop of his machete weeding the bougainvillea hedge. I did not alert my mother. I had a hundred and sixty-five dollars in my back pocket, enough now to buy the woodcraft construction kit from Maura's Lumber. I felt the outline of the bills with my right hand, looked up at the men's faces. I bit the inside of my lip.

Did I know him? Did he work here?

I shook my head, no.

They watched my face. You here by yourself?

I nodded.

And your name, Miss? They had the same dark skin as Mr. Lebreton. Their hair cut low to the scalp, like his. But their necks and arms were thicker, their shoulders square and straight.

Jamie. This was a lie. The name I was given was not Jamie, it was Maryann; but I had always preferred a boy's name.

Their eyes narrowed, looked past me into the hallway, at the living room beyond. My father had left earlier, but my mother was in her bedroom dressing for church.

Before they could ask more questions, I stuck out my hand with the hundred and sixty-five dollars in a tight roll. I do not know how I knew to do this. Maybe I had seen it in a movie. Maybe I had seen my father do it. Maybe I already thought anyone could be bought or sold. My heart hammered against my chest. The tall one in front hesitated. I stood on one foot then the other. He reached for the roll. He studied me, then the roll, counting it out, measuring us both. He glanced over his shoulder at the shorter officer. He grinned; the shorter officer chuckled, pursed his lips and motioned toward me with a lift of his chin.

All right then, the shorter one said. Sorry for the trouble, pretty girl. And they turned and walked down the steps, across the driveway to the van. I shut the door and watched them leave through the open window, the hammering in my chest so loud I could barely hear the van's engine whirring to life.

Who was that?

I spun around. My mother was standing behind me in her slip.

No one. I mean, they had the wrong house.

Who they?

I shrugged. Just some people looking for Mrs. Taylor. I told them hers was the blue house farther down.

Oh, my mother said. Well, draw the curtain. I don't want the sun fading the sofa.

The driveway was empty. I pulled the curtain to. I waited for her to head back to her room.

I rushed out to the porch searching the backyard for Mr. Lebreton. The cutlass was stuck in the dirt under the sapodilla tree. Yellow and black butterflies arced and floated in the air. Pigeons cooed in the eaves over the porch. The air conditioner droned. And hanging from the branch of a mango tree like the shadow of a strange fruit was Mr. Lebreton's cowboy hat, the silver spur swinging side to side from its leather cord and glinting in the sun.

A cold sweat broke over me. I ran back into the house, out the front door to the edge of the driveway. I stopped dead when I saw that a hundred yards away the immigration officers' van had blocked the road, sideways, and up against it, arms twisted behind his back, wrists shackled, was Mr. Lebreton. He looked small and thin and breakable. For the first time since I'd known him, I wondered how old he was, and if he was married. I wondered if he was somebody's father and who would worry about him not showing up for dinner. I had not thought about him having a family. I had not thought about anyone caring where he was when he wasn't at home. I crouched behind a croton bush and watched as the officer who had taken the money walked around the van to the driver's side, while the other roughly pushed Mr. Lebreton into the van and slammed the door. Behind the dark glass of the window, Mr. Lebreton's bare head fell forward, his shoulders slumped. Then, for a brief moment he raised his head and I thought he looked in my direction; I felt he could see me. My heart fell and I didn't know if I should turn and run, or stay behind the bushes, out of sight. I stood up instead, and walked toward the van.

Cowboy! I yelled. The officers looked over at me and laughed.

A crowd had gathered — neighbours and some of the ones who had congregated the day before. They whispered to each other, looking at Mr. Lebreton, then at me. I stood a few feet from the van, my legs suddenly trembling, my chest hot. Mr. Lebreton's head was facing the floor of the van, but he looked up again, and our eyes met for the third time. I didn't know what to say. I opened my mouth but nothing came. The van was reversing and taking Mr. Lebreton away, to a detention centre, back to Haiti, and I wanted to tell him I was sorry. Instead I said I know your name is not Cowboy.

Mr. Lebreton looked tired. He stared at me as if trying to see something very far away. He nodded, but I could not tell what he was nodding at, what he was saying yes to. Then he closed his eyes and the van lurched forward and it was too late. I watched the van until it had turned onto the main road and disappeared. I watched the sun fill the sky, and yellow and brown dogs wander away to find shade. I watched the empty road till my head ached, and my feet burned on the asphalt.

## KHADIJA MAGARDIE
# Elbow

The night they came, the old plywood he'd found at the Marlborough dumpsite and erected into a door complied with a crack as they kicked it down.

The rusted twist of wire he'd threaded through the door-frame pole as a lock betrayed him. With a clang it snapped and gave way.

As they moved about the shack, the frame of sheet iron clattered into the ochre dust, offering no resistance. The treacherous walls that had once sheltered him gave him up.

When they came for Thomas Moyo, there was nowhere he could hide.

◆

If you lifted his shirtsleeve and exposed his bony forearm, there was no tell-tale circular scar that the young men of his generation are supposed to have since babyhood. A badge of belonging in this great city — testifying that the subject had been weighed and given shots at the government clinic.

He wasn't up to date on who was sleeping with who in the country's most popular TV show.

And though his friend Mandla couldn't live without it,

Thomas Moyo didn't jive to kwaito at the local tavern, where they hung out every Friday night.

"The thing about you people, you're just here to take our women with your funny music and your long traditional weapons, heh?"

A fat kehla stumbled over to the two young men standing in a corner near the door. The smell of cheap liquor seeped through his pores, and oozed out of the sweat on his bald head.

He leaned in close, his eyes bloodshot but deliberate, and focused. Thomas could smell his sour breath.

He was typical of the last-Friday-of-the-month crowd. Men straight off the train from the city, pouring their wages down their gullets before sunset.

They'd return to their homes, and their women — spent, broke, and spoiling for a fight. This one wasn't going to wait.

The sweaty tormentor cupped a hand over his crotch, mimicking an obscene gesture.

"But it's not true, is it? There's nothing like my big Zulu weapon! You want to see it?"

He fumbled for his zipper. Behind him, one of the man's friends slurred encouragingly.

Thomas tried to look away. The intoxicated slug grabbed his arm.

"Hey, look at me when I'm talking to you, blackie!" The glass of stout in his other hand spilled onto his trousers. He swore and wiped at the stream of saliva from the side of his mouth. "Come, I'll show you a real South African weapon."

He shoved Thomas.

"Na, man, leave it, leave it, we believe yours is bigger." Mandla put his hand on the man's shoulder.

The man's cheerleaders remonstrated angrily with Mandla, seeing their fun had been cut short. He cocked his head in his friend's direction and gestured to the door. They put down their half-finished drinks.

"Gents, next time," Mandla said to nobody in particular.

"Sharp-sharp." They didn't turn around as the two men left.

Mandla elbowed his friend playfully. "Let's go home kwere-kwere!"

Thomas knew his friend, his keeper and protector, was joking.

They had grown up together, and lived side by side, on Burundi Street in Extension Two.

When twelve-year-old Sonto Mthembu pulled his hand to her breast behind the school toilet shed in Grade 6, Thomas told Mandla first.

And the cold April afternoon his young mother breathed her last on her cot in the shack they shared — it was on Thomas's shoulder that Mandla wept.

Even after the whispers began.

And the people of Extension Two averted their eyes when they saw the orphaned boy begging along London road. When his mother was alive, there were no fences between the shacks, and the women would invite him in to share a plate of pap with their own boys.

But after the ladies of the burial society had her safely interred, their tongues held back no longer.

Soon the gossip reached Mandla's ears.

That she'd died of that thing that was filling up Avalon Cemetery in Soweto — and now it was here — among the decent people.

The women said, with glee, that his quiet, churchgoing mother, who spent nearly half her life scrubbing the floors in the kitchens of the whites in Johannesburg, had got what she deserved.

She was *isifebe* — a drunken whore. How else would she have money, with no man?

Thomas and his mother fashioned another small bed out of crates and a used foam mattress, and put it in the corner of their shack.

They had planned, since they were boys, that they would go into business together. For three years they washed taxis at the rank until they had saved enough start-up money.

Now here they were; selling second-hand handsets and airtime to love-struck schoolgirls with heavy thighs and scandalous hems.

The tall, thin, and shy Thomas and the short, wiry, and brash Mandla were *bafowethu*: brothers.

◆

His father, Velaphi Moyo, had arrived in Johannesburg seventeen years ago, caked with dirt, and dirt-poor. He had walked for five straight days all the way from across the Limpopo.

Velaphi Moyo had left with nothing from that place where poverty and the pall of despair hung over the village in a perpetually dusty haze.

The people were starving. The rains hadn't come, and the children soon grew fearful of the worried faces of the adults — who knew what was coming, but said nothing.

The chimurenga had come, and gone. And as the village elder said, shaking his head bitterly, the speeches of the Leader in Harare would be tastier between two slices of bread.

He began saying the unthinkable; life was worse now than under the whites. At least they had work then, and could feed themselves.

But Velaphi Moyo had heard there was hope across the Limpopo, in the City of Gold. If he could just get to Johannesburg, he would be able to find a job, and send money home.

The night he left, he promised his grandmother he would return, and bring her a new Zambia cloth to tie around her waist.

"No, Grandmother, you mustn't cry," he said, cradling the old woman's head in his hands.

"At the end of July, I will send word through Sibanda's son for you to collect from the building society in Bulawayo."

Velaphi Moyo was never seen in the village again.

But every month on the last day, his grandmother would wake before dawn, and lay out her best clothes on her bed.

◆

Stolid and confident despite her eighty-four years, she would be on the main road at first light. Soon the thunder of dust and stones would announce the arrival of Sibanda's son in his pickup.

The skull-faced youngster with the sly eyes of his father had long smelled the old woman's desperation, and knew how much she would pay for the favour.

What he charged her was enough to fill his tank five times over. The thought of how much money he would make out of these trips was enough to make him smile, and hum tunes all the way to the city, tapping his fingers on the steering wheel.

It was always the same.

He'd usher the old lady into the building society, then go wait outside. He'd leave her waiting in line, and after an hour she would reach the front of the queue. She would hand over her frayed brown identity book, and be issued with the five hundred rand from her grandson in the City of Gold.

Half would go to Sibanda's son, and the rest to feed her family.

But before they got into the pickup and drove back home, the youngster would stop at the Athena Café on 14th Street downtown.

The grandmother waited in the idling van as he went inside and ordered the usual. A soft drink and two yellow sponge cakes for each of them. It was her only treat until the next month came again. There was food to buy, and school uniforms for the great-grandchildren.

But one day, the money stopped coming.

"I told you, it isn't here," said the clerk behind the glass, a young girl with stubborn eyes and a pouted lower lip.

"But there must be some kind of mistake, check again ..." The old woman's voice was plaintive.

"I've checked three times, maybe your son is dead," the girl said rudely. She rang the bell signalling the turn of the next customer, and turned away from the old woman.

The grandmother shuffled out of the building into the waiting car and sat there silently, too ashamed to tell Sibanda's son what had happened.

She knew they were all secretly jealous of her grandson. They'd start talking about how the Moyos thought they were better than everyone else, but they were really like the rest of them — poor and disappointed.

"Athena Café, Gogo?" he ventured, smiling.

"Not today, my child, I'm not feeling well." She folded her hands on her lap and looked out of the window, so he could not see the tears running down her cheeks.

His family couldn't have known, but the grandmother knew. Velaphi Moyo had found a woman.

A "Jo'burg" woman.

The type everyone in the village had heard of, who eats men's money and churns out fatherless babies twice a year.

They used powerful muti to ensnare men, and make them forget their true families.

Johannesburg women, the women of the village said — first in whispers then openly — were loose, and didn't take care of themselves. That's why they latched onto good men, to make them take care of them and their bastards. So he'll never be able to send money back home.

Until the grandmother died in her sleep many years later, she dreamt of the taste of that yellow sponge cake.

◆

A week after his birth, Thomas Moyo's mother wrapped him in a brown blanket in the custom of her people, and climbed into the taxi that would take her to register his birth at Home Affairs on Harrison Street.

There, in black ink in the ledger of births and registrations, the arrival of her firstborn was duly noted.

Velaphi Moyo stood at her side in the stiff grey suit his woman had bought on hire purchase from the Indian shops. He nodded gruffly at the clerk and, as per the laws of the land, was asked to sign next to the box on paternity.

Two months later, as was custom, a goat was slaughtered and a bracelet made of its skin wrapped around his right wrist. His proud mother would now be addressed by her title, ma-Thabo.

But as the weeks turned to months, despair at his long unexplained absences, and her own loneliness would draw the new mother away from Velaphi Moyo, and into the bosom of the church.

Soon after the child's first birthday, when the time came for him to be baptized, the priest told her she had to give her son a Christian name.

She had been reading the Bible and decided on Thomas: the apostle who doubted. As she too doubted the intentions of the boy's father.

The priest had also told her to stop living in sin.

It was asking too much of the boy's father, whose restless spirit at nights still carried him across the Limpopo to the dust of the village. He imagined the sight of the homestead, and imagined all the young girls he had loved and disappointed.

The lonely man, a tree without roots in the mighty Johannesburg, longed to hear their melodies of love in his own language again.

But he knew he would never go back. He was a lowly security guard, watching cars outside shopping malls, and hustling for tips. Nothing of the man the people at home imagined him to be.

He had a bastard son from a woman he was drawn to because he was a man, and a man had needs. But he knew he would never marry this woman who had given herself so eagerly to him, and may be just as generous with her favours when he was not there.

The day ma-Thabo came from church with her sisters, dressed in white and carrying the newly baptized Thomas, he was gone.

◆

Word of Velaphi came to the township every now and again. He was living with this or that woman. Or he had gone back to Zimbabwe. Or that he was dead. Every few years, news of him would reach ma-Thabo and her son. Someone had been drinking with him in a tavern somewhere. The drunken man, it was said, would rave like a madman, laughing and crying at the same time.

"My son, my son ..." he'd slur at them, stabbing a finger into his chest for effect. "My real South African son; he'll become something one day!"

Unlike his kwere-kwere father.

◆

Thomas Moyo got his first lesson on being too black on his first day of school.

The class of seven-year-olds was instructed to stand up, one by one, and introduce themselves. When it came to his turn, the shy, thin boy, despite his height, stood behind the desk, hoping the teacher would pass him by.

"What do they call you, boy?"

"Thomas."

"Well are you the Son of God, Thomas? What is your father's name?" The others tittered.

"Thomas Moyo, teacher ..."

"What's Moyo? This isn't a Shona kraal, boy!"

The teacher was enjoying herself, and was encouraged by the laughter of a group of boys.

"Are you a South African?"

"Yes, teacher."

"Where were you born?"

"East Rand Hospital. I mean, Alexandra Township, teacher."

"What's your father's name?"

The boy felt the blood rush to his cheeks. His father's name was forbidden from being spoken in his mother's house.

Besides the elongated face and mournful eyes of his son, there were no sign Velaphi Moyo had even existed. Like the rush of water polishing the stones of the riverbed, the father's image had faded from his son's memory.

"I, I don't know, teacher." Thomas felt the tears welling up, and fixed his eyes on the ceiling.

"Look at me when I'm talking to you, boy."

Sitting next to him, a short, squat, yellow-skinned boy with a huge gap in his front teeth elbowed Thomas painfully.

"So why are you so black? We South Africans aren't so black!" the teacher exclaimed, clapping her hands together.

The woman looked around the classroom for the affirmation that came in guffaws from the boys.

Thomas looked down.

Next to him, the yellow boy was laughing the loudest, poking at Thomas's back.

"Hey, myeke, leave him!" came a voice from behind Thomas. The yellow-skinned tormentor fell forward as he was shoved from behind. Thomas turned to see a stocky boy with dark skin.

Ever since that day, Mandla took it upon himself to be Thomas's protector. He, too, was fatherless, but anyone in the class who dared to ask knew they'd be asking for trouble.

"I can take care of myself," he bragged on the soccer pitch at break time. "I hope that bastard doesn't cross my path because I'll show him."

What Mandla lacked in the reading and arithmetic department he made up for in brawn. His mother and his now invisible father's people were from rural Zululand. He said he was "makoya" — as pure as they come — from a nation known for needing no excuse to use their fists.

Thomas responded to taunts with silence.

"Where did you get so black, have you been driving the sun?"

"Wena, Thomas, I've run out of shoe polish, can you lend me your head!"

It was worse when Mandla wasn't around. To support himself and his mother he sometimes ducked school to sell loose cigarettes at the taxi rank.

The boys would corner Thomas behind the woodwork classroom, and order him to speak Shona. But he'd grown up speaking the language of his mother's people.

Their language.

He'd once asked his mother if she knew any Shona from the days she was with his father. She clicked her tongue impatiently.

She never told him that Velaphi Moyo wasn't even Shona.

"Why do you want to learn that kwere-kwere language?"

He knew the boys in the playground wouldn't believe him, but he'd rather endure the beatings than pretend to speak a language no real South African understood.

◆

When Mandla finally decided, aged sixteen, that school was not for him, Thomas too packed his satchel for the last time and strolled out of the school gate. For weeks, his mother would beg and plead with them, but where Mandla was going, so was Thomas. She was sad, then angry. She blamed her son's friend for corrupting him.

"Typical Zulu, no brains!" she'd scream, as Thomas begged her to not make a scene. But she loved Mandla, and he loved his adopted mother.

Suddenly, without any real warning, everything changed in Extension Two.

His mother had read something about it in the papers, about trouble on the West Rand involving some miners and a local woman. The street committees in the township had gone on a rampage and burned their houses. He hadn't given it too much thought.

As Thomas walked to the taxi rank he passed a group of boys smoking at the street corner.

"Go home, kwere-kwere!"

But this was his home, his only home.

The very next afternoon as he tried to get into a taxi downtown, he felt himself being pulled out backwards. The unseen assailant grabbed his belt and yanked him out just as the taxi sped off.

He swung around to see two policemen.

"Hey kwere-kwere, where's your pass?" said the one, a heavy-set giant with watery yellow eyes.

Thomas Moyo didn't carry a pass. Or refugee papers. Or a passport. He was a South African.

He turned on the policemen.

"I don't carry a pass, this isn't apartheid!"

One of them grabbed Thomas around the neck. He yelped and tried to shield his head from the blow, but he felt the heavy thud as the policeman's knuckles connected with his skull.

All around them, in the busiest street in Johannesburg, people went about their business as though there were nothing wrong. Nobody turned around.

The policeman's sidekick brought his face up to Thomas's as he struggled to free himself.

"What's an elbow in Zulu, you black bastard?"

They'd received instructions from head office to root out the immigrants in town.

But many of the vermin had intermarried, impregnated local woman to get papers, and learned their language.

They were becoming harder to spot. But this word, *indolol-wane* — so old-fashioned nobody used it — would only be known by a true South African.

Thomas Moyo had no idea what the word elbow was in Zulu. Or in Shona. Or in the language he spoke every day.

The bigger policeman stuck his hand into Thomas's back pocket, and felt around for his wallet. He suddenly felt a rush of anger, and pushed the policeman.

The two fell upon him instantly, kicking him in the side and shoving his face into the dirt of the road. He flailed and kicked out, but he was no match for the truncheons of the two heavyset constables.

"You think you're clever, you think you're clever!" the one kept shouting.

Thomas tried to scream, but instead swallowed a mouthful of dirt. The policeman pushed him face down, to the ground. His arms were pinned behind his back. The bigger policeman aimed a boot at his head. He winced and tried to duck from the blow. But the boot landed at the side of his temple.

When he opened his eyes, two girls in school uniform were staring at him intently. He groaned. One eye felt swollen and bunged up.

People were walking by as though nothing had happened. He was bleeding in the gutter in the middle of Johannesburg, and nobody turned around. He felt around for his wallet in his back pocket. It was gone. So was his cellphone.

He got up and dusted himself off and staggered off down the street. It was a small price to pay.

After all, he was too black.

◆

When the trouble began, Thomas Moyo didn't think it would come knocking at his door.

Everyone knew who he was. His primary school teacher lived two streets down. There were at least three from among his mother's people in the township. And though she was away visiting her friends in Soweto, she was just a phone call away, in case they needed to check. She had his birth certificate.

Everyone had seen him at the stall where they bought airtime.

They knew that he was one of them.

But the night they eventually came for Thomas Moyo there was no escape.

The scrape of pangas on the asphalt, and the hammering on the doors were straight out of hell …

◆

Three days before, the street committees had a meeting outside the library in Extension 5. They began with fewer than ten people, but an hour later there were hundreds. Men, women and children.

The foreigners are committing crimes, they said.

"Yes," shouted a fat woman in a transparent blouse and a beige skirt. "My daughter was almost raped the other day by one of these cockroaches!"

Her voice turned to a shrill scream. The crowd roared. A man began striking the air with a whip.

"The barakas … they're selling bread for half price, and I'm losing business! They should go sell in Somalia, not here!" a man yelled.

Another man suggested marching on the foreigners' homes that very night.

"No, no," an old man implored. "The police will come."

But the crowd had smelled blood, and pushed the old man aside. Now would be the time they got their own back on the bloodsucking foreigners.

Just that morning, the Somali shopkeepers in Extension 5 were seen packing some boxes into their van at the back of the store. Then they came to roll down the metal gate and locked up, before speeding away.

"Look at them, running like rats from the Juksei in full flood." The women laughed.

◆

Thomas Moyo never got to explain the night they came.

He couldn't leave. Or go, as they constantly warned him, back to where he came from.

They beat down his door and fell upon him with clubs and knives. As they paused over his beaten and broken body, they were laughing. One lit a cigarette.

They — the sons and daughters of Mandela — had cleansed the township of another blood-sucking foreigner.

The two sisters in the shack next to his were screaming as they were pulled outside into the wintry air in their nightdresses.

The street committee had been told the women were sluts who had Nigerian boyfriends who bought them clothes and air-time for their phones. They would be whipped.

The younger girl sobbed and pleaded, grasping at the remaining shreds of her nightdress to cover her private parts.

She reached for her older sister, who was screaming as dozens of hands clawed at her, pulling her clothes from her body.

She was to be paraded naked around the township that night, as a lesson to other women who were thinking of committing similar crimes.

The women's screams was the last sound Thomas Moyo heard, as they drove the knife into the side of his neck.

He fell without a sound.

The wound gurgled. The body jerked in a last vain attempt to hold on to life. Then it stopped.

The men stood over their victim. One dragged on his cigarette, and flicked ash over the lifeless man.

They turned around, as they heard the footsteps of their leader.

From amongst the shouting and the screams, and the crackle of burning wood, came a voice: "Is the kwere-kwere dead?"

## A.L. MAJOR

# Antonya's Baby Shower on Camperdown Road

The first time I saw the boy, I thought, *Now who child is this?* Yellowman and the boy was standing next to each other, both wet and shaking cause they was so cold. The boy's face looked like mud paste. He had dark purple lips and eyes like he was past the point of ever crying again. He was thin, bony, and he smelt of oil, dirt and only God knows what else. He was wearing a black shirt slicked against his skin, and his shoulders was hunched. I didn't know anything about the boy, who was the boy people or how old he was, just that he was Haitian and the only one to survive.

Yellowman dropped the Haitian boy off the night it happened, when lightning burst open the sky and Yellowman boat sank. "All the Haitians dead themselves trying to swim back to shore," Yellowman said, and coughed. "Except for this one. I carried him on my back." Yellowman dried the boy off with my towel and pushed him toward me. "Ena," Yellowman said. "Stop acting like you don't need something to take care of." I tried not to be too ungrateful or ugly since Yellowman was trying to give me what we already lost. I told Yellowman I would look after the boy for one night only. Yellowman said one night was all he needed to figure out what to do next.

There was barely any space for me in my one-room house, let alone the boy. That first night I pushed my fridge up against my bed so I could sleep knowing the boy wasn't eating all my food while my eyes was resting. The boy spread out on the floor, wrapped up in an old bed sheet. A balled-up towel was his pillow. He slept in a fit. He was bawling a wail that could snap the branches on a guinep tree. I had to slap the boy across his face three times before he caught himself and woke up, but even then when he was staring at me, he had a scary look on him like he was still trapped in that nightmare.

◆

I couldn't leave the boy alone in my house. I know a preacher who hired a Haitian to mow his lawn. He gone off to do his errands, came back to his house and everything he owned gone. I used to tell Yellowman, "You shouldn't take them Haitians into Florida. Bahamians shouldn't get on the bad side of the U S of A." Yellowman never listened to me good. Right away I called the American woman whose house I clean every week, and I told her I wasn't feeling good in my belly. That woman so afraid of her daughter getting sick, she said, "Take as much time as you need, please," hanging up like she scared I could pass my sickness through my phone to hers. Her husband work at the embassy, not that he helped me get no visa. Embassy people like to live in houses behind pretty white gates.

The American woman. She not so bad. She just like everything clean and organic. My first day she gave me something called a Mommy Helper Kid Keeper Child Safety Harness, which I remember thinking must of been an American name for leash cause that what it looked like. She sighed at me when I asked her what it was for. "Taking care of a fidgety child is very hard, Ena. I hope you won't judge me." Then she showed me how to hook the thing to her daughter. She had the best begging eyes like she didn't know if she was a good mother and she just wanted me to say she was. "You have any kids?" she asked me. I shook my head no and that must have pulled tight on her heartstrings cause she took my hand into hers and looked at me with more pity than I could handle like she wanted me to prove my sadness was so much worse than hers.

If she could have seen me with the boy. I made up my mind he was eight, and I called him Boy when I had to call him something. Boy and I got into an easy routine. In the mornings, before the rooster crow and the sun up, I take him into the bush and I hose him off. He dance around the water like he never took a bath before. When I feed him, I break the bone off stew fish so he don't choke. We play checkers to pass the time. Any time I make a move that allow him to double-jump me, he shake his head and tap my hand and say, "Non, Mammie." Laughing too like he don't care if he won. When evening fall, Boy and I would sit outside and listen to Neighbour radio until night-night when I pull him on the bed with me and we sleep. His head right in my chest so close he could hear my heartbeat. For a short while, I was able to forget my loneliness.

I was kindest to the boy. I know plenty people who wouldn't have let him eat off their plate or sleep on their floor. The man who lived across the street from me. He hired a Haitian to move some bricks from the front of his house to his backyard. When the Haitian asked for a cup of water, the man said, "No man. Go drink from the hose." I even washed Boy's clothes the same time I washed mine. I was fine with taking care of Boy for a while but then a week passed by, and I was hanging my clothes on the line when Neighbour asked me if I was going to my niece baby shower. First, she said, "Isn't it a beautiful day." Neighbour was a tall, dark-skin woman who acted like she lived where we lived by choice. She started every day saying it was a good day, even if the garbage men forgot to come again and we had rats climbing over weeks-old garbage bags all day and night, and the sound of gunshots nearby made your heart beat so hard it rattle-rattle inside your throat.

I said, "It an alright day."

And Neighbour laughed. "You going to your niece baby shower this afternoon?"

I said, "What you mean? Eloise ain't tell me anything about a baby shower."

Neighbour patted her head and made the curlers in her hair wiggle. "I must of got it wrong," she said, and she rushed into the house with her dress hitched up and her pink panty showing she in such a state.

The next minute I in the house again, my phone ringing. I pick up the phone and sure enough it Eloise. "How you doing?" Eloise ask me, and I could tell from the way she ask she didn't want know.

"I right here. I doing okay. You know. Same old, same old. My man is off in Florida for work."

I only lied a little. Eloise don't like Yellowman 'cause he married to a bank teller and sweethearting me on the side.

"When he come back he say we can finally move out of this place. Lord knows the crime is up with the Haitians moving in next door."

"That's nice," Eloise say.

"And how you?"

"I good. You know Antonya shower is this afternoon? You coming? I thought I told you."

"No you didn't. Well, of course, I'll come. What time?" And a pause then like she sucking all the air into her belly. Nothing worse than a woman eight years younger acting like she only got to wait out your company till you die.

"You can come even this late notice?" she say.

"How would it look I the aunt not there at the baby shower?"

"All right…. Well, I'm happy you could come. Antonya is so big now. We having the shower right at her house on Camperdown Road. Ena, you should see this house, a two-storey with marble floor and her own pool, and she got white neighbours. My child live next to white people. I tell you this a surprise, right?"

I said, "What? The baby?"

Eloise didn't laugh. She never knew how to see the funny in anything. She my only family left alive, and you could always tell us apart by her broad nose and her fat lip and by the way we acted, like if I drew a rainbow, she had to paint one. Even after she gone off to that fancy American school, and I stayed in Nassau doing what work I could — scrubbing tiles, selling bottled water on the side of the road, serving daiquiris out at the fish fry — she never got out of the habit of making me feel less-than, never tired of making me beg for any bit of her kindness.

"I need you to pick me up," I said. "My car in the shop."

She yawned into the phone like the inside of her mouth was as hot as a dryer. "All right, wait outside. I be there eventually. And Ena? Please remember this is a baby shower."

She sighed again. "At least try to wear something nice."

◆

I hadn't had a reason to wear a dress at a party in a while. Last party was for Eloise friend baby birthday. I had me a time. The baby was only one years old, but they had the house decorated better than anything I ever had for myself. I drank sky juice. I played dominoes. I swang my hips and danced until my wind leave me, even when there wasn't no music playing. They had a whole cake with pink and blue frosting, and the baby picture was printed on top of the cake. When Yellowman and me saw that cake we burst out laughing, and I yell, "Now, who want eat a slice a chubby baby?" Only me and Yellowman got the joke. I was six weeks pregnant then and I made Yellowman promise we'd never get a cake like that.

I only owned two dresses that was good enough for Eloise, both so pretty when I wore them Yellowman said I looked better than a prize-winning horse. When Yellowman talked that way I felt like I was a star fruit and he was shovelling the seeds out of me.

I put the dresses next to my chest, and I pretended for a second I was somebody fancy. I was so busy picking between the two dresses, getting ready to prove myself to Eloise, I forgot all about the boy. What to do with the boy? I couldn't take him with me to the baby shower cause Eloise and her sip-sip loving friends would have a cat baby. They would sling questions at me I couldn't answer. And I couldn't leave him at my house, not only cause I didn't want him to steal all my stuff, but cause I liked to keep an eye on him. Sometimes he snuck out while my back was turned and I caught him walking around the street, just lost. He almost got ran over by a car one day. Lucky I caught him by his sleeve and slapped him upside his head so he could learn that wasn't right.

"Come," I say to Boy. I yank his hand and take him over to Neighbour.

"Neighbour," I say. "You could do me one favour?"

Neighbour only peek out the window like she didn't know who was calling.

"You could look after this boy for me," I say. "I got Antonya baby shower this afternoon. You know I the aunt. How it would look?"

"Who he is?" Neighbour ask.

"My cousin from Tampa child."

"How come you never mention no cousin before? And why the boy look like that?"

I look down at the boy, and he has his face twist up like he know I trying to get away from him. His hand was curled up in my mine.

"He a little under the weather," I tell Neighbour.

"Well, then why you gone leave him with me? I can't get sick. I sorry I can't help you," she said.

There wasn't no point in saying, "But please Neighbour." Her days was too pretty. She couldn't trouble herself for anyone. No one could help me. Everybody had a reason for why they couldn't watch the boy like they knew what he was. I ran all around the street, past the woman who sold guava duff and bottled sodas out the back of her car. She had a christening to go to later. Past the house of a man whose son chopped up somebody with a cutlass over a bad game of dominoes. He didn't answer the door. Past the couple who paid for bootleg Direct TV even though their car windshield had a spider-crack in it and a bent wiper. Past the woman whose grand-baby was found in a burnt-down church after her father put his devil in her. Old woman had a swollen ankles. Everybody have a reason for why they couldn't help me.

The boy held onto my hip the entire time like I was more to him than a lady he only met a week ago. When we got back to the house, the boy pointed to the Checkers board. This old checkers board the American woman gave me cause she bought an ivory one. People who have too much money is spend it on foolishness. The boy sat in the chair, and I bet he was thinking the game could fix everything. He set his eyes on the board. He pinkied one of the red checkers to its diagonal right. Then he looked at me, wanting me to make the next move. He started talking to me in that Haitian talk that sound like big bubbles and small bubbles bursting. I felt like shaking the boy until his eyes rolled back in his head and he just stayed tilted over.

"What you expect me to do?" I say to him, and, of course, the boy didn't understand me, and I didn't understand him.

Back when I was pregnant, Yellowman bought booties and bottles and blue socks for the baby. I told Yellowman it wasn't right to buy the baby things before the baby born. I said, "It seem to me like you telling God you know better than he does." Yellowman said, "Ena, calm your nerves. I's a man who take care of his son," he said. There wasn't no sense in asking if he would take care of his daughter. We had plenty fight over those booties, but then after all that, the baby just flushed out of me, down and dead like everything else. Yellowman had to return the booties and bottles and blue socks, and he only got store credit. I had to answer everybody questions when they asked me where my baby was. I remember when I told Eloise I lost my baby, she say, "It better off this way considering how you live." Not a "he" or a "she," just "it" like that's the only thing I could grow inside me or the only thing I could take care of. I waited until the boy wasn't looking, and I wrapped a pillowcase around his right wrist, tying him to the chair arm. I tied him to it tight so he couldn't move his hand. I tied him to it till he yelled so I could know it was tight enough. He kept talking at me and picking at the pillowcase but I know how to tie a knot. I smacked his hand so he would know to leave it alone. I tried to tell him this was the easiest way, he best way. I couldn't explain to the boy that like a lot of things in life the situation is mix-up, and I was just doing the best I could. He look at me with his wide eyes. He look at me like boys do, like he don't know if he wants me to leave or to stay. I left his left hand free. I put a bowl of water and an open can of sardines near him.

I put on my bright pink taffeta dress. It was so starched I could cut my finger along the hem. I put on my fuchsia hat with the gold fabric flower pinned into its side. I heard Yellowman whistling, from wherever he was, when I slipped my feet into my pink peep-toe shoes.

"Just be good," I told the boy. "I'll be back soon."

The boy still talking at me when I walked out the door.

♦

Antonya party went late into the night. I had to beg Eloise to take me home. When I got back, I rushed into the house and I prayed, "Lord, I didn't mean to be out that late."

I was half-expecting Boy to be gone. In my mind, I saw him pick and pick at the knot until he got his right hand free. I saw him taking my food out my fridge, running out the door and into the street, only God knowing where he went. After I lost my baby that's what I came to expect. A goiter-size feeling slipped down into my belly and rested. Yellowman had wanted to try again. I said, "Maybe God knew I wasn't supposed to be nobody mummy."

The boy was where I left him. Everything I owned was still there, but the boy had pee-peed himself and my house smelt sour. I said, "I sorry, Boy. I didn't mean to be out so late." The boy didn't look up at me when I called to him. He wouldn't let me help. His right arm looked limp and useless, but he shook it for a while and it finally woke up. He pressed his left hand against my chest and pushed me away so hard. He made me wish he had run away. I wanted to tell him, "Taking care of a fidgety child is hard," but I also didn't want to waste any more words. Instead I went to sleep on the bed and he slept on the floor, and in the morning, I walked him over to the Haitian shantytown and I left him.

## JENNIFER NANSUBUGA MAKUMBI
# Let's Tell This Story Properly

If you go inside Nnam's house right now the smell of paint will choke you, but she enjoys it. She enjoys it the way her mother loved the smell of the outside toilet, a pit latrine, when she was pregnant. Her mother would sit a little distance away from the toilet, whiff-ward, doing her chores, eating and disgusting everyone until the baby was born. But Nnam is not pregnant. She enjoys the smell of paint because though her husband Kayita died a year ago, his scent lingered, his image stayed on objects and his voice was absorbed in the bedroom walls: every time Nnam lay down to sleep, the walls played back his voice like a disc. This past week, the paint has drowned Kayita's odour and the bedroom walls have been quiet. Today, Nnam plans to wipe his image off the objects.

A week ago Nnam took a month off work and sent her sons, Lumumba and Sankara, to her parents in Uganda for Kayita's last funeral rites. That is why she is naked. Being naked, alone with silence in the house, is therapy. Now Nnam understands why when people lose their minds the first impulse is to strip off. Clothes are constricting but you don't realize that until you have walked naked in your house all day, every day, for a week.

◆

Kayita died in the bathroom with his pants down. He was forty-five years old and should have pulled up his pants before he collapsed. The more shame because it was Easter. Who dies naked on Easter?

That morning, he got up and swung his legs out of bed. He stood but then sat down again as if he had been pulled back. Then he put his hand on his chest and listened. Nnam, lying next to the wall, propped her head on her elbow and said, "What?"

"I guess I've not woken up yet." He yawned.

"Then come back to bed."

But Kayita stood up and wrapped a towel around his waist. At the door he turned to Nnam and said, "Go back to sleep. I'll give the children their breakfast."

Lumumba woke her up. He needed the bathroom but "Dad won't come out." Nnam got out of bed, cursing the architects who had put the bath and the toilet in the same room. She knocked and opened the bathroom door, saying, "It's only me."

Kayita lay on the floor with his head near the heater, his stomach against the bathroom mat, one end of the towel inside the toilet bowl, the other on the floor, him totally naked save for the briefs around his ankles.

Nnam did not scream. Perhaps she feared that Lumumba would come in and see his father naked. Perhaps it was because Kayita's eyes were closed as if he had only fainted. She closed the door and, calling out his name, pulled his briefs up. She took the towel out of the toilet bowl and threw it in the bath tub. Then she shouted, "Get me the phone, Lum."

She held the door closed when Lumumba gave it to her.

"Get me your father's gown, too," she said, dialling.

She closed the door and covered Kayita with his grey gown.

On the phone, the nurse told her what to do while she waited for the ambulance to arrive.

"Put him in recovery position ... keep him warm ... you need to talk to him ... make sure he can hear you ..."

When the paramedics arrived, Nnam explained that the only thing she had noticed was Kayita falling back in bed that morning. Tears gathered a bit when she explained to the boys, "Daddy is unwell but he'll be fine." She got dressed and rang a friend to come and pick up the boys. When the paramedics emerged from the bathroom, they had put an oxygen mask on Kayita, which reassured her. Because the friend had not arrived to take the boys, Nnam did not go with the ambulance. The paramedics would ring to let her know which hospital had admitted Kayita.

◆

When she arrived in Casualty, a receptionist told her to sit and wait. Then a young nurse came and asked, "Did you come with someone?"

Nnam shook her head and the nurse disappeared. After a few moments, the same nurse returned and asked, "Are you driving?"

She was and the nurse went away again.

"Mrs. Kayita?"

Nnam looked up.

"Come with me." It was an African nurse, "The doctor working on your husband is ready."

She led Nnam to a consultation room and told her to sit down.

"The doctor will be with you shortly," she said and closed the door behind her.

Presently, a youngish doctor wearing blue scrubs came in and introduced himself.

"Mrs. Kayita, I am sorry we could not save your husband: he was dead on arrival." His voice was velvety. "There was nothing we could do. I am sorry for your loss." He crossed his hands. Then the fingers of the left hand pinched at his lips. "Is there anything we can do?"

In Britain, grief is private — you know how women throw themselves about howling this, screaming that, back home? None of that. You can't force your grief on other people. When Nnam was overcome she ran to the toilet and held onto the sink. As she washed her face to walk out, she realized that she did not have her handbag. She went back to the consultation room. The African nurse was holding it.

Her name was Lesego. Was there something she could do? Nnam shook her head. "Is there someone you need me to call: you cannot drive in this state." Before Nnam said no, Lesego said, "Give me your phone."

Nnam passed it to her.

She scrolled down the contacts, calling out the names. When Nnam nodded at a name, Lesego rang the number and said, "I am calling from Manchester Royal infirmary.... I am sorry to inform you that.... Mrs. Kayita is still here.... Yes, yes ... yes of course ... I'll stay with her until you arrive."

Looking back now, Nnam cannot remember how many people Lesego rang. She only stopped when Ugandans started to arrive at the hospital. Leaving the hospital was the hardest. You know when you get those two *namasasana* bananas joined together by the skin: you rip them apart and eat one? That is how Nnam felt.

◆

Nnam starts cleaning in the bathroom. The floor has been replaced by blue mini mosaic vinyl. Rather than the wash basket, she puts the toilet mats in the bin. She goes to the cupboard to get clean ones. Instead she picks up all the toilet mats there are and stuffs them in the bin too: Kayita's stomach died on one of them. Then she bleaches the bathtub, the sink and the toilet bowl. She unhooks the shower curtain and stuffs it into the bin too. When she opens the cabinet, she finds Kayita's anti beard-bumps powder, a shaver, and cologne. They go into the bin. Mould has collected on the shelves inside the cabinet. She unhooks the cabinet off the wall and takes it to the front door. She will throw it outside later. When she returns, the bathroom is more spacious and breezy. She ties the bin-liner and takes it to the front door as well.

◆

Kayita had had two children before he met Nnam. He had left them in Uganda with their mother but his relationship with their mother had ended long before he met Nnam. On several occasions Nnam asked him to bring the children to Britain, but he clicked his tongue. "You don't know their mother; the children are her cash cow."

Still, Nnam was uneasy about his children being deprived of their father. She insisted that he ring them every weekend: she even bought the phone cards. When he visited, she sent them clothes.

Kayita had adapted well to the changing environment of a Western marriage — unlike other Ugandan men, married to women who immigrated before they did. Many such marriages strained when a groom, fresh from home, was "culture-shocked" and begun to feel emasculated by a Britain-savvy wife. Kayita had no qualms about assuming a domestic role when he was not working. They could only afford a small wedding; they could only afford two children. At the end of the month they pooled their salaries together: Kayita worked for G4S so his money was considerably smaller but he tried to offset this by doing a lot of overtime. After paying the bills and other households, they deducted monies to send home to his children and sometimes for issues in either family — someone has died, someone is sick, someone is getting married.

Nnam had bought a nine-acre tract of land in rural Kalule before she met Kayita. After decades in Manchester, she dreamt of retiring in rural Uganda. But when Kayita came along, he suggested that they buy land in Kampala and build a city house first.

"Why build a house we are not going to live in for the next two decades in rural Kalule where no one will rent it? The rent from the city house will be saved to build the house in Kalule."

It made sense.

They bought a piece of land at Nsangi. But Nnam's father, who purchased it for them, knew that most of the money came from his daughter. He put the title deed in her name. When Kayita protested that he was being sidelined, Nnam told her father to put everything in Kayita's name.

Because they could not afford the fare for the whole family to visit, Kayita was the one who flew to Uganda regularly to check on the house. However, it was largely built by Nnam's father, who was an engineer and the only person she could trust with their money. When the house was finished, Kayita found the tenants to rent it. That was in 1990, six years before his death. They had had the same tenants all that time. Nnam had been to see the house and had met the tenants.

◆

Nnam is cleaning the bedroom now. The windowsill is stained. Kayita used to put his wallet, car keys, spectacles, and G4S-pass on the windowsill at night. Once he put a form near the window while it was open. It rained and the paper got soaked. The ink melted and the colour spread on the windowsill, discolouring it. Nnam sprays *Muscle* cleaner on the stains but the ink will not budge. She goes for bleach.

After the window, she clears out the old handbags and shoes from the wardrobe's floor. She had sent Kayita's clothes to a charity shop soon after the burial but she finds a belt and a pair of his underwear behind the bags. Perhaps they are the reason his scent has persisted. After cleaning, she drops a scented tablet on the wardrobe floor.

◆

Ugandans rallied around her during that first week of Kayita's death. The men took over the mortuary issues, the women took care of the home, Nnam floated between weeping and sleeping. They arranged the funeral service in Manchester and masterminded the fundraising drive, saying, "We are not burying one of us in snow."

Throughout that week, women who worked shifts slept at Nnam's house, looking after the children then going to work. People brought food and money in the evening and prayed and sang. Two of her friends took leave and bought tickets to fly back to Uganda with her.

It was when she was buying the tickets that she wondered where the funeral would be held in Uganda, as their house had tenants. She rang and asked her father. He said that Kayita's family was not forthcoming about the arrangements.

"Not forthcoming?"

"Evasive."

"But why?"

"They are peasants, Nnameya: you knew that when you married him."

Nnam kept quiet. Her father was like that. He had never liked Kayita. Kayita had neither the degrees nor the right background.

"Bring Kayita home. We'll see when you get here," he said finally.

As soon as she saw Kayita's family at Entebbe Airport, Nnam knew that something was wrong. They were not the brothers she had met before and they were unfriendly. When she asked her family where Kayita's real family was, they said,

"That's the *real* family."

Nnam scratched her chin for a long time. There were echoes in her ears.

When the coffin was released from customs, Kayita's family took it, loaded it on a van they had brought, and drove off.

Nnam was mouth-open shocked.

"Do they think I killed him? I have the post-mortem documents."

"Post-mortem, who cares?"

"Perhaps he was ashamed of his family." Nnam was beginning to blame her father's snobbery. "Perhaps they think we're snobs."

She got into one of her family's cars to drive after Kayita's brothers.

"No, not snobbery," Meya, Nnam's oldest brother, said quietly. Then he turned to Nnam, who sat in the back seat, and said, "I think you need to be strong, Nnameya."

Instead of asking *what do you mean*, Nnam twisted her mouth and clenched her teeth as if anticipating a blow.

"Kayita is … *was* married. He has the two older children he told you about, but in the few times he returned, he has had two other children with his wife."

Nnam did not react. Something stringy was stuck between her lower front teeth. Her tongue, irritated, kept poking at it. Now she picked at it with her thumb nail.

"We only found out when he died, but father said we should wait to tell you when you were home with family."

In the car were three of her brothers, all older than her. Her sisters were in another car behind. Her father and the boys were in another; uncles and aunts were yet in another. Nnam was silent.

"We need to stop them and ask how far we are going in case we need to fill the tank." Another brother pointed at the van with the coffin.

Still Nnam remained silent. She was a *kiwuduwudu*, a dismembered torso — no feelings.

They came to Ndeeba roundabout and the coffin van veered into Masaka Road. In Ndeeba town, near the timber shacks, they overtook the van and flagged it down. Nnam's brothers jumped out of the car and went to Kayita's family. Nnam still picked at the irritating something in her teeth. Ndeeba was wrapped in the mouldy smell of half-dry timber and sawdust. Heavy planks fell on each other and rumbled. Planks being cut sounded like a lawnmower. She looked across the road at the petrol station with a carwash and smiled, *You need to be strong, Nnameya,* as if she had an alternative.

"How far are we going?" Meya asked Kayita's brothers. "We might need to fill the tank."

"Only to Nsangi," one of them replied.

"Don't try to lose us: we shall call the police."

The van drove off. The three brothers went back to the car.

"They are taking him to Nsangi, Nnam. I thought your house in Nsangi is rented out?"

Like a dog pricking up its ears, Nnam sat up. Her eyes moved from one brother to another to another, as if the answer was written on their faces.

"Get me father on the phone," she said.

Meya set the phone on speaker. When their father's voice came, Nnam asked, "Father, do you have the title deeds for the house in Nsangi?"

"They are in the safe deposit."

"Are they in his name?"

"Am I stupid?"

Nnam closed her eyes. "Thanks father thanks father thanks thank you."

He did not reply.

"When was rent last paid?"

"Three weeks ago: where are you?"

"Don't touch it, Father," she said. "We're in Ndeeba. We're not spending any more money on this funeral. His family will bury him: I don't care whether they stuff him into a hole. They are taking him to Nsangi."

"Nsangi? It does not make sense."

"Neither to us."

When Nnam switched off the phone, she said to her brothers, "The house is safe," as if they had not heard. "Now they can hold the vigil in a cave if they please."

The brothers did not respond.

"When we get there," there was life in Nnam's voice now, "you will find out what is going on: I'll be in the car. Then you will take me back to town. I need to go to a good salon. Then I'll get a good busuuti and dress up. I am not a widow anymore."

"There is no need …" Meya began.

"I said I am going to a salon to do my hair, my nails, and my face. But first I'll have a bath and a good meal. We'll see about the vigil later."

Then she laughed as if she was demented.

"I've just remembered." She coughed and hit her chest to ease it. "When we were young," she swallowed hard, "remember how people used to say that we Ganda women are property-minded? Apparently, when a husband dies unexpectedly, the first thing you do is to look for the titles of ownership, contracts, car logbook, and keys and all such things. You wrap them tight in a cloth and wear them as sanitary towel. When they are safe between your legs, you let off a rending cry, *Bazze wange!*"

Her brothers laughed nervously.

"As soon as I realized that my house was threatened — *pshooo.*" She made a gesture of wind whizzing over her head. "Grief, pain, shock — gone."

◆

As the red brick double-storied house in Nsangi came into view, Nnam noted with trepidation that the hedge and compound were well cared for. When the coffin van drove in, Kayita's people, excitable, surrounded it. The women cried their part with clout. Kayita's wife's wail stood out: a lament for a husband who had died alone in the cold. The crying was like a soundtrack to Kayita's coffin being offloaded and carried into the house. But then the noise receded: Nnam had just confirmed that Kayita's wife had been the tenant all along. She had met her. Kayita had been paying his wife's rent with Nnam's money. Nnam held her mouth in disbelief.

"Kayita was not a thief: he was a murderer." She twisted her mouth again.

Even then, the heart is a coward — Nnam's crumbled as her brothers stepped out of the car. Travelling was over. The reality of her situation stared straight in her face. Her sisters too arrived. They came and sat in the car with her. Her father, the boys, her uncles and aunts parked outside the compound. They were advised not to get out of their cars. The situation stared in Nnam's face without blinking.

People walked in and out of her house while she was frightened of stepping out of the car. She did not even see an old man come to the car. He had bent low and was peering inside when she noticed him. He introduced himself as Kayita's father. He addressed Nnam. "I understand you are the woman who has been living with my son in London."

"Manchester," one of Nnam's sisters corrected rudely.

"Manchester, London, New York, they are like flies to me. I can't tell male from female." The old man turned back to Nnam. "You realize Kayita had a wife." Before Nnam answered, he carried on. "Can you to allow her to have this last moment with her husband with dignity? We do not expect you to advertise your presence. The boys, however, we accept. We'll need to show them to the clan when you're ready."

The sisters were speechless. Nnam watched the man walk back to her house.

The two friends from Manchester arrived and came to the car where Nnam sat. At that point, Nnam decided to confront her humiliation. She looked in the eyes of her friends and explained the details of Kayita's deception the way a doctor explains the extent of infection to a patient. There was dignity in her explaining it to them herself.

◆

There is nothing much to do in the kitchen but she pulls out all the movable appliances to clean out the accumulated grime and rubbish. Under the sink, hidden behind the shopping bags, is Kayita's mug. Nnam bought it on their fifth wedding anniversary — World's Best Husband. She takes it to the front door and puts it into a bin. On top of the upper cabinets are empty tins of Quality Street that Kayita treated himself to at Christmas. Kayita had a sweet tooth: he loved muffins, ice cream, ginger nuts, and éclairs. He hoarded the tins, saying that one day they would need them. Nnam smiles as she takes the tins to the front door — Kayita's tendency to hoard things now makes sense.

◆

Nnam, her friends and family returned to the funeral at around 11.00 p.m. Where she sat, she was able to observe Kayita's wife. The woman looked old enough to be her mother. That observation, rather than give her satisfaction, stung. Neither the pampering, the expensive busuuti and expensive jewellery, nor the British airs that she wore could keep away the pain that Kayita had remained loyal to such a woman. It dented her well-choreographed air of indifference. Every time she looked at his wife, it was not jealousy that wrung her heart: it was the whisper *you were not good enough*.

Just then, her aunt, the one who prepared her for marriage, came to whisper tradition. She leaned close and said, "When a husband dies you must wear a sanitary towel immediately. As he is wrapped for burial, it is placed on his genitals so that he does not return for ..."

"Fuck that shit!"

"I was only ..."

"Fuck it." Nnam did not bother with Luganda.

The aunt melted away.

◆

As more of Nnam's relations arrived, so did a gang of middle-aged women. Nnam did not know who invited them. One thing was clear, though; they were angry. Apparently, Nnam's story was common. They had heard about her plight and had come to her aid. The women looked like former *nkuba kyoyo* the broom-swinging economic immigrants to the West. They were dressed expensively. They mixed Luganda and English as if the languages were sisters.

They wore weaves or wigs. Their makeup was defiant as if someone had dared to tell them off. Some were bleached. They unloaded
crates of beer and cartons of Uganda Waragi. They brought them
to the tent where Nnam sat with her family and started sharing out.
One of them came to her and asked, "You are the Nnameya from
Manchester?" She had a raspy voice like she loved her Waragi.

Nnam nodded and the woman leaned closer.

"If you want to do the crying widow thing, go ahead, but
leave the rest to us."

"Do I look like I am crying?"

The woman laughed triumphantly. It was as if she had been
given permission to do whatever she wanted to do. Nnam decided
that the gang were business women, perhaps single mothers,
wealthy and bored.

Just then a cousin of Nnam arrived. It was clear she carried
burning news. She sat next to Nnam and whispered, "Yours are
the only sons."

She rubbed her hands as if Nnam had just won the lottery.
She turned her head and pointed with her mouth toward Kayita's
widow. "Hers are daughters only."

Nnam smiled. She turned and whispered to her family,
"Lumumba is the heir. Our friend has no sons," and a current of
joy rippled through the tent as her family passed on the news.

At first the gang of women mourned quietly, drinking their
beer and enquiring about Britain as if they had come to the vigil
out of goodness toward Kayita. At around two o'clock, when the
choir got tired, one of the women stood up.

"Fellow mourners," she started in a gentle voice as if she was
bringing the good tidings of resurrection.

A reverent hush fell over the mourners.

"Let's tell this story properly." She paused. "There is another
woman in this story."

Stunned silence.

"There are also two innocent children in the story."

"*Amiina mwattu.*" The amens from the gang could have been coming from evangelists.

"But I'll start with the woman's story."

According to her, the story started when Nnam's parents sent her to Britain to study and better herself. She had worked hard and studied and saved, but along came a liar and a thief.

"She was lied to," the woman with a raspy voice interrupted impatiently. She stood up as if the storyteller was ineffectual. "He married her — we have the pictures, we have the video — he even lied to her parents. Look at that shame!"

"Come on," the interrupted woman protested gently. "I was unwrapping the story properly. You are tearing into it."

"Sit down. We don't have all night," the raspy woman said.

The gentle woman sat down. The other mourners were still dumbfounded by the women's audacity.

"A clever person asks," the raspy woman carried on. "Where did Kayita get the money to build such a house when he was just broom-swinging in Britain? Then you realize that *ooooh*, he's married a rich woman, *a proper lawyer in Manchester.*"

"How does she know all that?" Nnam whispered to her family.

"*Hmmm*, words have legs."

"He told her that he was not married but this wife here knew what was going on," the woman was saying. "Does anyone here know the shock this woman is going through? No, why, because she is one of those women who emigrated? For those who do not know, this is her house built with her money. I am finished."

There was clapping as she sat down and grabbed her beer. The mourning ambiance of the funeral had now turned to the excitement of a political rally.

"Death came like a thief." A woman with a squeaky voice stood up. "It did not knock to alert Kayita. The curtain blew away and what filth!"

"If this woman had not fought hard to bring Kayita home, the British would have burnt him. They don't joke. They have no space to waste on unclaimed bodies. But has anyone had the grace to thank her? No. Instead, Kayita's father tells her to shut up. What a peasant!"

The gang had started throwing words about haphazardly. It could turn into throwing insults. An elder came to calm them down.

"You have made your point, mothers of the nation, and I add it is a valid point because let's face it, he lied to her, and as you say, there are two innocent children involved."

"But first, let us see the British wife," a woman interrupted him. "Her name is Nnameya. Let the world see the woman this peasant family has used like arse wipes."

Nnam did not want to stand up, but she did not want to seem ungrateful to the women's effort. She stood up, head held high.

"Come." A drunk woman grabbed her hand and led her through the mourners into the living room. "Look at her," she said to Kayita's family.

The mourners, even those who had been at the back of the house, had come to stare at Nnam. She looked away from the coffin because tears were letting down her "hold your head high" stance.

"Stealing from me I can live with, but what about my children?"

At that moment the gang's confrontational attitude fell away and they shook their heads and wiped their eyes and sucked their teeth.

"The children indeed ... *Abaana maama* ... *yiyi*, but men also ... this lack of choice to whom you're born to ... who said men are human ..."

The vigil had turned in favour of Nnam.

It was then that Nnam's eyes betrayed her. She glanced at the open coffin. There is no sight more revolting than a corpse caught telling lies.

◆

Nnam is in the lounge. She has finished cleaning. She takes all the photographs that had been on the walls — wedding, birthdays, school portraits, Christmases — and sorts them out. All the pictures taken before Kayita's death, whether he is in the picture or not, are separated from the others. She throws them in the bin-bag and ties it. She takes the others to the bedroom. She gets her nightgown and covers her nakedness. Then she takes the bin with the pictures to the front door. She opens the door and the freshness of the air outside hits her. She ferries all the bin-bags, one by one, and places them below the chute's mouth. She throws down the smaller bin-bags first. They drop as if in a new long-drop latrine — the echo is delayed. She breaks the cabinet and drops the bits down. Finally, she stuffs the largest bin-bag, the one with the pictures, down the chute's throat. The chute chokes. Nnam goes back to the house and brings back a mop. In her mind, her father's recent words are still ringing: "We can't throw them out of the house just like that. There are four innocent children in that house and Lumumba, being Kayita's eldest son, has inherited all of them. Let's not heap that guilt on his shoulders."

She uses the handle to dig at the bag. After a while of breaking glass and the frames, the bin-bag falls through. When she comes back to the house, the smell of paint is overwhelming. She takes the mop to the kitchen and washes her hands. Then she opens all the windows and the wind blows the curtains wildly. She takes off the gown and the cool wind blows on her bare skin. She closes her eyes and raises her arms. The sensation of wind on her skin, of being naked, of the silence in a clean house is so overwhelming she does not cry.

## MICHAEL MENDIS

# The Sarong-Man in the Old House, and an Incubus for a Rainy Night

The wetness is really a celebration, when it hadn't rained in such a long time and the dust outside his house had stopped moving, with nothing to move against, nothing to stir it into swirls. And the smell, as the water comes hurtling through the sky, he sees it almost in slow-motion, speeding, in a hurry to meet the ground that has been dry for too long. The smell of it has always been homely to him, because he remembers a friend, a girl from his teen years, who always used to ask him, "Do you like the smell of the rain, Wijey? Do you like the smell of it on the dust?" and he would say "Yes," every time, while wondering if it was so. It must have been the change. The instant change in the air they had been breathing — its sudden freshness. It was a funny way to find hope, a groundless reason to suddenly feel better.

Wijey remembers being sixteen, how difficult it was. He is now at the very edge of his seventies, sitting on a sloping armchair with armrests that could swivel around to become footrests. And now, so many years after being sixteen, he thinks that the smell had also a note of innocence to it. Not in any way a symbol, but a memory. And this makes sense, actually. Because it's his own innocence as a boy who found hope in the smell of rain-on-dust that he remembers, that he associates with the smell of rain-on-dust today.

That girl, wherever may she be now?

Wijey brings his trembling, dying fingers to his lips, fiddling absently with the dry flakes of skin there, picking at them. A habit he carried to maturity from immaturity — like an old seller of wares, bringing back home a load he was supposed to trade away for something better.

◆

It was raining that night, more than half a century ago, when he sat in his bedroom, teaching algebra to Krishnan, a newfound friend.

Wijey remembers this now in the darkness of his corridor, with the green paint on the walls. And nothing else but the shadows.

The rainy day ghosts.

They were both still boys, and Wijey had no idea of the things he was about to discover beyond that night, but that's not what moves him the most about this memory. There is, in most of us, a stolid self-pity of sorts, when we think of things that broke our hearts when we were just children. But more, much more, when they break us somewhere else. A place without a name, for now.

◆

And Wijey taught him carefully, what he knew — navigating the various Xs and Ys, cautious not to overwhelm.

Wijey was a rich little boy, unlike Krishnan. With a lot of books lined against his bedroom wall, the Dickenses and the Flemings on two opposite sides. His shiny prefect's badge, although only of the middle-school, sitting primly on the dresser, next to the bottle of Old Spice he never wore because he didn't like the smell. They were all there: little pieces of imported wealth that he had arrayed around himself, in case anyone wanted to know why he was important; I think. Because he had no other answer to give of his own.

◆

When the lesson ended, Wijey's mother convinced Krishnan to stay the night, because it was not safe to drive in the storm all the way to Wattala, where he lived. She said it would probably last all night, the storm.

Their dinner was brought up to the bedroom in a large tray. The woman carrying it was quiet and brisk, and Wijey called her by name. While they ate, she laid out Wijey's spare pyjamas for Krishnan, and fresh towels.

"Do you want more parippu?" Wijey kept asking him, or "Shall I put some pol sambol?" And they talked about the radio shows and music, and Rukmani Devi, and the Hepburns. Krishnan looked up at the ceiling a lot as he talked, a funny habit he probably outgrew. But the Hepburns, he couldn't stop talking about: those two women, being so different from each other. He kept saying, "It's Audrey's body, machan … that shape," and he would have used a word like *exquisite*, had he had access to it, to describe what he meant.

Wijey didn't like being called *machan*. And Wijey didn't like talking about the Hepburns. But he didn't say anything. He sensed there was something to it, this dislike of the topic — but only in the way one sees soft tendrils of smoke seeping through a door. It wasn't a fire, an inferno, if he didn't open the door. It was just a stream of smoke, leaking. Harmless. At least for the time being.

They talked into the night, with the rain hammering outside, about things that only barely snagged Wijey's attention. Something else kept him talking, wanting to talk, but all of it was still shut behind the door that screened the streaming smoke.

He kept the windows open, and tiny vapours of rain sprayed into the room with the smell of dissolving dust, and soon it was time to go to sleep.

◆

Wijey's days stretch and inch into each other now, with hardly any movement in the house of green walls, except for the shadows, starting short in the mornings, and gradually reaching across the floors and furniture, along the route the sun took across the sky. Like a sundial: marking time and undulating memory.

But everything in the house seems alive, their movements all at an equal speed, an equal rhythm. The furniture, the shadows, the thick dust. The man.

Wijey climbs the stairs forever, a walking stick clutched in his fingers, his sarong held tightly in a clench of cloth around his waist — undone, slipping, unhelpful.

Nobody is here. Nobody has remained.

He sways.

The stairs, wooden as they are, creak. The walking stick seems to bend. He palms the wall to balance himself.

He forgets the sarong.

And he is naked, instantly. One hand on the wall, one hand on a bandy stick, in the middle of his stairs.

The sarong, a bangle around his ankles.

◆

Krishnan, Wijey remembered, had rather long hair that night. And, after his bath, before they went to sleep, his hair covered his ears, fell lightly on his forehead, curled along the curve of the nape of his neck.

Wijey was moving about, clearing his bed of books and debris, putting the Classics back in the places they were used to, straightening the textbooks edgewise on his desk. But it's the corner of his eye that was most clever, as he sees — almost accidentally but not quite so — Krishnan coming out of the bathroom in the gleaming white towel Prema had given him.

Wijey's forearms turn cold.

He begins to fuss even more with the books that are now geometrical on his desktop. Something had happened. There was the largeness of Krishnan's shoulders, wet, bubbles of bathwater still there. There was the shut bedroom door, and the sudden privacy between the two of them stemming from that fact, which hit Wijey the moment the door shut with a click. There was, maybe, also a nervousness in Wijey. A discomfort. An excitement. Shivers on his fingers that could have been named by any of those things, or all of them.

Krishnan dries his hair with a second towel, roughly, completely unaware that Wijey is suddenly uncomfortable. His shoulders, and the muscles on his arms, work furiously as he rubs his head dry — and Wijey, with his head lowered to his dresser, watches, gulping. One index-finger running absently, up and down, along the edge of his dresser-top.

He says, with some difficulty, "You — you shouldn't have bathed. It's late. Raining also."

Krishnan grins, shrugging. "Yes, but I can't sleep without a bath, machan. Amma says I'll be bald before I am twenty."

Wijey nods stiffly. And tries to smile.

Krishnan stops wiping himself. He only stands there, with one towel around his waist, another clutched limply in his hand, and Wijey doesn't know what to do, doesn't know why his breath is rising, and he tries looking everywhere other than at Krishnan.

"Well, let's sleep. I can't wait to sleep. Before the rain stops." Wijey's speech is discordant, and Krishnan squints at him for a split-second.

Immediately, Wijey regrets his suggestion — because no one sleeps in a towel. And as Krishnan picks up the pyjamas laid out neatly on the bed, Wijey wildly imagines that Krishnan is about to take his towel off in front of him, and panics inside, though only for that second. In the next moment, they both instinctively turn away from each other: one polite, the other private. But while Krishnan turns around to face a wall, Wijey has turned around to find the dresser-mirror right in front of him, and all of this is wild and spontaneous and happens very fast, much too fast to have been in any way premeditated ... but when it happens, when Krishnan inexpertly crouches forward on one leg to pull on his pyjamas and his towel slips — slyly or inadvertently — to reveal him, Wijey doesn't even think of looking away.

He is, admittedly, caught by surprise.

But, for the briefest second, he calms down.

Because in that quickly passing moment of an unknowingly revealed Krishnan, Wijey realizes that it was his beauty. This boy in his room with a slipping white towel was beautiful, and that was the cause for all this panic inside him.

◆

Upstairs, on the top of a long, old, dark-wooded cabinet, are frames of dusty photographs. Dark squares of history that don't receive even the shortest glance from Wijey now, because he no longer remembers them to be there.

But in any house that has been lived in for a long time, there are things that mark, or claim, the entrances and exits of travellers. Bits of history bigger or smaller, but more invisible than a framed photograph on a cabinet-top. Like the puddle of candle-wax hardened at the top of the staircase, where a twenty-something Wijey had sat entangled with someone he thought he loved, during a long power-cut years and years ago, reading books. He had left with a lot of explanations to Wijey, most of which explained nothing, except the vague possibility that Wijey, despite his wealth, and his fervent way of loving someone, was somehow not *enough*. Then there was the dent on the kitchen wall, a deep gash of wounded plaster, that marked the spot where a dinner plate had crashed, when the young boy who was madly in love with Wijey refused to accept his sheepish explanation of what had happened with the stranger in Pettah. He had gone, too. And there was the sticker of Mickey Mouse, now grey and slowly disintegrating, stuck to the bookcase in Wijey's small office upstairs: a remnant from a trip abroad, with a friend who was gone now, who had used to call every once in a while to make sure Wijey was still there.

There were the empty bottles of wine and arrack containing all the conversations that were poured into them as the drinks were poured out. And there was that ashtray someone else had given him for a birthday. The cricket bat another one had forgotten to pack in his haste of walking out, which Wijey, in a histrionic moment of self-consoling, had had mounted on the wall beside the dining table.

Houses are full of these things, little redundant witnesses to truths that need not bear reminding. The truths of loneliness, and the endlessness of our numbered days.

◆

The rain is now an easy drip out in the garden, keeping time with the *tic-tic* of the ceiling fan. The lights are out, there is darkness everywhere, and Krishnan is snoring comfortably beside Wijey, his bedsheets tangled somewhere near his knees, a pillow shoved under one arm.

Wijey is wide awake, his wide eyes stunned by the ceiling he couldn't see.

Beside Krishnan, his arms folded across his chest, Wijey was shivering — not from the cold, but because of the new and frightening weakness of his body, as it yearned, now indubitably, for the touch of the person sleeping beside him.

Krishnan stirs, and murmurs something in his sleep.

Wijey, mindlessly, crawls closer to Krishnan. Close enough that, without an inch between them, Krishnan's breath warms the ball of Wijey's shoulder.

And, if he closes his eyes, this minimizing-maximizing hotness on his shoulder would be the only thing linking him to the physical world. And the snoring, which was really just a low rumble; and the dripping rainwater outside. If he closes his eyes, he would fall asleep to these things. And, while he slept, there wouldn't be anything to touch the certainty of those few facts.

Even thinking this forms a lump in his throat.

Wijey shifts his body a bit more, carefully, so as not to disturb Krishnan's sleep, and allows his shoulder to touch, quietly press, Krishnan's half-open lips.

It's the quietest kiss Wijey will ever receive. Or *steal*.

In the darkness, with eyes at the ends of his fingers, Wijey finds Krishnan's hand, lying in the narrow gap between their bodies, palm upward. Slowly, like touching a freshly opened wound, tentatively, Wijey lets his finger touch Krishnan's palm: so gently that Krishnan will not know that his body was being discovered, and (in a rudimentary way) loved. So gently that Wijey does not feel Krishnan's skin beyond its stillness, its sleepingness. He lets them grow, the ovals of skin that were in contact.

Krishnan doesn't stir.

*Succubus, incubus, succubus, incubus.*

The words seemed to float toward him from his books, and he, in an unnoticed distraction, wondered which name would more accurately apply to him.

He stays this way for a very long time: his hand in Krishnan's palm, and Krishnan's lips on his shoulder. Both of them breathing, one of them sleeping.

◆

Soon, there will be the birds calling through the coming morning. And with it, a resignation. Failure, salvation.

There he will be, at the end of the race, knowing that this isn't how it is completed, and that this is in fact the way it is interrupted, prevented from being complete.

Krishnan was supposed to wake up, find Wijey there holding his hand, and kiss him, and tell him that this was not a forbidden thing to be wanting, that it was only natural that Wijey found him beautiful, and fascinating in the way that beautiful people are found. They were supposed to come together, and there needn't have been a question of what was to be done between them, what was to be found, what was to be taken home. What was to be remembered.

The biggest regret for Wijey was not that none of this came to pass, but that Krishnan would know nothing of what happened in their room that night. For Krishnan, when he woke up in a few minutes, an hour maybe, Wijey would still be just a friend: wealthy, quiet, good at algebra.

◆

The journey from a downstairs window to his bedroom is now a long one for Wijey, a trip through memory, through old lives that cannot be unlived.

Stories that will soon vanish into delirium.

But, for now, Wijey's thoughts are slow, measured, trained. And in a night with a rare downpour, and dust-smells and old memories, he wonders a lot of things.

His large empty house of green walls could be, right now, filled with grandchildren. A wife. She wouldn't know him to the last detail, but would still love him, and hold his elbow while he clutched the unhelpful sarong … he may have lied to her from time to time: slipped into the shadows of the night and made love with a boy in a neighbour's unsuspecting garden. But she would still be here.

Because, where, after all, does selflessness end, and selfishness begin? To a man who could have neither this, nor that, what does it all mean? He would have tried his best. Fairness, honour. To be certain and a refuge from her sadness. To be sufficient in every way he could help, and repentant for the ways in which he wasn't.

◆

But here is Krishnan, sleeping innocently beside him all those years ago. And here is Wijey, denied a newly found desire, and a resolution to find it again elsewhere.

There was no turning back for him.

## ANDREA MULLANEY

# The Ghost Marriage

I did not meet my husband until six years after he died. He comes to me now after dark, speaking only in the poetry he loved when alive:

*The beauty of night*
*The scent of jasmine flowers*
*Your long hair, unbound.*

I have often wondered how those six years might have changed him, whether Chonglin was always the gentle, kind lover that he is now or whether death has smoothed out the imperfections in his character, just as it has left his beautiful face forever unwrinkled. But I do not question him. I sense there are things he cannot say.

He did not come to me on our wedding night; it was almost three months afterwards that he first appeared in my room. Perhaps he felt shy, or was not able to until then — I do not know how he is able to come at all. And, because I cannot ask, I do not know if this is normal with marriages like ours. Perhaps there are many women in Shanghai who are visited at night by their dead husbands. I think, though, that I am the only Englishwoman.

Such knowledge of Chonglin's life that I have comes from Gao Bohai, my husband's brother and the one who arranged our ghost marriage. When he speaks of his brother, which is rare, Bohai's face becomes softer, less fixed and serious than when we talk of business, which we must discuss every day.

He will mention, perhaps, a village the silk boats must pass through and say: "Ah, my brother would often go there to fish. He said the waters were very good, very pure." Or, perhaps, there will be a letter from a certain merchant, complaining of the quality of our latest shipment, and he will say: "Chonglin never liked this man. He said he was like a cormorant who drops the food already in his mouth to pick up more."

I snatch up his words, eager for the simplest detail to remind me that my husband was once alive. Sometimes I feel that my morning conversations with Bohai are all that keep me from madness.

When Gao Bohai first asked if he might call on me, I had thought only that my father's young Chinese partner wished to extend his sympathies and, perhaps, to explain some of the legal affairs to do with the dissolution of their trading company. He had dined with us, displaying manners as good as his English, on two polite occasions during the six months I had been living in Shanghai.

When my father died I was already wearing half-mourning and had only to add more, but I did not feel it. He was almost as much a stranger to me as he had been when I arrived, sick and shaking from a difficult sea voyage and still in full black after the death of my mother.

She and I had lived a quiet life; we had no friends, few acquaintances, and no other living family. I had been trained for no profession and, being neither sufficiently rich nor beautiful, such suitors as were in prospect were not much agreeable to me. So for want of a better alternative I was shipped off to a man I knew only as an awkward figure to whom I had been briefly presented on his infrequent visits home — a stranger I soon forgot.

To welcome me in China, my father had prepared a room in his house filled with exquisite tapestries and expensive carved screens. But we had been too long apart; he knew nothing of my tastes and was a man too reserved to reach out and bridge the gap between us. And, for my part, I was too proud and resentful to try. Perhaps if we had lived together longer, the distance might have narrowed and we would have come to trust each other.

But we did not get the chance. He had lived through the Opium War and had been instrumental in brokering the treaty agreement which opened up the port to free trade, making him a target for those who resented the British settlement here. But in the end he was killed by a simple infection which flooded his lungs.

I was immediately the subject of attention from the residents of the colony, who came visiting to offer consolation and, with varying degrees of tact, to enlist me for various small commissions at home. They all assumed that I would, of course, be returning to England on the next available passage. As did I, though with no great enthusiasm.

But while I gathered my affairs, I replied to Gao Bohai with an invitation to tea, since I had learned that this was an important social custom here. He arrived promptly and waited with me in the drawing room while the maid carefully prepared the small pot, in the English fashion as I had shown her.

"I wish, Miss Keswick, to express my sorrow at the death of your father. He was a good man who did much to improve the relations between our empires and to bring prosperity to Shanghai," he began, as if reciting a studied speech. "I think, perhaps, you do not yet know what you have lost, but that is understandable. You did not know him as I did. He was against the opium smuggling, against the indemnity payment — he did much to lessen the humiliation of our officials here. He was loyal to his country always, but he loved China."

It was a view of my father I had not thought of, perhaps a fair one, yet I could not help but resent the implication of his words.

"Indeed, Mr. Gao, I can believe that he did. He certainly loved it more than England, or I would have known him a deal better."

He inclined his head, respectfully, but answered me firmly. "I believe that he wanted very much for you to come to understand him. Do you like Shanghai?"

I hardly knew how to answer. "I have not seen very much of the city. But — yes. I shall be sorry to leave."

"Would you wish to stay?"

"Perhaps, but that is not possible, Mr. Gao."

"You have friends in England, you have a place to return to?"

"No, I have not. But I can hardly stay here alone."

"You could stay here if you were to marry. And if you remained, the company would not have to be sold, as there would still be a British director, which is required under the Treaty. This would be very good for Shanghai, for our trade is growing very well, and I think that soon the company would be worth far more than it could be at present disposed of."

I reached for my teacup to try to hide the astonishment which must have flooded my face. It was an extraordinary proposal. I knew it was not a personal one, since I was well aware both that Gao Bohai was a married man and that, unlike some of the more primitive cultures I had learned of in school, the Chinese did not allow polygamy. Several of my British visitors had attempted to inquire whether I had any matrimonial plans — Mrs. Nye had even tried to subtly put forward her half-witted son Charles — but I had not come halfway around the world to marry someone for the mere sake of it. If I had wanted to do that, there were half-wits enough at home I could have suffered. For Mr. Gao to advise me so openly to marry seemed a wholly unwarranted intrusion.

My feelings must have shown. He leaned forward, anxiously, and continued: "Miss Keswick, I hope you will forgive my pre-sumption. I merely make a suggestion, a way that, if you wished, you could remain here in Shanghai with full status."

"And whom do you suggest that I marry?"

"My younger brother, Gao Chonglin."

"I was not aware that you had a brother," I said, in some confusion. I was sure that my father had mentioned that the entire upkeep of the Gao family, including his widowed mother and his sisters, rested on Bohai.

"He is not living," he said quietly. "He was caught in a fire during the occupation and was killed. It would be a ghost marriage."

Later, when Bohai had left, I found that my hastily-given assurance that I would think over his proposal — a promise given purely to hasten his departure — was, indeed, something I could not avoid. Although it had sounded preposterous and barbaric at first, I was prepared to understand a strange logic to the practice as he had described it among the clans, where in certain situations a young woman would be married to the dead son of another family. It was a business arrangement, he explained, to seal a dynastic truce or contract. Such things could be undertaken with living grooms, too, as he understood also happened in the West, but then the young couple were obliged to live together whether their tastes and inclinations agreed or not.

These "ghost marriages" sounded disturbing, but I had to concede that perhaps they were less onerous for the woman than the uncertain potential of a life given over to a husband not of her choosing.

"Indeed," Bohai had said, almost eagerly, "there are many women in Shanghai who work in the silk trade and who wish to live independently rather than take a living husband, so they ask the priest to find them a ghost to marry. Their families are satisfied that she will not die unmourned, as it is the custom that a woman is remembered only by her husband's family, and they in turn are then able to adopt a grandson to continue their line."

That, he was quick to add, was not what he intended in offering his late brother as a potential bridegroom; I presumed, though he did not say so, that he himself could continue his family's line. He understood that our customs were different, he hoped that I would not be offended by his proposal, he wished only to suggest a possibility which might serve both our interests, allowing me to remain here in my father's house without need of chaperone and allowing him to continue running the company that they had begun together.

It was, of course, ridiculous.

"Has any Englishwoman ever contracted one of these ghost marriages?" I had asked. And he had answered that he was unaware of any. Though I had not been close to my father, he was a respectable gentleman and I was his daughter: such an improper undertaking was not to be considered.

And yet the very act of rejecting the idea so decisively meant that I admitted the possibility of accepting it; from there, perhaps it was inevitable that I should slowly admit the desirability of accepting it, and within a week, without knowing how, I had made up my mind to do it. In the end, I believe, what finally swayed me was the prospect of another miserable voyage home, with constant *mal de mer* and nothing to look forward to in England but its cessation.

Once I had conveyed my shift in opinion to Gao Bohai, he acted swiftly. The documents were drawn up, the necessary ceremonies were arranged — most of which, I was glad to find, could be conducted in my absence — and shortly I found myself before an altar, opposite a paper effigy meant to represent my dead groom. Surrounded by solemn Chinese faces, including the entire Gao family and other notables from the city, I went to some pains to maintain my composure, for we were in what they considered to be a temple and I did not wish to give offence. But when a hunched old woman crept forward waving sticks above her head — they swayed like winter branches in a strong wind — I had to bite the inside of my cheek to keep from erupting in unseemly laughter. She had lit them from a lamp and they issued a strange, sweet scent. I believed she was my new mother-in-law.

Perhaps, if it had not all been so peculiar, I might have dwelt on the situation, or become discouraged: this was hardly the wedding my own mother would have wanted for her beloved only daughter. But she was not here and as it was, it passed in a sort of haze as I was paraded through an event I could not understand.

After the ceremony there was a banquet, with endless rounds of unfamiliar delicacies passing before me and unintelligible talk all around me, and after the banquet Gao Bohai accompanied me back to my father's house, now truly my own home in law for the first time. At the gate, under the jasmine tree, he paused and offered me his hand.

"As I am now your brother," he said, awkwardly, "I would be honoured if you would address me as Bohai and accept my sincere wish that this marriage may bring you what you require."

It was an odd form of congratulations, but I understood: he could hardly wish me joy. It must, I realized, be strange for him also; this could not have been the wedding that he had once hoped for his younger brother either. I gave him my hand, but instead of raising it to his lips in polite salute, he simply raised it toward him and seemed to study it.

It was dusk and the moon was low in the sky; I was fatigued from the day and wished very much to be alone, yet something impelled me to ask: "Chonglin ... what was he like? Did he work with you?"

I could not yet read Chinese faces as easily as Western ones, but the sadness which seeped through Bohai's staid expression was clear. "No. My brother was ... young. The baby of the family. He had no interest in business. He loved to be outdoors, he loved all things in nature. We thought there was time to ... indulge him, until he joined the company, so we allowed him to study and to write."

"What did he write?" In truth, I was really asking, who have I married?

"Poetry." Bohai breathed out the word, very slowly. "Chonglin had a strange fancy. He did not care for Chinese poetry. He became a student of a Japanese form, hokku. Do you know it?"

I did not. The poetry I knew was Tennyson, Southey, Miss Barrett. But as I wished Bohai good night and retired inside, it comforted me somehow to know that this ghost husband had been a man once, a man who disliked business and liked poetry. It made him more substantial, less alien. Perhaps, in time, I could eventually come to think of him as my true husband, who had died, leaving me a true widow. It might make my peculiar situation feel less of a masquerade.

But as the news began to disseminate, it became apparent that no pretty form of words would alter the case for the residents of the British Settlement, who made it known with varying degrees of subtlety that my paper marriage had put me firmly beyond the pale. Mrs. Hamilton averted her head when I passed her on the Bund, the heart of the Settlement; Mrs. Nye and Miss Farrell ostentatiously exchanged their seats when I took my place at Sunday service in the consul building; the Reverend Liddell took me aside afterwards and suggested that perhaps the service in the newly formed American Concession might be more suitable for me. The message was clear: marrying a living Chinaman would have been bad enough, but a dead one was quite repulsive.

Their feelings did not concern me. I had no friends there; I did not miss the tedious chatter of the colony with their fretful complaints about the climate, the inefficiency of the Chinese customs men, or the ingratitude of those at home for the sacrifices they were making for the Empire — sacrifices which involved the accumulation of great wealth. With relief I shed the round of visiting which I had felt obliged to adopt since coming to join my father's household.

I found, instead, that my position allowed me the luxury I had longed for since my mother's death: to be left alone. My servants were quiet and respectful; my visitors were few. Bohai came every morning for an hour to discuss business matters, a kind formality during which I merely nodded assent to everything. Occasionally his timid sisters or his quiet, pretty wife would pay a call, a courtesy matter, I assumed, but with little common language between us, these visits consisted of virtually silent tea-drinking sessions. I found them rather calming.

The rest of the time was my own, to read, to walk in the gardens, and, as my confidence grew, to explore Shanghai. I hired rickshaws, and once I managed to convey to the drivers that I did not want merely to be taken to the Bund and back, was carried hither and yon across the city, marvelling at the abundance of people and the makeshift buildings springing up everywhere as trade flourished.

There seemed no part of the city which was not in flux: though I saw no signs of the late war, it was apparent even to my untutored eyes that it was a time of great change. And everywhere, the Chinese, swarming in from the countryside, swelling the population of the city to numbers I had never imagined from the cocoon of the Settlement.

Once or twice I was drawn to the incredible noise and activity of the docks, where the tall masts of the ships waiting to be loaded loomed above like a high forest. Men swarmed around me, carrying what seemed to be tremendous burdens, yet hauled as lightly as if they contained only air. With their identical queues, their woman-ish, beardless faces, and drab costumes, they at first appeared like so many interchangeable ants, intent on their curious business. But as I watched, I began to see the differences between them: one wiry man with a friendly, open face, joking with his comrades as he slipped between them: I imagined he was taunting them for being slow. Another, serious and sad-eyed, but moving as precisely as a cog, efficiently placing himself through the crowd. It was like a dance, a dance of industry, in which each movement led to the next, from the weavers of Nanking all the way to the ladies of London in their silk dresses. I wondered if I would ever see London again.

There were women, too: old women, stirring evil-smelling pots from which they offered cups to the men as they worked. And young women, at whom I was careful not to look too closely, offering the men something else. But they also, perhaps, had their place in the dance: I was merely an observer.

I tried to express something of this to Bohai, clumsily, for he was the only person I talked with. We were in my father's study, a place I went only for these morning consultations, for I felt a fraud sitting behind the large leather desk and nodding uncomprehendingly to his precise reports.

He frowned a little, rubbing the blotter before him with his finger.

"Miss Keswick," he said, in his formal way, "I must advise that the docks are not a safe place for you — for any lady. It is a rough place, of rough people; your purse could be taken in the crowd. And then, accidents are common there. I fear that the dockworkers' lives are cheap and the masters do not have great care for their well-being. I do not think that your father would have encouraged you to frequent that place."

"Perhaps not," I said — bridling a little at the implied rebuke — "but I am quite untouched and, indeed, I did not leave the rickshaw. But it does seem a place of danger — I saw a poor man whose foot was quite crushed when a heavy crate fell on it as it was being loaded. He howled in some distress, but the work around him paused only for a moment as they moved him aside and then resumed. I suppose that human sympathy is a luxury in such a world."

"That is partly true," said Bohai, "but such things are the way of any great enterprise and the men are glad of the work. It is their labour which is changing the city, yet so many choose to avert their eyes from its harsher side. Though I do not urge a return visit, I am glad that you have seen something of our trade. Did you find it impressive?"

"Truly," I replied, surprised, yet pleased, that he had called it "our" trade. "I had not realized just how vast the enterprise is. It is — I find it almost thrilling."

"Your father found it so," he said, rising from his seat and beginning to pace around the study. "As do I. Miss Keswick, I believe that Shanghai is becoming a great city, a new kind of city which will rival any and which will lead a new China. For too long we have closed ourselves from the rest of the world, secure in our self-satisfied, ancient traditions, but we cannot continue to be bound by them. The world is changing too fast, there are new discoveries, new frontiers of knowledge: China must embrace them if she is not to be left behind.

"The silk trade is but the start — Shanghai is but the start — we must open ourselves to these new ideas, open ourselves to the world. There is a great future ahead, I am persuaded, and it is my privilege to play some small part in it."

It was a passionate speech such as I had rarely heard from any man, let alone the reserved Bohai. But he did not seem embarrassed afterwards, as an Englishman might do if his enthusiasms carried him away; he merely smiled.

"And you, you are part of this change also," he said, more gently. "It is impossible for anyone to stay the same amid such transformation. You are of Shanghai now; you are of my family and of the company. If it would interest you, I could show you more of what we are doing — indeed, as a partner, it is your right to know all."

My right! Certainly this was a strange place. I could not imagine an Englishman offering to discuss business with a woman. And yet I did not think it was exactly the Chinese way, either, but merely a curious consequence of the unnatural situation in which I was placed — in which Bohai had placed me.

The thought disturbed me and I gave him no direct reply, merely turning the conversation to other matters, but I could not deny my genuine interest in the subject. In the succeeding days, I began, cautiously, to ask simple questions. He seemed to seize upon them and so he began to teach me about tariffs and profits, trade routes and importers, so many matters that I had never expected could be within my province.

It soon began to seem as if my days were filled with new ideas and sensations; at night my head was too full for sleep and I lay awake in the bedroom, still furnished with my father's attempts to please his strange daughter, my thoughts running for hours. I felt that I was waiting for something — I knew not what, but something which was coming inexorably. Yet I was not anxious. I felt content to wait, even gleeful, as if I was summoning something by my own power.

And then, nearly three months after my ghost wedding, my husband finally came to me.

I should have been shocked, but I was not even surprised, for I thought at first that it was simply a dream.

It seemed as though I was lying happily half-asleep, listening to gentle autumn rain outside of my open window, too pleasantly warm to close the shutters.

A voice, low and tense, came out of the night and it seemed like the language one hears in a dream, where everything is known and understood and nothing need be explained.

He said:

*I have come, my love*
*I felt a pull from your heart*
*Do you wish me here?*

It was dark in the room but I knew him at once. He was beautiful: his face resembled that of Bohai, but younger and oddly more vital. I was not frightened. He was my husband; how could I wish otherwise? I sat up in the bed, looked at him clearly and named him formally: "Chonglin. You are just as I knew you would be. I am happy to meet you at last."

He started to speak again, but I stretched out my arms to him and, just as in a dream, there was no distance between the time he was there and the time he was here; we were united. There could be no wrong in it. He was my true husband.

When I awoke in the morning, alone in my silk sheets, I knew by certain signs on them that it had been no dream. I had one brief moment of panic, my throat closing as I thought of a grave, a coffin, of dirt falling. The thought of him leaving me as dawn broke to climb back into a deathly cold bed was horrifying, and I felt I, too, could not live.

But then I remembered his cool hands stroking mine; the fine bones of his face, the delicacy of his brown eyes. If he was a ghost, he was my ghost. I could not truly fear him, nor do anything but pray he would return again.

And so he has, most nights, a faithful spouse whose visits have transformed my life. I am still free to pass my days as before: discussing business in the morning, wandering the city, reading in the quiet gardens.

But the nights, ah, the nights are something outside of it all. They are like a secret space in which I am no longer my mother's daughter, or my father's, no longer even an Englishwoman in Shanghai but simply myself. It is nothing like the dull, dutiful marriages I came to China to escape, a life I had known would bury me in misery. As the wife of a ghost, I feel so very alive.

Yet there is still something more to come, I know. A secret to be revealed or a sentence to be spoken, a step in the dance which will change its direction.

I asked him only once how long our time could go on, if he would always be able to come to me, if a ghost marriage could have a future. His answer, of course, was couched in the poetry that thrills yet frustrates me as it veils his true meaning.

*Cricket's life is short*
*One summer and one winter*
*But sings many songs.*

He speaks in English, but still I do not understand him.

Yesterday, I risked asking Bohai about hokku; I reminded him of what he had said on the day of my wedding and asked him why Chonglin had been drawn to this product of another culture.

At first it seemed like he would not answer. Then he said: "It was a thing I never asked him. Do you not know?"

"I? How should I know?"

"I thought, perhaps … perhaps it was the same thing that draws you to Shanghai."

And perhaps he is right. Perhaps Chonghai, in life, was impelled to escape his country, to find his spirit's home somewhere else. Then why, I wonder, does he linger here now, instead of going on? Perhaps he is waiting for me to join him. Perhaps he is waiting to be reborn.

This morning, Bohai did not come for our meeting. The rhythm of my day was broken, but he sent a gift to occupy me instead: a little pamphlet in English about the art of the Japanese hokku. I have been reading it in the garden by the jasmine and I have learned so much. The book says that hokku are meant to express a single moment, a revelation in one thought that cannot be said in any other way.

I have been trying, clumsily, to write my own hokku, so that I can speak tonight to my ghost lover in his veiled language and he will tell me what to do. For there is a fearful suspicion growing within me and there will come a time when it can no longer be hidden. And I cannot imagine what will become of me then.

Is it possible that I have been mistaken … is it possible that I have allowed myself to be mistaken? No, it cannot be — he is my true husband, he is Chonglin — but it frightens me to think that my mind is not clear, that I am not seeing clearly. Bohai said that there was a line which must continue, he said that I would not die unmourned, he said … there are times when he looks so like his brother.

My poem is a poor thing, but it tells what I cannot express in any other way and I hope that by the morning I will have my answer. I will say to him:

*After winter, spring*
*Joy and sorrow of new life*
*Buds from a dead tree.*

## CARL NIXON
# If These Walls Had Ears

On his first night in the house, Andy lies on a mattress in the empty lounge with the windows wide open and listens to the neighbours beating their son. It sounds to Andy as though they are right in the room with him. There's no driveway between the sections, only a sagging, paling fence, four metres all that separate the two houses. The temperature must still be up in the mid-twenties even though it's after eleven o'clock. Not even the ghost of a breeze moves the tips of the kowhai trees, which have been planted one to a house all along Tern Street.

At first he could only hear the noise of their TV: theme songs; hollow canned laughter; the surge in volume as the adverts for post-Christmas sales are recycled every fifteen minutes.

And then the boy starts up. Andy guesses he's maybe, what, eight or ten? Around that anyway, by the sound of him, a bit whiny and demanding.

A woman; irritated, screechy as a parrot. Andy listens to her move through the gears from grumpy needling to threats, and then she's at full throttle. It's all, "You do what I say!" and "Screw you, you spoilt little shit!"

The kid yells back at her over the tinny laughter from the television.

Andy lies on his back in the dark room. There's no furniture at all unless you count the mattress. Dust hangs in the warm air. It's rising up into his nostrils every time he rolls over. He tries not to listen to the shouts and the swearing being flung over the fence.

Then he hears the clear slap of flesh on flesh.

The boy cries out sharply.

A new deeper voice, male, a volcanic rumbling. Short, hard sentences like explosions.

Andy rolls over again, his back to the noise, and stares at the dark shadow that is the brick fireplace. One of the first things that he's planning to do is rip that out. If he can be bothered, he might even clean up the bricks; use them to make a paved area down the back of the garden.

Christ, half the neighbourhood must be hearing this.

The boy's voice manages to stay defiant for a while, yelling, mimicking, lobbing back the curses and obscenities that are being hurled at him by the man.

Crash. Shatter. Sounds like glass.

And the male voice erupts, goes right off, loses it. The sound of another whack comes through clearly over the shouts and then another, louder, harder.

The boy's voice fades into choking sobs.

Fades into silence.

Andy listens, straining to hear. The whole neighbourhood seems to catch its breath. Even the normal sounds of the suburban summer night are temporarily hushed. For a moment:

the television next door is switched off,

there are no passing cars on the street,

the chained German shepherd down the road is mute, for once,

a droning car alarm that has been going off in the distance for the last twenty minutes suddenly stops.

Andy lies on his back, staring up at the chipped plaster rosette on the ceiling. It occurs to him that he could actually reach over the sagging fence between the two properties, reach right through their open window, and touch these bloody people.

◆

Soon after dawn he begins to demolish the internal wall between the living room and the hallway. According to the LIM report, the bungalow, which he bought by tender only the week before, is seventy-three years old. The walls, predictably, turn out be lath and plaster. His crowbar bites into the wooden batons between the studs in the living room, levers and cracks the thick, dry plaster, scattering chunks across the floor, throwing clouds of dust into the air.

By mid-morning it is stifling in the room, even with the windows open. He wears only an ancient T-shirt and paint-splattered black rugby shorts, running shoes with no socks. He drinks so much water from a plastic Coke bottle that he needs to go to the loo every half-hour.

By 11:30 Andy is starving. Breakfast was two cold, stiff pieces of Hawaiian pizza left over from last night and there's no more food in the house. Part of his plan for the afternoon is to take the car down to the supermarket and get enough supplies to see him through for at least the next few days. Some stuff he'll get for the long haul — toothpaste, shampoo, detergent, Jif for cleaning the loo. He's budgeted that the house will take him twelve weeks to do up completely.

Andy decides to knock off for lunch a bit early and brushes most of the dust out of his hair, walks in the sunshine down to the café by the bridge. The young woman behind the counter is heavily pregnant, thick black dreads piled into a tangle on her head.

"That's a bad case of dandruff you've got there," she says, dark eyes flashing.

He grins sheepishly and rubs at the plaster in his hair, turning his head as he habitually does when talking to people he doesn't know so that his wonky left eye and the pale lattice-work of scars is obscured.

When his coffee is ready he carries it and a bag with a pie down to the river. He eats sitting on a graffiti-scrawled bench on the bank. Here, the water is shallow, brown and sluggish. A gull finds him and soon there are half a dozen circling him on the grass. Someone has pushed a Countdown shopping trolley off the bank on the far side and three wheels poke up out of the slow current.

For the first time in years Andy thinks about the man who sometimes turned up at their house when they were kids. He would chase Mark and him around, shout and rant, make loud, scary noises. The best place to hide was among the pines in the domain that bordered their section. The man would mostly stay in the house, wouldn't normally bother chasing them between the big trunks of the pines. Most times they were safe in the trees.

Andy breaks off a piece of hot pie, the mince threatening to slop from the pastry. The gulls watch with pale, red-rimmed eyes, and edge closer.

"Screw you," he says and eats the pie too quickly so that the meat burns his tongue.

◆

The rubbish skip that he ordered two days ago has finally turned up. Andy sees the truck driving off as he walks around the corner, the skip left poking out of the driveway like a lost landing craft from the Second World War. As he walks past his neighbours' house he stops and studies the place; hadn't really looked at it properly before. Actually, it's not that bad, not as rundown as he'd imagined it would be. It's an ex-state house: a box with a concrete-tile roof, probably a rental, but he could be wrong.

As he stands there, a soccer ball comes bouncing down the drive and onto the road. Andy walks over and retrieves the ball from the gutter with his foot. He dribbles it back to the footpath. The ball is faded and scuffed, one hexagonal panel threatening to peel right off, the whole thing close to being completely munted.

A boy of about nine appears, a pale, skinny kid with hair cut so short it makes him look like an apprentice crim, or someone who's just had a bad case of nits. There are several white nicks in the dark stubble covering his head. Despite the heat the boy is wearing jeans and a long-sleeved shirt.

"G'day," says Andy. The kid stares at the ball at Andy's feet and mumbles what could be a reply.

"Do you play football?"

"Yeah," the boy says.

"What club?"

He shakes his head. "Nah, just after school."

Andy flicks the ball up into the air with the toe of his right foot. He stops its descent with one thigh, pops it back up, and catches it on the other, lets the ball fall to the top of his foot and then juggles it six times before he loses control. The ball spins away and lands on the dry grass. Andy retrieves it and pushes a gentle pass back to the kid.

"That's cool."

"I used to be a soccer poofter." The boy looks blank. "When I was your age, that's what they called you if you played soccer."

"Can you show me how to do that juggling thing?"

Andy licks his lips and looks over at his house. "Maybe another time. Right now I'm really flat-out next door."

"Okay." He doesn't appear disappointed, just resigned, as though he was expecting the knock-back. "You gunna live there?"

"Just for a few months."

Andy can see the kid looking at his eye. Sometimes he catches kids looking or overhears them asking an embarrassed parent, *Mum, what's wrong with that man's eye?* But his eyelid still works fine. He winks and the boy starts.

"An old war wound."

"Really? Were you in the war?"

"Nah, not really, just an accident. I better get going. See ya."

"Yeah."

The boy turns and dribbles his clapped-out ball up the driveway and onto the front lawn. He begins to kick it against the foundation of the house. Andy can still hear the sound of the ball hitting the concrete ten minutes later when he picks up his crowbar and gets back to work.

♦

The man who chased them around the house was their father. That business began after their mother walked out. She packed a suitcase one day and never came back, a Wednesday in April. Andy was eight and his brother, Mark, was eleven. That day their mother had left Samantha, who was only just starting to walk, with one of the neighbours. He and Mark came home after school, to the big draughty villa where they lived, to find the house empty and a note on the kitchen bench. Before that, it had been just another school day. He still remembers being surprised that something so life-changing could happen on a day that had started off so normal.

At first their father seemed to hold it together. He organized for a succession of teenage girls who lived in the neighbourhood to come to the house after school, while he was still at work. They were supposed to keep an eye on things, make sure the place didn't burn down. Mostly the girls were there for Sam. Andy suspected that if it hadn't been for their little sister, their father wouldn't have spent money hiring a babysitter at all.

Most days he and Mark disappeared after school anyway. When it wasn't raining hard they took their bikes or their eel spears, shanghais tucked into the top of their pants, and went through the gate in the fence, fading away into the domain like Indian trackers among the pines. Other days they took off on their bikes to meet their respective packs of mates. In gangs of four or five they would cruise the streets, making their own fun, but mostly just trying to outride boredom.

None of the teenage girls lasted very long. Andy doubts that his father could afford to pay them very much, not enough to keep them coming for more than a few weeks. When the pool of girls ran out, Mrs. Sullivan from down the road came after school. She was better than the girls because she also cooked their dinner. For almost a year they stopped living on canned spaghetti and poached eggs, or on Andy's macaroni cheese. But then Mrs. Sullivan discovered that she was pregnant — with twins. She inflated like a puffer fish until he and Mark were sure she was going to burst right there in their kitchen. And then one day she said goodbye. Mrs. Sullivan and her husband were moving to a bigger house in a better part of town. The three kids lined up in front of her and she hugged each of them in turn, tears in her eyes. Andy remembers that she straightened up and turned slowly away like a heavy ship fighting a current, before walking out the door.

After that, their father arranged for a local woman who ran a small informal crèche to keep Sam at her house until he finished work. Mark started going to Kieran Hart's place every day after school. There were long stretches of time — months on end — when Andy would let himself into their big dim house using the key hidden in the hollow under the brick by the cabbage tree. He would always stand in the hall, the open doorway behind him, and listen to the house:

the mice running in the walls,

an overgrown tree branch scraping on window glass,

on windy days the gusts getting up under the rusting roof, flexing the iron,

the metronome drip ... drip ... drip of the kitchen tap.

Their father's drinking slowly went from two or three nights a week to every night. He would start at the pub after finishing up at the sections he was supposed to be developing. When he came home he'd carry on, sometimes with Ed Tanner, but mostly by himself, sit watching television, the beer bottles lined up at his feet like small brown dogs, obedient and alert.

After three beers he'd grin lopsidedly and start to go on about all the plans he had for the business and for overseas holidays and how once the subdivision took off they would move to a brand new house. When Andy brought in the dinner on a tray the old man would always say, "You're a great kid."

But sometimes alcohol took the old man by the throat and dragged him through a black doorway. It was on those nights when the mask came out. Andy could see it being slipped slowly on; not a real mask, but a leather-hard, twisted sneer that their father wore.

Andy would always try to stop it when he saw the mask coming. He would tiptoe around, keep his voice down, act happy-as, ask how high when the old man growled jump. But the mask made Mark reckless, almost crazy. It was as though his brother couldn't help but taunt it, dare it to do its worst. On those nights the best Andy could do was to quickly put Sam to bed, lock her door, hide the key. Then he would stand in the hall and listen to Mark and their father. Get ready to run.

When it was all over, usually hours later, he would sneak back in to the house and start to clean up the broken glass, or the thrown plate of food fanned out over the living-room wall, repair the door or the chair the best he could, mostly with duct tape, or at least get the worst of it out of sight.

The next day, when their father eventually came out of his bedroom, he was inevitably cheerful. He'd offer to take them to the movies. There were fish and chips for dinner and Boston-buns with icing half an inch thick. Usually he stopped drinking for a few days.

The old man lives up the coast now, Ross Point, in what used to be his family's bach, a clapped-out little place, barely better than a hut, just out of the township. He's not retired exactly, but apparently still does some maintenance work at the district high school. Andy knows all this because Sam keeps in touch with the old bastard — even drives up and stays with him occasionally.

Well, good on her, he thinks, as he rips a fresh section of lath and plaster from the wall with the crowbar. It crumbles and washes across the bare boards, lapping against his shoes. Yeah, good on her.

Personally, he can think of a million other things he'd rather do.

◆

On Saturday morning Andy strolls out to check the letterbox. After two weeks a trickle of redirected mail has started turning up. The work on the house is coming along okay. There's been no repeat of the beating next door, not that he's heard anyway, just a few times when voices have been raised. There's a baby over there that he didn't hear on the first night. He often hears it crying and its clothes hang on the line visible above the fence. On a couple of occasions he's seen the older boy's head poking above the palings. But he's found that if you ignore him the kid gets bored and goes away.

The woman from next door is standing at the end of her path, smoking a cigarette, flicks it way into the bushes when she sees him coming. He is surprised at how young she is, in her late twenties, maybe thirty, tops. Her voice made her sound older.

"G'day," she says. "How ya going?"

He can see her looking him over, noting his bad eye and the scars. "Fine, thanks."

"Happy New Year."

"You too," he replies.

"How was ya Christmas?"

"Quiet." A phone call from Sam in Wellington and a card from Mark that arrived two days ago.

"You doing a bit of work on the place?"

"Yeah."

"You going to live in there?"

"No, I'll sell it once it's done up. Or maybe rent it out for a while. Depends."

She is short and slim, wearing tight black jeans and a singlet top. Her hair is long and straight and so dark that he thinks it must be dyed. Although it's ten o'clock on a Saturday she's got on makeup. In the sunlight her face is a different colour from her neck, almost orange, her eyebrows plucked, drawn back on in black. There's a small tattoo on the top of her left breast, a red rose with a single drop of blood falling from its thorny stem. Andy has to make a conscious effort not to stare at it, which, he guesses, is the idea.

"Mind if I come over and have a quick look?" she asks.

Days without seeing anyone have made the part of his brain in charge of talking shrivel. He can't think of a plausible excuse fast enough. "Sure."

As they walk up the path along the side of the house he notices the boy slip in behind them. Today the kid is wearing a T-shirt and shorts. What looks to Andy like the remnants of bruises on his legs could just as easily be yesterday's dirt.

Andy leads them around the back to where he's just finished putting in French doors. "Eventually, there's going to be a deck back here."

She nods. "Yeah, that'll be nice, with a table and chairs for eating breakfast in the sun and stuff."

Andy has completely gutted the whole rear of the house. What had been a poky, dark kitchen full of cabinetry left over from the sixties and separated from the living room by a narrow hallway is now a large open-plan space.

She tells him that her name is Sheree. "With three Es. And this is Tyler." She gestures toward the boy, who is hanging back.

"Yeah, I've met Tyler before."

She shoots her son a hard look. "He hasn't been giving you any trouble, has he?"

"Nah. We just talked about soccer."

She relaxes. "'Cause he's been getting in a bit of trouble at school."

Tyler ignores her, walks past them, and goes through the door that leads to the front part of the house.

"Don't you touch anything in there," she calls, then turns to Andy and rolls her eyes conspiratorially. "Boys, eh. You got any kids?"

"Not that I know of."

It's an old joke but she giggles like a twelve-year-old. "Tyler's been in some fights lately at school. Pete and me don't know what to do about it, but Pete works shifts so mostly it's me who has to deal with it. I don't think his teacher knows how to handle him properly."

Andy wonders if handling him *properly* means beating him until even his voice sounds bruised. He could say something about what he's heard, but what's the point? Undoubtedly, she'd go septic and he'd end up copping a load of abuse. In a couple of months the house would be finished and he'll be gone. None of his business.

"You do all this yourself?" she asks, looking around with wide eyes. With Tyler out of the room she's suddenly standing in close, looking up at him, the rose moving in its own breeze.

"Apart from the electrical and plumbing."

"Aren't you clever." She touches the top of his forearm. "Is this what you do for a job?"

"At the moment."

"Were you born up here?"

"No, I go wherever I can get a bargain."

"Sounds a bit lonely."

"It suits me."

Tyler comes back into the room carrying something black in both hands. Andy knows what it is straight away. The boy's mother takes a few seconds before she lets out a scream, only half stifled.

Tyler grins. "I found it in the other room."

It's the mummified cat that Andy disinterred from under the floor on the third day. The space under there is perfectly dry. Over God knows how many years all the water had been sucked out of the dead animal's body, leaving nothing but hard leather and fur.

"Put that down!" says his mother. "It's disgusting."

"It's okay," says Andy. "It's not dirty. It's completely dried out."

The eye sockets are empty, gums permanently pulled back revealing rows of yellow needle-teeth, whiskers stiff as wire. Must've been a big cat because its remains are surprisingly heavy.

She looks from Andy to the boy. They can both tell that she is torn between her disgust and wanting to appear to be relaxed and tolerant, a cool mum.

"Can I keep it?"

"No. Anyway, it doesn't belong to you, Tyler."

"He can have it if he wants. I don't mind. I was probably just going to throw it into the skip." Andy knows he's stirring but can't help himself. It's the first time that he's seen the boy smile. Tyler is transformed from the type of kid who makes old ladies clutch their handbags closer to almost good-looking.

Tyler doesn't wait for his mother to put her foot down. "Thanks," he calls, already moving toward the French doors. "I'm going to take it to show Gem." And he's off. Andy has a glimpse of him as he runs past the kitchen window. Tyler is holding the mummified cat up as he runs so that for a second their two heads are visible above the sill, both with short dark hair, both grinning.

"Sorry, I know it's a bit disgusting."

She sniffs. "Nah, it's all right. I better get going, eh. The baby might've woke up."

"Boys his age love that macabre stuff."

"I guess."

"He'll probably be over it in a week and then you can just biff the ugly thing into the skip if you want."

She sniffs again and is gone.

◆

That night he works late, trowelling white plaster onto the kitchen wall, smears and smoothes. The evening air is taut with heat and sweat runs down his back beneath his overalls. All the lights are on, including the work light, which he's attached to the extension cord and hung off the top of the ladder. The brightness reflects off the white Gib board and off the wooden floor, which in a few weeks will be sanded down and polished. Without any furniture the big space is an empty drum in which sounds bounce around.

They're starting into it again next door. As he works he hears them winding up like a rusty engine: the first angry shout of the evening, the first slammed door. The fight is about the cat. She yells that it's "not bloody staying in my house!"

Tyler yells back, calling his mother an "unfair bitch" and a "cow."

The baby begins to cry.

He hopes like hell that the guy, Pete, has left for work. But almost as the thought comes to him, Andy hears the rumbling voice. It makes his gut bunch and turn acidic.

He keeps plastering, concentrates on the sound of the plaster going onto the wall. It has a rhythm — *scrape scrape ... scrape scrape ... scrape scrape.*

After a long time the sound becomes footsteps on pine needles.

◆

He was running through the domain in the dark. It was a cold winter night and it had been raining, behind him angry shouts, the flash of a torch beam through the trees. He sped up, couldn't really see where he was going, the trunks of the pine trees jumping out in front of him, swerving to avoid hitting them, feet scraping and slipping on the wet needles. He thought Mark was somewhere off to his left. He could hear him before, but now there was only the sound of his own footsteps running over the pine needles, the rasping of his breathing.

He'd been sure that they were caught back there. The last big wind must've blown the pine needles round, the gate in the fence jammed; he only just pushed through the gap in time. Now the curses and threats of his father had dropped behind. Andy was still running fast but dared to look back.

And that was when there was a sudden blow to his head and a bright red flash that went off like a Roman candle behind his eyes.

Silence.

He woke up lying on his back. He had the impression that time had passed but he'd no idea how much. He was looking up at the pine tree that he had run smack into. Low down were the jagged stumps of broken off branches poking out of the trunk. Above him the dark clouds were drawn back and a three-quarter moon appeared. Andy realized that there was something wrong with his eye. He tried to focus on the moon but one eye floated slowly off by itself, drifted lazily toward the ground. When he reached up and felt his face there was a lumpy swelling covering pretty much the whole left side. He gingerly prodded with his finger. The skin felt numb and squishy, like a half-filled water-balloon, and there was a flap of skin into which his finger disappeared. He looked at his hand. It was black with blood.

He lay still, listening, wondering if he was going to die.

Heard the sound of the night wind in the treetops.

Swollen drops of rain plopping from the branch above him onto the needles close to his head.

And later, Mark moving through the darkness toward him, saying his name in a hoarse whisper.

◆

Something hits the side of the house with a solid bang. Andy starts and the work light sways. He quickly climbs down from the ladder and goes out into the hot night. The guy next door is still yelling, the baby crying even louder.

At first he can't see what's hit the house, but then in the spilled light from the kitchen window he spots the mummified cat, lying half underneath a bush. When he picks it up the body is hard and spiky.

The man is yelling louder. It's clear that the kid's about to get another beating.

*Whack.* There it is.

The boy lets out a sound like an animal.

Without thinking about what he's doing, Andy climbs up onto the fence. He is still holding the dead cat in one hand. The old paling fence leans away from him and when both feet are on the lower rail he can stand without using his hands, thighs pressed against the top railing.

In front of him is the lighted window of their kitchen. The man is standing with his back to Andy, a piece of rubber garden hose in his hand. Tyler is lying on the floor curled into the fetal position and Andy sees the man's hand go up and whip down, hears the sound of the hose landing.

Raising the stiff dead cat above his head in both hands, Andy throws it as hard as he can through the window. The glass shatters loudly, exploding inward. The bristling black body clears the pile of dirty dishes on the kitchen bench and hits the man in the back of the leg. He swears and jumps back. His head swivels and his mouth gawps as he tries to grasp what has happened.

Yelling, the woman rushes into the room. She stops when she sees the cat and stands swaying slightly.

The man's shoes crunch on the scattered glass as they both move in for a better look. They stare down at the bared teeth, at the sunken eyes. The dead cat stares accusingly back at them.

Forgotten, Tyler slinks away.

The man is still clutching the hose when he comes and looks out through the shattered window into the night. But Andy is gone. He is back inside, heart pounding, listening. He hears nothing, only a long silence that has settled over the whole neighbourhood:

the baby is quiet,

in the lucky houses with heat pumps set to cool, the machines stutter and then pause in their breathy cycles,

no dogs bark,

no cars growl through the patches of light out on the street,

the trampoline and vegetable-patch lawns, all are pools of darkness. In that moment they are undisturbed even by a hedgehog's snuffling progress, or the fall of a cat's paw on the grass.

JULIAN NOVITZ

# Tenure: An Informal Reflection on the Hunting of the Squid and Its Impact on Higher Education

## 1. Introduction

Students sometimes ask me why there are no old scholars in our department. Or why, for that matter, are there none in any department? Why, in all the schools and faculties of our university, is there no Dean, Reader, or Senior Professor older than fifty say, or fifty-five at the most? It will often be a first-year student who asks me this, a scholarship boy or girl raised on one of the farms or ranches in the untamed interior of our country, far from the universities, far from the sea. Occasionally I will wonder why they have not heard the answer to this from their peers, for it is no great secret, and yet I also suspect that the subject is instinctually approached with a degree of tact and reticence, because the question is never raised in a seminar, but always during an individual consultation when we are secluded in my study. At such times I will stop leafing through their latest essay or assignment and peer at them keenly from over the rim of my spectacles, in the way that all good professors eventually learn to do, and ask them, why do *they* think that there are no old scholars walking these halls?

A lot of the time they will simply shrug and look away, but occasionally some thought or idea will spark within them, and they will lean forward eagerly to relay the theories that must have already been fermenting in their heads. Do the aging scholars relinquish their positions, stepping gracefully aside to permit a new generation to step into their roles, thus allowing the wheels of thought and discourse to spin onward, unencumbered by old dogmas and disproven theories? No, no, I always have to chuckle when they give me that one. Well then, the student might continue, perhaps they simply tire of the tedium of classes and the babble of students. Perhaps they turn their backs on it all and go inland, seeking the silence of the plains, the solitude of the steppes? Again, I will shake my head. It is not like that, I tell them. Perhaps that is how it should be, but no. It is not like that at all.

The sad truth of the matter is this. When an academic reaches their middle years, a strange and terrible yearning will inevitably take hold of their heart: a haunting call that neither conferences, nor seminars, nor articles can sate. It may be resisted for a semester or two; perhaps time enough to set one's affairs in order; to complete a supervision or grade one final batch of exams, but sooner or later they will forsake their offices and their grants, their distinguished fellowships and their graduate students. In small yet sturdy boats — one-mast crafts that they take to with the instinctual aptitude of an old sea hand — they will sail away from city and campus, down through the gulf of Saint Corentien and out onto the rolling waves of the open ocean. From there they follow the Southern stars as best they can, plunging fearlessly into uncharted waters, always with a singular purpose, their every thought fixed on hunting and slaying the *Mesonychoteuthis hamiltoni*, the fabled colossal squid.

## 2. Theoretical Perspectives

Inevitably the student will lean forward at this point. Does the squid even exist? they will ask, and I can only shrug in response. Who knows? There have been sightings and reports, of course: tall tales from drunken sailors and fishermen; what may have been unspeakably large sucker marks found on the decaying corpse of a

whale beached in Dunwich Bay; the frantic yet garbled radio trans-
missions from ships that vanished without a trace in the night.
Indeed, the Department of Cephalopod Studies has long debated
the plausibility of this specimen, concluding that while there is still
ample room for speculation, there can be no definite proof that
the vast gulfs of the sea hold any creatures of such magnitude. In
the middle years of the last century, Professor Fredrick Untert⊠ble
(renowned at the time as the founding father of Austrian Neo-
Formalism and the most austere philosopher in Europe[1]) delivered an acclaimed lecture in which he argued that our belief in the
squid was merely a result of the hysteria produced by the perpet-
ual fracturing and re-fracturing of the neological boundaries of
Anglocentric scholarship that divide our subjective and objective
object choices, our activity and simultaneous passivity as essential
actors in the discourse that surrounds primary movement. The
applause generated by this conclusion was only slightly dampened
by the fact that this was Untert⊠ble's final lecture — he was last
sighted five days later, walking resolutely toward the harbour, a
harpoon in hand. His theory remains persuasive to this day.

An alternative perspective was later offered by Untert⊠ble's
pupil, the notorious Marcel Zargoné, who postulated that while
the squid may lack the property of *a priori* existence, it might
nonetheless exist in the space created from the liminal momentum
generated by our constant penetration of an essentially gendered
discursive hinterland, one that works to comprise and contain the
public existence of the so-called "academe." Zargoné went on to
speculate that the nature of the squid could not be determined by
the reflecting on the squid per se, but rather by reflecting on the

1. As a side note, the second volume of Sören Drassberg's *Viennese Memoirs* (recently
republished by the University of St. John and the Holy Ghost Press) contains some
charming anecdotes about the late professor's eccentricities, particularly his insistence
on never sitting or reclining during waking hours (from dawn to dusk he would always
read, take his meals and dictate his dialectics while standing upright), and his steadfast
refusal in the last five years of his life (maintained, one assumes, through the sheer force
of his iron will and steely resolve) to allow his mind to slip into a state of subjective
judgement with regard to any person, place, or concept.

formal order of the actions that surround and construct the concept of the squid itself, thus allowing us to adopt an unmediated stance toward it and removing the need for its pursuit. These ideas were encapsulated in a brief yet fascinating essay that was sadly eclipsed by the furore surrounding Zargoné's very public feud with his former colleague and lover, the famous Marxist Lactationist Louise Shoudonger, who denounced his attempts to define the boundaries of ontological scholarship by exposing them as just another re-articulation of the phallo-digestive tropes of Western epistemology. Indeed, Zargoné was a largely discredited and ignored thinker by the time he began his own long march to the sea.[2] Suffice to say, however, that any proof or disproof of the squid is immaterial. Academics will eventually sharpen their harpoons and raise their sails regardless. The idea of it is enough. That is all.

But what happens to them? The student will inevitably ask at this point. What happens to the academics that go? And, of course, if they are clever enough, they will have already surmised from the indeterminate nature of the squid what my answer must be. Nobody knows. Attempts have been made to track those who embark upon the hunt, by radar at first, and then later by satellite, but sooner or later their blips always fade away into the unknown depths of the ocean. I have stood by the harbour and watched them all depart over the years, my supervisors and professors, and now, gradually, my colleagues and peers. Nobody knows why this happens, save for the departing academics themselves, and their need is not something that can be put into words. It may come slowly or suddenly, it may subsume them in an instant or be briefly resisted, but sooner or later the call must be heeded. That is how it has always been.

---

2. Though I would refer interested readers to my colleague's recently published investigation into this fascinating area of Zargoné's thought: Damaz, A.Z. (2014) "Processing, Voicing, Constructing: the Marginal Territory of the Tetaphysical Supplement in Marcel Zargoné's 'The Ineffable Kraken.'" *The Canadian Journal of Symbology 28 (6)*, 37–49.

### 3. Case Studies

Of course, the curious thing is that, although the call comes every time and to everyone, no one really believes that it will ever come to them. How could they? When I was a young lecturer none of my friends ever imagined that they might end their careers as distant specks on the southern horizon. To them it was self-evident that all the paradigms of the past (squid hunting included) could be overturned by rejecting the false radicalism of neo-formalist discourse in order to devise a model of scholarship based on the geo-cosmic semiotics of Valestién and Cosvonté. When we gathered for pints in one of the pubs atop the sheer coastal cliffs of our university town, my friends would mockingly refer to senior members of our department as "the old harpooners," and much laughter would ensue, though I would never join in. Unlike the others, I came from an old academic family and I knew that the hunting of the squid was no matter for jests. In any case, we grew older, more senior and respected, more secure in our positions, and before too long the first of our coterie departed for the sea. We began to shun the haunts of our youth, no longer gathering for drinking or merriment, but burrowing away in our offices, digging through journals and monographs, working frantically on our research papers, as if the weight of texts and the buzz of ideas would be enough to keep the call from our heads.

Even now some of them still cling to shreds of false hope. Occasionally one of my colleagues will excitedly report meeting some lecturer on another campus who had reached the age of sixty or sixty-one without showing signs of any seawards inclination, though usually it will be only a few months before they slink sadly into the common room to announce that they have just heard word of that same lecturer's departure. I still remember Professor Husstunt, who had reached the ripe age of sixty-two when I received my first lectureship. She was the oldest academic on this side of the coast, a brilliant, generous scholar who had produced one of the first truly seminal commentaries on Cosvonté's

*Apocryphal Epistemologia,* and everyone believed that she was comfortably past the age of the call. During my first two years in the department, Husstunt's career and publication record was constantly presented as a model for graduate students and junior academics to follow: engage with these theories, publish with these presses, attend these conferences, and you will never need to worry about the hunt for the squid. This level of certainty had reached the point where some colleagues felt it safe jokingly to present her with gifts of harpoons and nautical maps at the departmental Christmas parties, saying "Don't you think it's time you were getting along now, Professor?" — jests that she always took with her customary good humour. I last saw dear Husstunt on a crisp autumn after-noon, when she stopped by my office and tapped on my open door. I was with a student at that moment, but I asked if I would see her later to discuss a grant proposal that we were due to submit.[3] I remember that she smiled sadly and mouthed the word *No,* and then, with a graceful inclination of her head, indicated that she was heading in the direction of the harbour.

In previous eras, particularly the nineteenth and early twenti-eth centuries, a departure was seen as an opportunity for ritual and ceremony, a way of cementing the ties between university and town. The departing academic would be paraded through the streets on their way down to the harbour, accompanied by the faculty in full regalia. People would line the streets to clap and cheer; speeches would be made on the docks about the rigours and sacrifices of scholarship, before the academic would be helped into their boat by the closest of their colleagues and sent on their way. Such dis-plays have now fallen out of favour, as they are considered to be in poor taste by many (though I believe some of the more traditional colleges in Europe still have their own practices and observances). These days it is more common for university administrations

---

3. Even now, after all these years, I still feel a burn of frustration when I think of this lost project. To have so narrowly missed the opportunity to co-author a series of research pa-pers on the cognitive impact of Valestién and Cosvonté's *The Hermeneutics of the Interior* with a scholar as esteemed as Emila Husstant remains the abiding regret of my long career.

not to involve themselves directly in the departures of their staff, preferring to leave their timing and manner in the hands of the academic concerned. Some scholars will try to give their faculty plenty of notice (though there is seldom any formal requirement that they should do so) and will enjoy a final, sombre evening with friends and family before they embark on their journey. Others simply vanish from their offices and classrooms, taking to the sea without a word or gesture to any. It is commonly held that no two departures are ever quite the same (though I have been informed that an ethnographic study being carried out by researchers at the Steenstrup Institute may cast new light on this claim).

A few years ago, we had a vice-chancellor who was determined to stamp out the long tradition of departure and hunt. He had come to academia after many years in business and had made it his mission to modernize the university, to reshape and restructure it into a gleaming model of twenty-first-century efficiency. The new vice-chancellor viewed the hunt for the squid as an embarrassingly dated practice — akin to the division of male and female students into separate colleges, or the ridiculous pageantry of wearing caps and gowns to classes — or perhaps even something worse, like the unwholesome rituals from the university's savage and barbaric past (few now remember, much less speak of, the Mid-Winter Bacchanal, the Running of the Undergraduates, or the Endowment of a Chair in Literature). The broad aims of the vice-chancellor's agenda had generated hostility in many quarters, but his specific views on the squid were warmly embraced by both staff and students. The campus had recently been shocked by the entirely premature departure of a doctoral student, Joseph Owens, who had taken to sea at the age of thirty-one. The speculation was that he had not genuinely heard the call, but had embarked on the hunt to avoid further embarrassment after his dissertation was returned to him with requests for major corrections.[4]

---

4. As one of the many who briefly served as a co-supervisor during Joseph's long and unfortunate candidature, I regret to say that this is most likely the truth of the matter.

In any case, none would dispute the rousing success of the Squid Awareness Month organized by the office of the vice-chancellor. Seminars were held to discuss the traumatic impact of the squid hunt on families and communities, as well as the damage that it caused to the university's yearly research output, not to mention the frequent disruption of class schedules. Committees were formed to identify at-risk staff members and refer them to appropriate counselling. For a time, the campus was designated a harpoon-free zone. These might have been only the first of many measures, had the vice-chancellor himself not vanished from his office one afternoon, leaving only a long black arrow scrawled down the length of his whiteboard to indicate his intended direction. South.

After hearing these stories, most students will quickly conclude that this is all madness. They will complete their degrees and leave the university, finding jobs in the professions, in the civil service, in politics, or the arts. They will die in accidents, in hospital beds, or in their homes, far from the brine of the waves. But I will see a strange glint enter the eyes of just a few of my students, as if they were already contemplating how they might be able to embrace this madness and live with the dire certainty of sea and squid. I know what this feels like: the rush, the thrill that comes when one considers the inevitable and yet still plunges in, headlong and heedless.

### 4. A Personal Narrative

I had not been there when my father departed, as I was only ten years old at the time and it was a school day. When I returned home that afternoon I found my mother sobbing in the kitchen, having only just heard the news from Claude Lamont, the head of department and my father's closest friend. It was not something that either my mother or I could have anticipated. My father was still relatively young, only a few months shy of forty-five; the department could have rightly expected another decade of

teaching and research from him. He had been a strong scholar,
not exactly well-liked by his peers, but generally respected, perhaps even admired by a few. His was not a slow, gradual departure,
where the first hints could be seen months in advance, with that
look of wistful distraction during a seminar, or those long weekend walks by the sea. The call had seized my father unexpectedly,
when he was at the very height of his powers.

It had had come to him during the weekly departmental
meeting. An argument had been raging for over an hour about
whether an undergraduate course in eschatology could be added
to the timetable in the second semester, or if that material was
more appropriately covered in graduate-level seminars, and my
father, though animated at first, gradually fell silent, his head
bowed and his long fringe falling down over his face. Then, quite
suddenly, he scraped his chair back from the table and climbed
to his feet, his eyes wide and fixed. "Colleagues," he said, his voice
hoarse with emotion. "It has been an honour and a privilege to
have taught alongside you for all of these years. But now I must
leave to hunt the squid."

For a moment, there was only stunned silence. Then someone down the back of the room began to clap, slowly at first, but
with increasing force and frequency. One by one, the assem-
bled academics joined in, and soon even my father's most bit-
ter enemies rose to their feet, some even leaning over to pat his
back and shoulders. He acknowledged the applause with a grim
smile, before making his way around the conference table and
out of the door. As one, the department followed him, not even
pausing to collect their notebooks and pens. They walked with
my father across the hallway and down the stairwell, out of the
Untert⊠ble Memorial Centre for Advanced Semantic Theory and
across the main quad to the gates of the university. It was a cold
winter morning in the last week of semester, and the campus
was under-populated, but the few students who were present all
stopped and watched as my father and his colleagues passed. The

small troupe of academics gradually wound its way down through the narrow streets of the city; not some triumphant, ceremonial parade of the older days, but a solemn procession of a dozen men and women, walking together in silence beneath an overcast sky. There were no speeches when they reached the harbour, no prolonged goodbyes. My father stopped alongside one of the small, well-provisioned boats that lay moored there for just such a purpose, then turned back to his peers and nodded. At the head of the crowd, Lamont struggled for a moment to say something, anything, but then embraced my father compulsively, kissing his cheeks, before handing him a harpoon. My father climbed into the boat to raise its sail while Lamont unwound the mooring line and cast him off. Without a backward glance, my father guided his craft out into the gulf, picking up the swift southeasterly wind that had blown in from round the coast. With throat-clearing, coughs, and murmured, shuffling apologies, the members of the department gradually drifted away until only Lamont was left, standing at the end of the pier as the sky dimmed and my father vanished over the horizon.

As for me, it took a long time to accept that my father was not coming back. Against my mother's wishes, I took to lingering by the quayside on afternoons and weekends, watching the rolling waves and listening to the distant cries of gulls. I remember thinking that if I waited there for long enough, then someday I would see my father sail back out of the thick sea mists, returning triumphantly to safe harbour, towing the corpse of the squid in his wake. Even when I was older I would sometimes spend the anniversary of my father's departure sitting on the pier, staring into the inky black water. The last time I did so was when I was twenty-one, three nights after I had sat the final exam of my bachelor's degree. I had no idea what I was going to do, or where I would go, and as I sat there, my eyes closed, listening to the distant roar of the waves far out in the gulf, I finally gave up on my old dream. My father was not coming back. At best I could hope that he had not succumbed to the elements or starvation, that he had followed the stars long enough to see the squid's vast, hungry beak and ready his harpoon. A month later I walked back up the hill to the university and filled out my application for graduate school.

## 5. Concluding Remarks

All of this was a long time ago, and now I am a Doctor of Philosophy myself, with lectures to deliver, students to supervise, papers to write. There was a time when I thought that I would never depart. But in my dreams I see the tentacles rising up from beneath the waves, a writhing undiscovered country of abyssal giantism, and the smell of salt seems to linger at my door.

## BRIDGET PITT

# Next Full Moon We'll Release Juno

Long before we released Clarence on the Plains of Camdeboo, it was well known in Oupoort that Jonah was soft in the head.

It was also well known that anyone who had a problem with that could sort it out with me. Jonah sometimes made me want to run up the *koppie* behind the Ouport and scream so loud that all the boulders would roll down the hill and bury the whole damn town. But he was my cousin and I had to keep him safe.

Jonah was always different. Ouma Saartjie said it was because he was born just as the blood-red midsummer Karoo moon was rising on one side of Oupoort, while the angry orange sun dipped below the ragged-toothed mountains on the other side.

Auntie Jenna said we shouldn't question God's creations.

If he hadn't been different, I might have been jealous of him. Not only did he snatch my place as the youngest cousin, but, as our relatives never tired of remarking, he also "looked like an angel." Oh, how those aunties would babble on about his green eyes, his curly hair bronzed with gold, his "tawny" skin.... Any kid who "looked white" was admired (and also despised) in our neighbourhood, although Jonah didn't look white so much as like a whole new breed of human, whereas I was just your standard issue Karoo *laaitie*.

But when the aunties tried to cuddle him, Jonah would go rigid and silent, as if listening for instructions from a distant planet on how to manage a life-threatening situation. And they would put him down, puzzled and a little afraid. When I saw that, I understood that Jonah needed someone to stand between him and the world. It seemed that he'd rather be squeezed by a python than hugged by an auntie, and I soon learnt to put myself in the path of relatives bearing down on him.

Keeping him safe at school was a trickier business. On Jonah's first day, Willie Kleinhans knocked him down in the playground and sat on top of him, pummelling him into the red earth like a secretary bird stomping on a snake. Jonah just lay there staring out at some dark star, and when I dived in and persuaded Willie to beat me up instead, he picked himself up and wandered off as if the whole thing had nothing to do with him. Every other day I had to punch someone for calling him spastic chicken brain or fish puke (which some genius coined after a Sunday school lesson about Jonah and the whale). Jonah never seemed to care about the insults, and never thanked me for defending him, but he was family. What else could I do?

Even Mrs. Carelse couldn't get to him. She was the Grade Two teacher at Oupoort Primary, a tiny gnome embittered by years of the Karoo wind and trying to ram knowledge into the heads of her reluctant charges. Even the toughest guys in Oupoort, like Boetie Galjoen (who they say once broke a bullock's neck with his bare hands), would shiver when they recalled her teaching methods. Jonah was in her class for four years, before his knees grew past his ears as he crouched at the little desk, and they had to promote him to Grade Three. Teachers weren't allowed to cane us anymore, but Mrs. Carelse was inventive when it came to cruelty: She would grind spelling and arithmetic into Jonah's head with her knuckles, or twist his ears and peer into them, claiming he had *boontjies* growing there.

"Why does your mother plant her boontjies in your ears?" she would yell, and all the kids would snicker, and run after him at break, shouting "boontjie ears." Then I'd have to beat them up, and get hauled off to the principal's office and clean the school toilets as punishment.

But Jonah just gazed past her at the flickering shadows on the classroom wall — spurring her to ever more furious persecution. Until the day he was tall enough to look her in the eye. He stared at her like he could see everything she'd ever thought, and growled. She left him alone after that.

The only things Jonah cried for were animals. He cried when Auntie Jenna twisted the necks of chickens for the pot. He cried when Bra' Zollie's dog got its ear chewed off in a fight. That dog was the meanest dog in town — even Bra' Zollie was scared of it — but Jonah could stroke it through the fence and it would lick his hand as if it was a little poodle. He cried when we used our catapults to drop starlings and robins and weavers. He'd scrabble to where they'd fallen and kneel on the red dirt, cradling their light-boned, feathered corpses against his chest. But even his crying was different. No tears, just a low mournful howl that blew through your guts like the winter wind and made you feel like you'd never know happiness again.

◆

When Jonah turned eighteen, he was kicked out of school, even though he was still in Grade Four. "We just can't keep him anymore," the principal told Auntie Jenna when she came to enrol him in January, with my ma and me tagging along for moral support.

"Can't keep him any more …" Jonah murmured as we walked away from the school, him still clutching his plastic Shoprite bag with its brand new exercise book, a *naartjie*, and a sharpened pencil. The merciless summer sun beat down, curling the edges of Aunty Jenna's white raffia church hat that she'd worn, hoping, perhaps, to so dazzle the principal with its purple ribbon and organza rose that he'd overlook Jonah's enormous size.

"That means no more school, my boy …" said Aunty Jenna. A slow smile broke out across Jonah's face. His eyes lost their drifty look and sparkled like the clear mountain waterfalls.

"No more school…?"

"… now it's time for you to find a job," Aunty Jenna continued. And his smile died.

"A job …" Jonah tasted the word reluctantly as if it were a boiled turnip. "A *job* …" His face went slack as his eyes flew off again into the faraway clouds.

A job? Who'd give Jonah a job? No one, obviously, and for months Jonah was happier than he'd ever been. All day, in all weathers, he'd be out, doing God knows what. Sometimes you'd come across him lying on his stomach in the veld watching the dew evaporate on a funnel spider's web; or digging into the black sticky mud at the dam with both hands and rubbing it over his face; or creating patterns out of the purple petals of wild *vygies* on the rocks by the stream, dipping each tiny strip in water and carefully sticking it down to form spiralling circles, then laying his cheek against them and singing to himself.

Auntie Jenna might have just let him be. But when Jonah walked down Main Road one Saturday morning wearing nothing but a coat of mud and a crown of plaited reeds, the town busybodies started to mutter about Social Welfare and a "protected environment," which we all knew meant a padded cell in the Oudtshoorn Sanatorium. Jonah needed a job to keep them off his case, but it would take a miracle to get it.

The miracle happened when Jonah's sister Desiree walked into Gerhardt de Wet's taxidermy shop and asked him to give her brother work. Gerhard had so little expression, we used to joke that his old man must have had him stuffed. Even the mouldering owl on his desk looked livelier. But when his glassy gaze fell on Desiree, some spark inflamed his sawdust heart. He'd do anything to win her — so I guess giving her idiot brother a job sweeping out the store seemed a small price to pay for her good favour.

I don't know what Desiree felt — she must have sometimes found it hard to forget that Gerhardt spent his day boiling skulls and ripping skin from flesh. But when Dawie Fortuin suggested it was Gerhardt's gold Mercedes Benz and family game farm that persuaded Desiree to overlook his flaws, I gave him a good punch to put him right. I knew that Desiree would walk a long, hard road to help her brother. And if riding in a gold Benz helped to sweeten her sacrifice, it was none of Dawie's bloody business.

Gerhardt's store was regarded as one of the seven wonders of Oupoort. Tourists would come from miles around with the victims of their hunting trips for Gerhardt to "restore to life" (which made you wonder why they'd killed them in the first place). "Oh, how life-like," they'd squeal, when they came to collect their impala or springbok. But to me, nothing could look more dead, and I found the shop an eerie place — a ghoulish gathering of the ghosts of caracals, leopards, eagles, buck; some whole, some just heads poking through the wall like they were trapped in two different worlds. Or zombies sent to spy on us with their glazed eyes, to take notes of human cruelty and stupidity to pass on to the God of abused beasts.

It seemed unlikely that Jonah would take to it, as Aunty Jenna pointed out when Desiree told her. "Jonah working with all those dead animals? You're mad."

"Let me talk to him," Desiree said. And the next Monday, there was Jonah waiting outside the glass doors of Safari Taxidermy at 7.00 a.m., skin glowing and scrubbed, wearing the new checked blue-and-white collar-shirt that Aunty Jenna bought from Pep Stores to honour the event.

Desiree was a very persuasive woman.

"What did you tell him?" I asked her later.

"I told him he was the guardian of their souls."

Well, that was asking for trouble, I thought. And Reverend Olifant would definitely have condemned it as blasphemous. But it made Jonah attend to his work like a high priest in a cathedral.

He would stroke the linoleum floor with the mop as if it were the finest marble; he would brush and vacuum the animals, sprinkle them with insecticide, and rub their horns and eyes with a duster as reverently as a bishop preparing holy vessels. Once when he was polishing the horns of a buffalo head beside me, I heard a soft, rumbling purr. It must have been coming from Jonah, but it sounded so much like it was coming from the buffalo that I caught myself staring at it to check. It returned my gaze coldly, a scornful glint in its beady eyes.

Gerhardt was impressed with Jonah's dedication, but nervous of his strange manner. After an awkward incident in which Jonah fell to his knees and howled when a customer brought in a dead lynx for stuffing, it was decided that perhaps he should work after hours. He'd arrive just before closing time, and I'd come past at eleven, help him lock up, and drop the key through Gerhardt's bathroom window on the way home.

All was well at first, and soon Auntie Jenna's face lost that look of a wrung-out *lappie*.

"Ja," she could announce triumphantly to the busybodies: "Jonah's on his own two feet now."

One moonlit night, after Jonah had been working a few weeks, I came to collect him after a few rounds at the Karoo Carousers Bar. The lights were off, but there was an odd flickering movement in the shadowy interior. I quickened my steps. Where was Jonah? Had someone broken in? Should I call the police?

I reached the shop, and peered anxiously through the window. Something was moving, leaping, twirling, and flashing through the dim light…. Had a real animal got in somehow? No … it was Jonah. What *was* he doing? And why was he *naked*?

Then I got it. Jonah was dancing. And for a second, as his pale body whirled amongst the silent animals, some trick of the moonlight made it look as if they were all dancing too.

I tried the door, but it was locked. I tapped on the glass. The animals froze into their customary and eternal poses — the leopard snarling on his plaster rock, the cobra rearing up at the meerkat, the lion leaping on the zebra's back. Jonah froze too, his eyes skittering around the room in panic. I waved reassuringly. He came toward me slowly and unlocked the door.

"Jonah, for God's sake, put some clothes on!" I said as I came in. "The whole bloody town can see your *piepie* in this moonlight."

But Jonah just glared at me.

"Busy ..." he said.

"Yeah, you're busy alright," I muttered. "Come on bra', get your clothes on, let's go."

He began unhurriedly to pull on his jeans and T-shirt. The animals' eyes and teeth glittered in the cool grey light. I shivered.

"Jeez, this is a spooky place in the dark. Why are all the lights off?"

He ignored my question. Instead, he gestured to the full-size kudu that stood in the centre of the room, and solemnly announced: "Mikey, we must release Clarence."

"What are you on about, Jonah?"

He walked over to the kudu and laid his hand lightly on its forehead like a priest baptising a baby. "Release Clarence," he said, slowly and carefully as though *I* was the brainless idiot in the room. "On the Plains of Camdeboo."

"Jonah, even by your standards that idea is *mal*. Clarence is a stuffed kudu. How'd you plan to release him?"

He looked pained. Jonah hated having to explain anything, and never did unless it was, in his opinion, a matter of life and death.

"Next full moon. We take him to the Plains of Camdeboo. So he can come alive. Release Clarence."

"The 'Plains of Camdeboo'? Where do you even get this shit? You've never been past Mr. Hendrik's dam."

He didn't answer that. "Next full moon," he said. "You'll take us there. Me and Clarence."

"Jonah," I said, wearily. "Let's be real now, okay? First of all, how do we get Clarence to these Plains of Camdeboo? Secondly, you know how Gerhardt De Wet is about this buck — what do you think he'll do if you 'release' it? And number three, Clarence will *never ever* come alive because he's just a pile of sawdust, animal hide, and glue made to look like a kudu. Now let's get your skinny arse out of here and home to bed."

Jonah looked through me as if he was having a much more important conversation with someone I couldn't see, and I knew he hadn't heard a thing I'd said. He stretched his broad hand between the kudu's eyes, and laid his own forehead onto it, as if sealing a promise. The kudu glared at me through his fingers, challenging me to disobey its wishes.

We left the shop and dropped the key at Gerhardt's place, then walked in silence back to our street. As he went in to his house, he turned to me and said, "Next full moon. Release Clarence."

I didn't mention it to anyone. It would have worried Auntie Jenna and would probably lose Jonah his job if Gerhardt heard about it. And it definitely would have brought the busybodies sniffing around with forms for Auntie Jenna to sign. I just hoped he'd forget the whole thing.

◆

By the time the next full moon came around, it'd gone completely out of my mind. I was at the bar again, drinking with Kelvin Meyer. Kelvin was dismal company, on account of having his heart broken by Desiree, whom he'd loved since third grade. When he came back from working in Cape Town with a second-hand Isuzu bakkie and his wallet stuffed with cash, he thought Desiree would just fall at his feet. All evening I'd had to put up with him whining on like a rusty windmill about "That *fokking* Gerhardt de Wet," and his "*fokking* Benz" and "*fokking* game farm," but at least he was employing his hard-earned fortune to keep me from getting thirsty.

Just before I set off to fetch Jonah, Dawie came in. "Hey Mikey," he said. "That *domkop* cousin of yours says to tell you that he's waiting for you to come and release Clarence."

"Release Clarence?" asked Kelvin. And with my tongue loosened by the beers, before I knew what I was doing I'd told them the whole story.

As I spoke, a sly smile slid across Kelvin's sour-lemon face.

"Gerhardt de Wet's kudu? Let's do it," he said.

"Kelvin, don't be *fokking mal*," I said. "Clarence is worth about forty grand, and Gerhardt loves that thing almost as much as he loves Desiree. He'll have *us* stuffed and put on display in his bloody shop."

Kelvin nodded, "*Ja*, it'll piss him off nicely. But he couldn't prove it was us."

"We could just borrow it," suggested Dawie. "It's hardly going to gallop away, is it? We'll take it out, show old Jonah that we tried, then take it back before Gerhardt notices."

"*Ja*," said Kelvin, getting up. "Or just leave the bugger out there in the Plains of Camdefuckingboo. Let's go, chinas. We can't let poor old Jonah down."

"Kelvin, fuck it man, sit down …" but he was halfway out the door. Nothing would stop him now. If he couldn't have Gerhardt's woman, he was determined to deprive the man of his stuffed kudu. I hurried after them — no one was taking my cousin kudu-releasing without me to keep him safe.

We piled into Kelvin's bakkie and headed down main road, with Kelvin demonstrating a creative interpretation of driving in a straight line. The lights of the shop were off.

"Perhaps he's gone home," I said hopefully, because however drunk I was, I knew this was a bad idea. But Jonah was waiting in the shadows, and as we pulled up, he stepped out.

He'd dragged Clarence to the entrance and tied Aunty Jenna's lilac scarf over its eyes. We hustled it out of the door and down the stairs, cursing and giggling and tripping over each other as we tried to manoeuvre its stiff, awkward limbs onto the bakkie. Jonah didn't giggle — he never giggled. He was as solemn as Rev Olifant at a church elder's meeting, and hissed furiously every time Clarence was bumped or dropped.

At last we got Clarence and Jonah loaded onto the back of the bakkie, and the rest of us squeezed into the cab. The effort seemed to have sobered Kelvin up a bit, at least, and we drove in a more orderly manner out along the R63 — too fast but within the lines — then turned off on a dirt road just before Graaff, heading through the Valley of Desolation toward the low, craggy mountains. The black rock towers of the surrounding hills watched us suspiciously, like the dark sentinels of some secret world. The road ran straight, then twisted and wound up through the mountains, bringing us up onto the escarpment. The plains stretched out to the distant Sneeuberg, carpeted by pale buffalo grass that shone like snow in the moonlight.

Jonah banged on the roof of the bakkie and Kelvin pulled over. We climbed out.

"This is the place," Jonah said.

We off-loaded Clarence. He looked pretty fine, even with the lilac scarf tied over his face, as he stood tall in the grass with his great spiralling horns and the silver tips of the thick fur ruff below his throat catching the light. He seemed to raise his head higher, as if catching the sharp, dry scent of the buchu plants and grass, of the red Karoo earth with its longing for rain. His ears seemed to quiver to the songs of the crickets and nightjars; to the eerie howl of a distant jackal.

"Stay there," Jonah instructed us, waving toward the bakkie with such authority that we all meekly obeyed.

The moon had retreated behind a cloud and we could only just make out Jonah in the darkness as he removed his clothes and laid them neatly on the rock. He bent low to touch his forehead to the earth and sang a long, grieving, wordless song, the high notes rising like the pale moons of his buttocks to the sky. He let the song fade slowly into the night sounds, stood up and pulled the lilac scarf from Clarence's eyes, then drew some symbol on the kudu's forehead with his finger. Then he stood beside it, one hand lightly resting on its back, and waited.

"What's he doing?" grumbled Kelvin. "Let's just leave this fucking buck here and go home. I'm cold."

"Shut up," I hissed. "You're the one who wanted to do this. Get back in the bakkie if you're cold."

Kelvin climbed into the cab and slammed the door. Jonah remained unmoving through this conversation, seemingly oblivious to us, his body drawn tight and alert.

The moon moved out from behind the cloud, flooding us with light. As the moonbeams fell on it, for a moment it seemed as if the kudu had leapt forward and was racing out away from us, its flanks and horns gleaming as it galloped through the sea of silver grass. But it was just Jonah, running with his arms outstretched, the scarf in his hand flying out like some strange night bird behind him. He ran swiftly but easily, loping with the effortless power and unbounded ecstasy of a wild animal. As if it were he, not Clarence, who'd been trapped in some sawdust and skin version of himself, and now, at last, could express his true glory. Clarence seemed to stare after him wistfully, and I wished that he could run too. I didn't want to see Jonah's face when he realized that Clarence hadn't been released after all.

Jonah completed a wide circle, and ran back to us.

"Did you see?" he yelled as he approached. I'd never heard him yell. "Did you see Clarence run?"

Dawie, who has the sensitivity and imagination of a pipe wrench, gave a snort. "Old Clarence never moved!" he said. "Look, he's still — *eina!*"

He broke off with a squeal of pain as I stamped on his foot.

Jonah glanced at the stuffed antelope. "That's not Clarence," he said. "That's just ..." he grappled with the words. "Like a bird ... when it comes out its egg ..."

"You mean this is like Clarence's shell?" I suggested.

"His shell ..." he considered the word, and nodded. "His shell. The real part is ..." He gestured widely out across the plains.

"So, can we take what's left of Clarence back to the shop now?"

He didn't answer that, just walked toward his clothes.

"Next full moon we release Juno," he announced, as he began to get dressed.

"Juno?"

"Juno. The leopard."

*Oh fuck.*

◆

I went to the bakkie to call Kelvin to help load Clarence. He'd passed out in the driver's seat with an almost empty brandy bottle clamped between his knees. Dawie and I yelled at him and slapped him and chucked the remains of the brandy in his face, but we might as well have tried to wake up Clarence.

"Fuck it," I said, kicking the tire and bruising my foot. "What'll we do now? If we don't get this bugger back before Gerhardt gets there, we're in deep shit."

"You'll have to drive," said Dawie.

"I don't have my licence."

Dawie shrugged. "*Ja*, but you know how. I never drove in my life."

I glanced up the sky. The pale flush of dawn was already breaking above the eastern wall of mountains. In a few short hours Gerhardt would be waking up and looking for his keys, then arriving at his shop. If Clarence wasn't there, Jonah would lose his job. And the men in white coats would come to take him away and lock him up forever.

Dawie was right — I had to drive.

We loaded the kudu and Jonah onto the back, and wrestled comatose Kelvin into the passenger seat besides Dawie, although I'd like to have shoved him out of the bakkie and invited the jackals to chew on him. I climbed into the driver's seat, feeling nauseous and apprehensive — but at least the alcohol had worn off, leaving only a sour taste and a pounding headache. I offered a silent prayer to the God of foolish boys, turned the key in the ignition, and released the brake.

As we bumped down the track, my fears faded a little. The bakkie ran smoothly beneath us, the steering wheel sat lightly in my hands. The cool morning breeze brushed my face, leaving me alert and wakeful. *It'll be fine,* I promised myself. *We'll get Clarence back in time, no one will know.*

I didn't panic when I hit the big loose patch of gravelly sand as we came around a bend. The bakkie wheels were sliding out from under me, but it was all happening quite slowly. But Dawie went berserk. "Turn into it," he yelled, suddenly Mr. Driving Expert. "Accelerate and turn into it."

I pressed the accelerator just as comatose Kelvin, dislodged by the skid, fell hard onto my lap, wrenching my hands off the steering wheel and jamming against it so it wouldn't turn. And suddenly we weren't going slowly but careering off the road as I clawed frantically at the wheel, blundering through the bushes and lurching sharply into a ditch, then a sickening revolution as we rolled down the slope, before landing the right way up in the veld. I sat for a moment, trying to gather my thoughts, my eyebrow streaming blood from where I'd smashed it against door frame. *JONAH* ... The door was jammed shut. I wrestled myself out through the broken window and hurtled through the scrub, shouting his name. As if speed mattered. As if I could reach him in time to catch him before he fell.

I saw the kudu first, a little way from the bakkie, one horn broken, its four legs extending stiffly into the dawn chill. Jonah lay beside it, with a small smile on his face, angelic in the pale light. His hand stretched out toward its face, as though to comfort it. As I knelt beside him, a small breeze ruffled his hair, giving the illusion of life. But when I put my ear to his chest, I could hear only the thin, high keening of the wind in the grass.

◆

I didn't go to his funeral. It was made clear that I wasn't welcome. I lay in the long grass outside, my face pressed against the gritty hot sand, and listened through the window. The way they all went on about Jonah as if he was suddenly everybody's darling, even those people who beat him up and mocked him, even the busybodies who wanted to lock him away. Even his father, who walked out on him when he was three.

It was so easy to be kind to him now that he was dead.

Auntie Jenna will probably never talk to me again. Nor will Desiree, although she did persuade Gerhardt not to press charges. I was his cousin, and I should have kept him safe. Everybody hates me these days. But I know Jonah wouldn't hate me. If he could come back, he'd just look at me with that rare, sparkling-eyed look and say, "Did you see Clarence run?"

Clarence's broken neck was easier to fix than Jonah's. He is back in his prized place in Safari Taxidermy. I can't go in there, obviously. But sometimes I come past late at night and press my face against the shop window.

The key to the shop digs in my hand. I told them that it was lost, that it fell out of Jonah's pocket in the accident. But I kept it.

Clarence looks back at me and winks. He knows that one of these days, when I have a car and the moon is full, I'll be coming to release Juno.

## JACK WANG

# The Night of
# Broken Glass

Before the war, when we lived in Vienna, I made a habit of greeting my father when he came home from work. The Steiner School let out at three o'clock, which gave me time to walk the good half-mile from the Graben in the First District to our townhouse in the Third, change out of my uniform, ask the cook for something to eat, and read a Sanmao or Tintin comic, all before my father returned. My reward for standing at the door was usually little more than a nod or a grunt of approval. Still, I met him every day because I loved and respected him and felt it my duty.

One day in November my father came home with a deep-furrowed look. Now that the world was topsy-turvy, he often returned from the legation — or rather, since March, the Chinese Consulate General of the German province of Ostmark — with a harried expression, but that day his face was grave, almost ashen, and my greeting went unacknowledged. Reflexively, he asked our manservant for the day's briefing. With eyes downcast, Old Chen reported that the American had visited again. My father remained calm, but the hat travelling from his hand to Old Chen's hitched in mid-air. The American, whom I had never met, was an old high school classmate of my mother's, apparently in Europe on business. When my father had proposed dinner, my mother had said, "He's not so important. Not like one of your dignitaries," in a tone that left me unsure who was being slighted. So I was surprised, as my father must have been, that the man had come calling for the second time that week.

Over dinner my parents said little. Curiously, my mother made no mention of her friend, and my father did not deign to ask. He did, however, make a show of reading the paper. At the end of the meal, in an overflow of irritation, my mother criticized the cook for the profiteroles. Too soggy, she said. The cook, an old hobbled woman they had brought with them from China, listened with head bowed before backing out of the room.

My father set down his paper. "Why do you ask her to make things she doesn't know how to make?"

"Because I want to eat them."

"But there's no need to scold."

My mother smiled, as if at a child's fanciful idea. "You coddle them."

"No, I consider them."

My mother lifted her eyes, then left the room, and my father shook his head, trying to understand how, with so much going on in the world, his wife could possibly fret over profiteroles or, as she put it in her American way, cream puffs.

◆

I met my mother for the first time when I was six. I say "mother" because that was what I was expected to call her, and did, though in fact she was my stepmother. My real mother died of tuberculosis when I was five. A year later my father came home with a new wife. He had been studying international law in Chicago despite already having a Ph.D. in political economics from the University of Munich. While he was gone I received a series of brightly coloured linen postcards of the World's Fair: the Hall of Science, the Avenue of Flags, the iron lattice towers of the Sky Ride. The theme of the fair was *A Century of Progress*. That's where my father met Grace.

It was a windless, thick-aired summer day in Changsha when a motorcar saddled with steamer trucks pulled up in front of our house and a woman in a white blouse, wide-legged trousers, and large round sunglasses climbed out. She was beautiful, which made me sad for my mother and scornful of my father, and she looked too fair to be Chinese. As it turned out, she was half Chinese, born of a Chinese father and a German-American mother. That, along with her clothes and her beauty, made her unlike any woman I had ever seen.

My father had secured a large two-storey house on the outskirts of town and staffed it with half a dozen servants, all in an effort to make his new wife comfortable, but as soon as they arrived he was stricken by all he had not foreseen. The house had no running water, and despite the need, Grace refused to use the privy, which had no seat and emitted an audible drone. After pleading with Grace in hushed tones, my father ordered Old Chen into town for a portable commode, a trip of at least three hours. For the rest of the afternoon my new mother paced the courtyard, smoking one Lucky after another, which made her seem feral and caged.

If I kept my distance that day and in the first appraising weeks to come, it was because she didn't speak a word of Chinese and I didn't yet speak English. My father hired a tutor, but she only learned to say a few innocent things, and only in the toneless way of foreigners. Our only hope, then, was if I learned English, which I did soon enough, through sheer exposure. Grace spoke in torrents and only paused to teach me phrases like *Hot diggity dog!* and *Now you're on the trolley!* which, when repeated, elicited barking laughter.

Needless to say, Grace was unhappy in China. Though my father had no particular desire to leave, he began to eye the Foreign Service. When the Governor for whom he worked recommended the post of First Secretary in the Chinese legation in Austria, my father accepted for Grace's sake. We arrived in Vienna in June of my tenth year, and at first everything did seem better. The city was glorious with summer, and everywhere open air orchestras paid homage to the old masters, which made our lives seem set to music. Many nights my parents put on tails and gown and went to balls and receptions, living at last the life for which they were meant.

But it wasn't long before Grace again felt stranded. She could no more distinguish *der*, *die*, and *das* than she could first and second tones. Then in the spring, German troops goose-stepped through the Ringstrasse, just blocks away from our townhouse. The crowds that greeted them were lusty, adoring, as was I, my schoolboy fantasies of soldiers and guns come to life. My father did not raise his arm but he didn't stop me from raising mine. That night, in a scene that would soon become commonplace, hoodlums took to the streets, smashing the windows of certain homes and shops. Thereafter, walking to and from school, I passed shop fronts marked *Jude* and *Nicht arisches Geschaeft* and blocked by baby-faced men in jackboots and flared helmets. As a visible foreigner and part of the diplomatic corps, my father felt undeterred and often went into these shops despite the piercing glares — and once, an arm held stiffly against his chest. For my mother, annexation was yet another rung of descent in a private tragedy. She chided my father for bringing her to a Nazi-occupied country. His answer: *Better the Germans than the Japanese.*

At the end of October, thousands of Polish-born Jews were rounded up and sent back to Poland. When one seventeen-year-old boy living in France learned that his family was among those languishing at the border, unwanted by either side, he walked into the German Embassy in Paris and pumped five bullets into the viscera of a minor German diplomat. Two days later, Ernst vom Rath died of his wounds. The seething of the Germans, checked so long as their countryman clung to life, would now be unleashed. This was what my father knew when he came home that afternoon.

◆

I have little memory of the rest of that night. I feel I should have more, given all that happened. I have a half-formed memory of waking in the night to the sound of breaking glass, but this may be a superimposition of what I learned afterward. Even if memory can be trusted, I don't recall anything else, which means I must have simply gone back to sleep.

By the time I awoke, my father had already left and made clear to Old Chen that I was not to go to school — or to leave the house, for that matter. When I asked why, Old Chen wouldn't say. Miserable with curiosity, I slipped out the door as soon as I found myself alone. On the Beethovenplatz, I was met by the air of something charred and ashes wafting like blackened snow, but it wasn't until I turned onto the Ring that I realized something was terribly wrong. It looked as though a violent storm had blown through in the night. Every other shop front was shattered and their wares strewn about, as if contents under pressure had exploded, and everywhere shards of glass lay glinting in the morning light. Amidst the wreckage, women and children rummaged, pocketing whatever they pleased. Eventually I came upon an odd scene: a group of what looked like patients standing in a crude circle in the middle of the street, white-haired and rheumy-eyed and still in their nightclothes, as if they had just come from bed. Despite the apparent difficulty, they were made to perform calisthenics — slow-moving knee bends, jumping jacks — by men in brown shirts, black ties, and red armbands. All the while, boys my age in replica uniforms circled about manically, pointing and shouting and laughing, and this, more than anything, struck me with fear.

I ran home.

◆

Over the years, in fits and starts, my father told me his side of the story, until at last it resolved itself and came to seem my own. That morning, he caught his usual streetcar, eager to get to where he was needed most. Earlier that fall, a line had begun to appear every day outside the consulate. Word had spread through cafés and synagogues: the Consul General of China signed visas for those who asked. However, to my father's surprise, there wasn't a single person outside on this of all mornings.

"Hasn't anyone come?" he asked Zhou, the Vice Consul, who lived upstairs.

"Some were here earlier, but they were … taken away."

"Why didn't you stop them?"

Zhou looked stricken. "How?"

My father sighed. He imagined himself dashing out, throwing up a diplomatic shield, but perhaps he, too, would have watched from the safety of his second floor window.

That morning's papers were scant. According to one, last night's events had not disturbed *the hair of a single Jew*. But over the course of the morning, news came in by cable, telephone, telex: dozens dead, countless terrorized, and everywhere, mass roundups.

In the afternoon a black Buick Eight with small Chinese flags flapping on either side of the hood appeared in front of the consulate, and from it emerged the only person who could be in possession of such a car: Chen Chieh, the Chinese Ambassador. Or rather the Ambassador-designate. Hitler had so far refused to let him present his credentials. Germany's only interest in the Far East was containing the Russians, a task for which Japan now seemed much better suited.

Nonetheless, when the man entered, my father said, "Your Excellency."

Chen appeared pleased as he took off his coat and hat and handed them to Zhou, who left the room sheepishly. "I heard that you were a smart man, Consul General Ho. You haven't disappointed."

He took a seat across from my father, chin short, earlobes long, and hairline receded to the top of his head like a Manchu. He wore a three-piece suit and thick round glasses and spoke in the haughtier Shanghainese way, without nasal inflection. My father waited for him to begin. Instead Chen picked up the leather-bound copy of the

Luther Bible on my father's desk. My father had grown up attending the boys' school on the campus of the Norwegian Lutheran Mission in Changsha, where he learned both English and German. It irked him that the Ambassador had palmed the book so blithely.

"You're a believer, then."

When my father said nothing, Chen's smile crimped, faded. He set the book down.

"I understand you've been signing visas for ... those in need."

"Yes, that's right."

Chen tented his fingers and nodded. "You're entirely in the right, of course. But perhaps we ought to be more cautious. We know how the Germans feel. Especially now. We don't want to risk ... upsetting them further."

My father sat upright. "But we have our orders."

The Ambassador fleered. "We know the motives of the Executive Yuan."

It was true that by offering passage to Jews the government hoped to raise funds for the war of resistance. It was also true that my father wanted in some way to join that war, haunted as he was by the carnage in China, Nanking especially, and by his guilt that he was safely beyond its reach. But these were hardly his only motives.

"Where are they supposed to go?"

"They may go to China if they wish, but they don't need visas. Shanghai is an open port. There's no passport control under the Japanese."

"But they need proof in order to leave."

"A steamship ticket is sufficient."

"A visa is better."

"Germany is our ally. We don't want to damage our warm relations."

My father had once had great affection for Germany, but it was Germany that had advised Generalissimo Chiang to abandon Nanking.

"Perhaps we should consult the Vice Minister."

"You needn't worry about that," Chen said, suddenly short. "I will speak to the Vice Minister. In the meantime, I suggest you do as I say. We all know what happened this morning. It's no longer safe. For you or anyone else."

This gave my father pause. Maybe in trying to help he would only be baiting the trap.

"Perhaps you're right."

The Ambassador studied him cautiously. "So we're clear, then."

My father drew a breath. "Yes. Your Excellency."

◆

Shortly after the Ambassador left, the telephone rang.

"Feng-Shan, it's Ruth."

My father started. Ruth and Max Blumberg were two of the many friends he had made since arriving in Vienna. His circles were wide as a matter of course, immersed as he was in the life of the city, but he was also an affable man versed in the art of conversation. He often held court in our sitting room, everyone staying up late until the room was miasmic with smoke (everyone, that is, except Grace, who always retired early). He last saw Ruth at a dance attended by Nazi officials. He couldn't tell if they knew the Blumbergs were Jewish — Germans seemed to condescend to Austrians in general — but when one of the otherwise solicitous officials took a leprous view of Viennese women, my father made a point to dance with Ruth. It wasn't the first time they had danced. The previous winter they had been part of a group that had gone to Semmering, where they skied by day and danced by night. Ruth was a frank and witty woman who sympathized with Grace — "Must be hard to hear only gibberish" — in a way that meant she also felt for *him*. At some point that night they stepped out for air and wound up leaning against a wall, she with one knee raised and her arms tucked like wings, and something about her pose and the strangeness of the evening made him lean in for a kiss. Halfway, he stopped, drew back, from decency or fear, he could never decide, but she hadn't flinched, not in the slightest, which meant she wasn't opposed or simply hadn't realized. He was never sure which.

"Where are you? Are you all right?"

"I'm at home. I'm fine, we're fine. We've been spared so far, thank god. But it's terrible, what's happening."

The Blumbergs were among those who had held out, stayed on. They couldn't imagine living anywhere else, least of all the Dominican Republic, the one country that had opened its doors. But perhaps the time had come to leave.

"Have you changed your minds?"

"Yes."

"Good."

"Can you come tonight?"

It took a moment to realize what she was asking.

"We can't leave the house."

"No, of course not."

"Will you come, then?"

Decades later, on the balcony of the apartment on Russian Hill to which he had retired, my father admitted to weighing the risks. What if he were found out, relieved of his duties, sent back to China? What chance would he and Grace have then?

"Feng-Shan, please. I'll do anything."

Perhaps it was just a turn of phrase corrupted by the memory of his own lust, but it sounded like a proposition, which startled and shamed him.

"How many should I bring?"

◆

After my foray into the streets, I expected to be met at the door and berated. Instead I found Grace in her robe, one hand spread at the base of her throat, listening to Old Chen in the kitchen. Soon after, through the floor of my room, I heard her having a one-sided conversation, which I took to mean she had called my father. She asked how he was and how soon he'd be back and even offered to meet him, but by the sound of things he wouldn't let her.

I was lounging in my room with my comics when the doorbell rang. Footsteps emerged from my parents' room and pattered down the stairs. Then a voice I had never heard wafted up in English. When my father had guests, I was expected to greet them, but something told me not to in this case. Part of me wanted to see the American for myself, but another part was afraid, as if seeing him would betray once and for all what was happening.

For a while they talked in the sitting room. Then they came upstairs. I waited for a knock, expecting to be introduced, but all that came was the sound of a door shutting, then murmurs, then nothing. Ten, maybe fifteen minutes later they went back downstairs, where the front door closed with a snap.

When my father came home I was there to greet him as usual. In my mind I had worked out ways to forewarn him, but when the time came I had no words. I simply watched as Old Chen delivered the news, only this time my father could no longer hide his feelings. "Grace, where are you?" he shouted. She appeared at the top of the stairs and clipped down in heels, fastening earrings as she went, as if merely running late. What was he doing here again? My father asked. He wanted to say goodbye, Grace replied. Why didn't he do that yesterday? Because he didn't know he was leaving. It was a different world yesterday.

For every question, she had a cool reply. He's an old friend. He speaks *English*. How can you begrudge me someone to *talk* to? All of these ready answers left my father flustered until he finally said, "You're being unfaithful."

Grace looked strangely satisfied. "You're one to talk."

My father's face slacked. I didn't know what this meant, only that Grace had parried and struck a blow. I kept waiting for him to reply, but he only looked at us plaintively. Then he opened the door and left.

◆

I don't know what my father was thinking or feeling as he walked away from our townhouse and through the Inner City. I can only imagine that what he saw mirrored in the wreckage around him was his own life, which steeled him to his real purpose in leaving.

The Blumbergs lived in the Second District. After crossing the inky waters of the Danube Canal, my father came to the Leopoldstadt, also in shambles. On the Leopoldstrasse he passed the remnants of a synagogue: Torah scrolls scattered like so much newsprint and the temple itself reduced to a blackened husk. He burrowed into his coat and pressed on.

After scanning left and right, he entered the Blumberg's building, rapped on their door. He was greeted by silence, then shuffling, the stuttering scrape of a chair. A single scouring eye appeared at the door before the chain fell.

"*Grüss Gott*," said a young woman. The maid.

Ruth crossed the room. "Feng-Shan," she said, embracing him.

My father couldn't help noticing a coil of perfume. "Where's Max?"

"He's been taken away. For interrogation."

"My God."

"At least it was someone who works for him. You know Max, always good to his own. I think he'll be fine. He'll probably be back tonight." She smiled stoutly.

"This will get him out," my father said, extracting papers from his coat.

She took them, examined them, then looked up, eyes gleaming. "Stay awhile."

Max was an executive with the Standard Oil Company, and his home looked the part, especially the grand piano and the small tabletop radio — a novelty at the time. Ruth offered a cigarette and the maid brought coffee and schnapps and for a moment being there almost seemed pleasant. But after a bit of politesse — "How's

Grace? And that sweet boy of yours?" — Ruth underscored the occasion by describing things she had seen and heard: friends beaten in the streets, a rabbi made to shout obscenities, a man forced to clean the sidewalk with his beard. "I have to applaud the Nazis," she said, "for the sheer inventiveness of their cruelty."

She rose and smoothed her brown housedress. "Come with me."

My father's pulse quickened when she led him to the bedroom. After closing the door, she crossed the room to a low-slung dresser and pulled out a jewellery box.

"I want Grace to have these," she said, plucking out jewellery as if pinching coins from a change purse.

"No," my father said, moving decisively toward her.

"I have more. We can't take everything."

My father put a hand on hers. After a long moment she dropped her things and gripped the edge of the dresser.

"It's not as if I have anyone to leave this to."

Toward the end of his life, after being widowed a second time, which put him in a rare confessional mood, my father described being struck by the wild idea of gifting her with a child, one she would carry with her all the way to Shanghai. Unlike that night at the dance, he no longer felt bound by his vows.

"Do you know what I want?" she asked, turning to him fiercely. "I want to come back and find everything as it was. I want to walk into my kitchen and take out my kettle and make myself a cup of tea. As if I never left."

She was hardly finished before they heard urgent knocking on the door. She and my father exchanged looks, then returned to the living room where the maid was already approaching the door. Soon a brusque voice said, "What do you mean 'God greet you'? *Heil Hitler.*" Then two men in plain clothes barged in.

"Firearms search," one of them announced.

"We've already been searched," Ruth replied calmly. "Twice."

"Then we're searching again."

The man turned to my father. "Who are you?"

"A friend," he replied.

"What are you doing here?"

"Waiting for the man of the house."

The plainclothesman frowned. Among the reasons must have been my father's impeccable German. "Show your identification."

My father, sitting again, released a veil of smoke. "By rights we should see yours first. Unless we're no longer following protocol."

The man's face contorted. "Our leader has said you foreigners no longer have special privileges. So you have no right to be so impudent."

The other man, gangling, pocked, and impatient with the scene, began to stalk the apartment. Soon drawers were yanked, overturned, menageries of glass swept to the floor. Ruth tensed.

"You foreigners have taken what is rightfully ours," the first man continued. "What you saw last night was the outraged soul of the German people."

The man went on, grandiloquently. Eventually the other returned, having failed, it seemed, to discover anything. "Who are you?" Without waiting for an answer, he reached into his great-coat, pulled out a revolver, and aimed it at my father, who stared with a mixture of curiosity and awe.

"Who are you?" the man repeated, voice rising.

The maid closed her eyes, mumbling.

"Who *are* you?"

This time my father detected a pleading. For the chance to put the gun down honourably.

"I'm the Consul General of China."

The two men looked at each other in dismay. "Goddamn it. Why didn't you say so?"

With that, the men left as abruptly as they came.

◆

That night I ate dinner alone, wondering if Grace was right about my father. Once, in Changsha, I found a silver dollar on my way home from school. When I got home I showed Grace, who promptly took it for "safekeeping." Feeling the money was rightfully mine, I took a dollar from my father's coat. When the money was discovered in my room, my father thrashed me with his belt, then fell to his knees begging me not to steal, which I found even more terrifying. All the while, I expected Grace to intercede, but she didn't. So despite his guilt-ridden look, I decided my father believed too much in character to be unfaithful and that the only one capable of deception was Grace.

After dinner I went upstairs, brushed my teeth, and changed into my nightclothes, all with a crude self-sufficiency that made me feel lonely. Then I shut off the lights and lay awake listening for the door. Eventually I was drawn to the window by tramping, shouts, the blare of klaxons, but all I could see through a scrawl of branches was the square in repose.

When the telephone rang, I startled. Grace came padding out of her room and down the stairs, but Old Chen, efficient as always, reached the phone first. From the top of the stairs I heard her asking who it was but didn't catch the answer.

Before long, the handle to the front door joggled and my father appeared, surprised by the sight of Grace standing with her arms crossed. They greeted each other with the same look of injury and hauteur. Without removing his coat or hat, my father strode into the sitting room. From my perch on the stairs, unobserved, I saw him pour a drink.

"Ruth called."

My father looked up.

"Max is home. She said you would know what that meant. You went to see her, didn't you?"

My father sat down and took a vacant sip of his drink. Slowly, haltingly, as if searching for ways not to, he recounted his day. It was at best a sketch whose details took decades to fill in, but that was the first time I heard about the Ambassador and the visas, the Gestapo and the gun. At the first mention of Ruth, Grace scowled triumphantly, but by degrees she looked concerned, astonished, and finally chastened. When my father was done, he pinched the corners of his eyes, and Grace sat down beside him. When at last she touched a hand to his shoulder, he turned and they looked at each other, and it seemed they had reached some kind of truce; whatever the reckoning, it wouldn't be tonight. I was glad my father had been vindicated but pained to think that Grace might be forgiven, that our lives might simply go on as before.

◆

Three months later we found ourselves at Vienna West Station, under plumes of smoke and ash and a canopy of iron and glass. In the weeks and months after those two nights of chaos, my father had continued to sign visas until he was found out and a black mark placed in his file. That's when he decided to go back to China. Grace, however, wasn't going with us. She was going back to America instead, and we were there to see her off. The three of us formed an awkward circle on the platform, next to an arcade where soldiers with dogs stood sentry. We didn't hug or kiss, much less cry. We simply waited for the moment of release, for the frayed tether to finally snap.

As we stood there, a line of children shuffled past, large man-ila labels dangling from their necks. Each carried a suitcase save for the ones young enough to be carried themselves. Their parents watched resolutely from the other side of the arcade, unwilling to give the soldiers who kept them off the platform the pleasure of a scene. Grace turned, tracked the children, then looked at my father, eyes bruised, squinting. To be parting now, as others were being parted, was the final measure of their failure. As if cleaved by the thought, she hurried onto the train.

Clouds of soot issued from the smoke box, and with a slow-waking lurch the train began to move. As it left the station, I thought of the time after my mother's death when my father left me for Chicago. He was gone a long time, nearly six months, and

.each day I would go to the window, wondering when he was coming back. Now those children, too, would have to wait. That day, the war not yet begun, I believed what their parents had said outside the platform: *Be good. We'll see you soon.*

The train slowly dwindled, and I thought we would go. I was ready to go anywhere, do anything, now that I had my father back. But he stood where he was, escorting the train to its vanishing point, hat pushed up in a tousled way. Only then did I stop to wonder what he must have been feeling, coming to the end of something that had had its beginnings, however inexplicably, in joy. Even when the train became little more than a wisp of smoke, he kept staring. I see him still, gazing into the distance, mourning all that couldn't be saved.

# ABOUT THE AUTHORS

**DANIEL ANDERS** was born in America, moving to Australia at the age of seven. After university, he embarked upon a writing course while he worked at a local bookstore. As a new writer just entering the literary scene, the Commonwealth Short Story Prize was the first writing competition he entered. He lives in Melbourne with his wife, two children, and a cat.

**EVAN ADAM ANG** is a recent graduate of the National University of Singapore, majoring in history. He has had a keen interest in writing fiction for many years. As an emerging writer keen to make his mark in the literary world, the shortlisting of *A Day in the Death*, one of his first stories, is a major milestone in his career.

**YU-MEI BALASINGAMCHOW** lives in Singapore and writes about history, travel, and culture in Asia. She is the co-author of *Singapore: A Biography* (2009), which received a gold prize at the Asia Pacific Publishers Association Awards in 2010 and was named a Choice Outstanding Academic Title 2010. Her work has been published in *The Epigram Books Collection of Best New Singaporean Short Stories* (2013). She is working on her first novel, with funding from Singapore's National Arts Council. Her website is www.toomanythoughts.org.

**HAZEL D. CAMPBELL** lives in Kingston, Jamaica. She is a published author of both adult and children's stories. She also freelances as an editor and teaches an occasional outreach writing class at the Philip Sherlock Centre at the University of the West Indies at Mona. Her publications include *Singerman* (Peepal Tree Press), four e-books on Amazon, and eight books for children. In 2011, she was awarded the Silver Musgrave Medal from the Institute of Jamaica for her "contribution to children's literature and the encouragement of new writers in the island."

**MAGGIE HARRIS** is a Guyana-born writer and artist who migrated to the U.K. in 1971. She has taught creative writing in universities and the community, and is a former International Teaching Fellow at Southampton University. She performs her poetry across the U.K. and has been involved in a number of artistic collaborations. She has published several books of poetry and was awarded the Guyana Prize for Literature in 2000 for her collection *Limbolands*. She is the author of two short story collections and a memoir.

**ALEXANDER IKAWAH** is a writer and filmmaker living and working in Nairobi. He is a founding member of the Pan-African writers' collective Jalada Africa. His work has been published in magazines *Jalada*, *Kwani?* and *Lawino*.

**ANUSHKA JASRAJ** is a fiction writer from Bombay. She holds a BFA in film production from NYU, and an MFA in creative writing from the University of Texas-Austin. Her work has appeared in *Granta* online, *Internazionale*, and the *Four Quarters* magazine. She currently lives in Austin, Texas, and is working on a short story collection.

**HELEN KLONARIS** is a Greek-Bahamian writer living in the Bay Area, California, where she teaches creative writing. She is co-editor of the forthcoming anthology *Writing the Walls Down*, and has been published in numerous journals, including *SX Salon*, the *Caribbean Writer*, *Poui*, *ProudFlesh*, and *Calyx*, and several anthologies. She is working to complete her debut collection of short stories.

**KHADIJA MAGARDIE** was born and lives in Johannesburg. She is a journalist by trade, but a writer by aspiration. Inspired by the short story traditions of the south of Africa, "Elbow" was her first attempt at fiction. She is currently working on her first novel.

**A.L. MAJOR** is a Bahamian-born writer. A graduate of Vassar College and of the University of Michigan's MFA fiction program, she is the recipient of a University of Michigan Hopwood award and the Ann E. Imbrie Prize for Excellence in Fiction from Vassar. Her work has been published in *Subtropics* and *Vice* magazines. She is currently working on her first novel.

**JENNIFER NANSUBUGA MAKUMBI** is a Ugandan novelist, short story writer, and poet. She has a Ph.D. in creative writing from Lancaster University and her doctoral novel, *The Kintu Saga*, won the Kwani Manuscript Project in 2013. The novel was published in 2014 under the title *Kintu*. Jennifer teaches creative writing at Lancaster University and is currently working on her second novel.

**MICHAEL MENDIS** is a law graduate living and working in Colombo, Sri Lanka. The winner of the 2013 Commonwealth Short Story Prize (Asia Region), "The Sarong-Man in the Old House and an Incubus for a Rainy Night" was published on *Granta* online in May 2013.

**ANDREA MULLANEY** is a journalist, university tutor, and writer based in Glasgow, Scotland. She has been the TV critic of *The Scotsman* newspaper since 2006 and has written for many other publications. She has had stories published in a number of anthologies, and has performed her work in Glasgow, Edinburgh, and Paris.

**CARL NIXON** lives in Christchurch, New Zealand. He is a full-time writer of plays, short stories, and novels. His collection of stories, *Fish 'n' Chip Shop Song and Other Stories*, was published in 2006 and was number one on the New Zealand bestselling fiction list and was shortlisted for the Commonwealth Writers' Prize, South East Asia and South Pacific region. His stories have appeared in numerous anthologies, and several have been broadcast by Radio New Zealand. He is also the author of three novels.

**JULIAN NOVITZ** is a short story writer and novelist from New Zealand. He lives in Melbourne, Australia, where he is a lecturer in writing at the Swinburne University of Technology. His latest novel, *Little Sister*, was published by Random House in 2012. His first award-winning collection of short fiction, *My Real Life and Other Stories* (2004), was followed in 2006 by his first novel, *Holocaust Tours*. He was awarded the 2008 Katherine Mansfield Short Story Award for "Three Couples."

**BRIDGET PITT** is a Zimbabwe-born South African writer. Her first published writing was for the anti-apartheid *Grassroots* newspaper in Cape Town; she also produced media for a number of organizations and has written educational material for NGOs, school text books, poetry and fiction. She has published poetry, short stories, and two adult novels, *Unbroken Wing* and *The Unseen Leopard*, which was shortlisted for the Commonwealth Writers' Prize in 2011 and for the Wole Soyinka Prize for Literature in Africa in 2012. Her next novel will be published by Umuzi in 2015.

**JACK WANG** grew up in Vancouver, Canada. He earned an MFA in creative writing from the University of Arizona and a Ph.D. in English with an emphasis in creative writing from Florida State University. His fiction has appeared or is forthcoming in *Joyland Magazine*, *The Humber Literary Review*, and *The New Quarterly*. He is an associate professor in the Department of Writing at Ithaca College in New York and holds the 2014–15 David T.K. Wong Creative Writing Fellowship at the University of East Anglia in Norwich, England.